THE EMERALD SORCERESS

Sherry Bessette

ISBN:978-0-9977948-0-9

First Edition: 2009

Manufactured in the United States of America
Printed by CreateSpace
Cover design by Novel Graphic Designs

For
The Girls!
Jacque, Cookie and J.J.
You are Kacie's magic.

CHAPTER ONE

Fierce winds rampaged the dark forest, viciously whipping each naked branch. Ancient trees bent and contorted, defending themselves against the gale. Casting grotesque shadows high into the raging sky, they danced in rhythm with the violent lightening.

Blinded by the stinging rain, a woman ran through the storm. She cast a fearful glance behind her, but saw nothing in the blackness of the night. Pausing to catch her breath, she heard the sound of a horse crashing through the forest in pursuit. In her panic, she stumbled to the ground. With a cry, the woman placed a protective hand on her swollen belly and pushed herself to her feet, urging them on.

A blinding flash of emerald fire split the night. For one fleeting moment, hope flared in the woman's breast as the Emerald Sorceress suddenly appeared beside the great stone arch ahead of her. Raising her arms to the heavens, the sorceress spoke the words\ of power, and the space inside the arch shimmered, bathing the night in a rainbow of color. The woman moved faster, concentrating on reaching the safety of the arch. Only a few more paces . . .

Out of the blackness, triumphant laughter reverberated around her, cutting through a roll of thunder as if the boom were nothing but a whisper. Her blood ran cold as she felt the hot breath of the animal on her neck. A bolt of green fire exploded behind her as the Emerald Sorceress sought to give her time. The scream of the horse spurred her forward. With her last ounce of strength, the woman reached the arch.

Breathless, she placed one hand on the cold, wet stones, holding her heaving belly with the other as her lungs hungrily drank in the damp air. She looked up at the beautiful sorceress standing between her and certain death. A smile passed between them.

"Go," the sorceress urged.

Without a second thought, the woman stepped through the arch, into the rainbow of light. As she vanished from sight, the colors shattered like a mirror, leaving only the black night and the storm.

The Emerald Sorceress slowly lifted her eyes to the wizard towering above her on his black stallion, his thin face blazed with anger. He was too late. A calm satisfaction crept over her as she gazed at the raven blazoned across his chest. "You've lost, Jozef. This one, you shall not have."

****

Kacie Miller bolted straight up from the mattress, eyes wide. Her heart hammered in her chest as she clutched at her blankets, still seeing the terrifying images of the nightmare flash before her. She forced her hands to relax their death grip on the medallion around her neck as her eyes traveled around the familiar bedroom. She focused on the thin line of daylight seeping around the edges of the heavy linen curtains on the far side of the room and drew a ragged breath. Letting it out slowly, Kacie tried to dispel the dream's terror with the comforting sight of light.

She reached up to wipe the perspiration from her face and frowned at her shaking hands. It was just a dream, she told herself.

A disturbingly real dream.

She shuddered, once again hearing the howling wind and feeling the rain sting her cheeks as she ran through the dark forest. Kacie frowned. No, she realized, it wasn't her cheeks that stung. She wasn't the woman in the dream. The woman looked like her, but something was different. She bit her lip. If it wasn't herself she was seeing, then who was it? But, the woman eluded her, just as she had the man on horseback.

Kacie shook her head, sending her long black hair cascading around her shoulders. *Jeez, Miller, get a grip. It's only a dream*, she admonished herself. "But, it's a very scary one," she argued back. *You're twenty-two, for goodness sake,* the logical part of her insisted. *Are you gonna let a little nightmare turn you to jelly?* She made a rude sound to silence her inner voice as she tried to calm her jangled nerves and collect her wits.

Stretching to release knotted muscles, Kacie glanced at the clock beside the bed. The display glared 9:30 am. She did a double take.

9:31

"Crimeny! I'm late!"

The dream and her fears were pushed aside as she jammed her feet into black and white cow slippers and waved a hand in the general direction of the curtains. Not even a thread stirred. *So much for my powers of telekinesis.*

She snorted and padded to the windows, oblivious to the moos coming from her feet with every step. "You don't have time for fantasies today, Miller. You have to be at work in twenty minutes."

She flung open the dark red curtains, relieved that for once there was no coastal marine layer shrouding the sun as bright morning light flooded the room. Kacie raced into the tiny kitchen and pulled open the fridge. Grabbing the remains of a double pepperoni pizza, she tossed it into the microwave. She slammed the door shut and started to point at the oven, caught herself and keyed in 2:00 and hit the start button. Today was not the day to play make-believe.

As a child, Kacie was convinced that buried deep within her was the ability to do things others couldn't. A wave of her hand should turn on lights or pick her clothes up from the floor and put them away. Of course, none of these things ever happened, but that never stopped her from trying. As she grew older, the habit became a game she continued to play. Usually, she just laughed at her private childhood joke. Today, it was a nuisance.

Kacie frowned at the microwave and raced back to her bedroom. She grabbed the first hanger she laid her hands on and slipped the blouse over her head, half hopping, half stumbling into the bathroom while she stepped into her long skirt and pulled it up.

Kacie put in her contacts, pulled her thick hair into a quick ponytail and slid several golden bangles up her arm. She gave herself one last look in the mirror and decided she looked semi-normal. In the other room, the microwave beeped. Kacie zipped in, grabbed her breakfast and headed for the door. *I wonder if pepperoni pizza before bed causes nightmares?* She shook her head at the thought. She'd only had pizza three of the five nights she'd had the reoccurring dream. With a sardonic laugh, Kacie rushed out of her apartment and waved the door closed as she charged down the wooden stairs.

The door stayed open.

Kacie threw her head back and let out a wordless cry of frustration. She stomped back up the stairs, yanked the door shut and raced down again. Casting a guilty eye at the big Tudor house adjacent to her

2

garage apartment, she grinned and hopped onto the polished wooden railing and slid the twelve steps to the driveway below. "Aunt Mary would kill me if she saw this." A peek up at the master bedroom confirmed her suspicions; her aunt was scowling down at her. "Oops." Kacie's grin widened. Unrepentant, she waved to her aunt.

Mary Miller shook her head and waved back. Kacie blew her a kiss and jumped into her red convertible Jeep C.J. and peeled out of the driveway.

Oblivious to the residential quiet, she jammed the gearshift into drive, stomped on the gas and raced down the tree-shaded street. Two blocks down, a red light threatened to stop her progress. Kacie glared at it as she sped closer.

"Change," she commanded, snapping her fingers and pointing at the light."Yes!" She pounded the steering wheel with delight when the light turned green. She down shifted and with tires squealing, made a quick right onto the freeway. The gas pedal went to the floor and the speedometer hit 80 mph just as she reached the end of the on-ramp. She pushed a strand of hair out of her face and cranked the stereo, directing slower moving cars out of her way with a wave of her pizza slice. Kacie pretended it was her powers of manipulation parting traffic like Moses at the Red Sea, not the fact that she was swerving in and out of lanes like a woman possessed by demons. Whatever the reason, traffic complied and she made the twenty-minute drive into downtown Santa Monica in ten.

Licking her fingers, Kacie found a parking spot behind The Dreaming Tree and patted the C.J.'s bright red fender for a job well done and headed into the metaphysical bookstore. "Now if I can just make it to the crystal room with out being seen," she told herself. She sneaked in the back door, past the incense counter and around the last bookshelf. The door to the crystal room was in sight and she was about to congratulate herself, when a voice stopped her in her tracks.

"Over sleep, Miller?"

Kacie swore under her breath. Pasting a saccharin-sweet smile on her lips, she turned to face her short, round, annoying co-worker. "Just pretend, Jon, my sweet, that the big hand is on the twelve and the little hand is on the ten." She cocked her head to the side and slowly drew an imaginary circle in the air as if moving the hands of time backwards.

Jon's eyes widened.

Kacie snickered and disappeared into the other room.

"Witch," Jon mumbled, not quite, under his breath and Kacie sent an evil cackle drifting through the store.

Like a perfect, conscientious – on time- employee, Kacie was dutifully dusting crystals when the store manager caught up with her five minutes later. Loren looked pointedly at his watch. Kacie shrugged.

"What happened to you this morning?"

Loren's light tenor voice would never match his muscular, 6'4" frame, but for once Kacie didn't notice the incongruence. "I had that dream again last night." She focused on the crystal in her hand. "It was so real, Loren. I honestly thought I was there." She glanced up at her friend, the night's terror still churning in her stomach.

Loren threw a sympathetic arm around her shoulders. "Kacie, you have got to get yourself another job." He waved a hand around the room full of crystals and other metaphysical objects. "This place is gettin' to you, Girlfriend," he teased. "Maybe you should lay off the pizza before bed."

"Thanks." Kacie made a face at him.

"And turn some lights on. You're gonna turn into a mole."

Kacie waved a hand at the lights. Nothing.

Loren pulled his glasses down his long nose, and looked over the rims at her. Without a word, he withdrew.

From behind a bookshelf, Jon piped up. "Use the switch, Miller, it works better."

"There are such things as sensor switches, you know," Kacie retorted.

"Not at The Dreaming Tree. Not in the entire year you've worked here, Miller. You have to switch the lights on and off by hand in this place."

"I'd like to switch you off," she grumbled and picked up a large crystal, gently wiping off the needle-like points.

"Oh, by the way," Loren popped back in. "Mr. Weatherby's back." Kacie gave him a blank look and he added, "You know, the guy that owns the store."

"I know who Mr. Weatherby is. I've just never met him, is all."

"Well, this is your lucky day." And, he was gone again.

"Great." Kacie threw down her dust rag and settled the crystal back in its place on the display shelf. "Why today? I'm a basket case today."

A shimmer of light in the corner of the room caught her eye and Kacie crossed the room to stand before a large antique mirror. "Just my luck, isn't it, Gueran?" she asked the dragon carved into the wooden frame. "A Suit. And I look like a holdover from a hippie convention."

Kacie twirled back and forth looking at the reflection of her long, tie-dyed, gauze skirt and low cut, muslin shirt. She smiled at herself and shrugged. "Oh well, you still love me don't you, Gueran?" She patted the dragon's head and could have sworn he winked his one eye at her. Kacie shook her head and laughed at her own foolishness.

She began to dust the intricately carved frame, running her hands over the exquisite sculpture. The mirror felt magical under her fingers, almost alive, as she admired the incredible craftsmanship that went into making this work of art. She loved the way the dragon draped itself over the top and down one side, while he curled his tail around the blade of the sword etched into the other side. She touched the large wooden gem in the hilt and imagined it to be real. "What an incredible thing you'd be," she whispered, leaning forward enough for the gold medallion around her neck to swing loose from her blouse and hit the mirror. A spark arced from the mirror into the necklace, giving Kacie a slight shock.

"Ow." She rubbed her tingling chest. "Okay, since when can you get a shock from glass?"

"Kacie."

Kacie heard Loren call her name, but she stood transfixed by the rainbow of colors that swirled across the mirror's surface. *Wow.* She tore her eyes from the kaleidoscope long enough to see if the display of crystals across the room were prisming in the mirror. No, their colors were dormant, shrouded in the morning shadows. Kacie frowned and turned back to the mirror.

"Kacie," Loren called her again.

"Loren, check this out." Kacie moved aside giving Loren an unobstructed view of the Dragon Mirror.

"Check what out?" Loren scratched his bald head as he inspected the mirror and then Kacie.

Kacie glanced back at the now clear, reflective surface. "How weird. There were all these gorgeous colors dancing in the mirror a second ago. It was awesome." She looked up at Loren again and shrugged. "Oh well. What's up?"

Loren just shook his head. "I need you to inventory that shipment of books that came in yesterday. I'd like Mr. Weatherby to think we do work around here once in a while."

"Sure." She gave the Dragon Mirror a final look and then dismissed the whole incident as just another in the growing list of weirdness in her life and headed for the back room.

Checking inventory wasn't her favorite job, but at least it should keep her safe from the Twilight Zone for a little while. Kacie turned on the radio – remembering to use the knob this time – and let the back-beat of the rhythm take her. She danced around the room, emptying boxes and applying price tags in time with the music. Very shortly a teetering tower of books sprang up in the center of her dance floor. She eyed them for a moment. "I think you should go over there." She directed her finger to a spot on the floor out of the way. The books didn't move. Kacie sighed. "Okay, fine." She made a face, grabbed an armload and walked them to where she wanted them. She flicked her fingers at the uncooperative books and began to sing with the radio.

She was dancing around a mountain of empty boxes when an elderly gentleman invaded her sanctuary. Kacie stopped singing. "Excuse me, Sir, customers aren't allowed back here. Can I help you with something?" She watched him wander around the room, obviously lost.

What a strange old guy. She eyed the snow-white ponytail hanging half way down his back. It was a perfect match for the short white beard he was stroking as he gazed about the room. Kacie raised an eyebrow at the bright, flowered shirt tucked into banana yellow Bermuda shorts, held around his bony hips by a woven tan belt.

Check out that buckle. Her gaze riveted to the golden, three pointed sunburst radiating out from a huge emerald. *That has to be the biggest emerald I've ever seen. I wonder if it's real? No way, it can't be.* She shook her head in awe as she continued to survey the strange little guy.

But, I tell you what, if he's wearing shoes and socks, I'm gonna die. Kacie suppressed a laugh and sneaked a peek at his feet. Huaraches. She sighed with relief. He was wearing sandals – without socks. *Well, that's a step in the right direction.* She wrinkled her nose and groaned at the pun.

He had to be seventy, if he was a day, and he looked like the poster boy for a Fijian travel guide. She let her gaze wander back up, and found herself staring into twinkling gray eyes.

The man smiled, waiting for her to finish her inspection and Kacie's face reddened. "I'm looking for my desk," he told her.

"Excuse me?" *His desk? The poor man's off his Twinkie. He shouldn't be out on his own like this.* Kacie gave him her best reassuring smile. "I don't think we have your desk, Sir. Um . . . is someone looking for you . . . maybe?"

Understanding flashed in the old man's eyes and he reached out and patted her hand. "It's all right, child. I'm Mr. Weatherby. Loren said my desk was back here somewhere," he shrugged. "Every time I leave, Loren moves things around so that I can't find a thing when I return."

"Mr. Weatherby?" Kacie jumped, snatching her hand away. *Terrific.* She stepped back into the stack of empty boxes and lost her balance. Boxes tumbled all around her as she fell into the middle of the avalanche.

From underneath the rubble she heard Mr. Weatherby's barely contained laughter. "Are you all right, child?"

I will be if I don't die of embarrassment first. This was not how to impress your boss. Kacie groaned. *Oh, I certainly impressed him all right. I'll be lucky if I don't get fired.* She buried her face in her hands. Who else would imply to their boss' face that he was senile?

Above her, Kacie heard boxes being shifted and then a hand reached down to help her up. "Are you all right, child?" Mr. Weatherby repeated and her yes was so rueful he began to laugh. His laughter was infectious and in spite of her embarrassment, Kacie found herself laughing with him.

"What in the world . . ." The concern on Loren's mobile features as he rushed into the room changed to shock and then understanding as he saw Kacie standing hip deep in empty boxes.

Mr. Weatherby winked at Kacie. "We were just introducing

ourselves when this poor child was attacked by that pile of boxes," he explained, sober faced. "It's lucky I was here or she might have been killed."

Loren looked at Kacie, who shrugged and held out her hand. "I'm Kacie Miller, Mr. Weatherby," she grinned and he winked at her again, clasping her hand in both of his warm ones. Kacie excused herself and slipped out of the room.

Okay, so he's a little eccentric. What's wrong with that? She looked down at herself. *The world needs a few more eccentrics.*

****

A bolt of lightning split a thick wet oak, spooking the great war horse, causing him to dance sideways. The Raven Wizard took a firmer grip on the reins, controlling his frightened mount. Jozef regarded the woman standing before him, taking in her deep chestnut hair and the tall frame, slender and straight under the sodden green velvet cloak.

"You are as beautiful as ever, Lady Emerald." Jozef bobbed his head to her. "Even after all this time." She continued to stare up at him, and a lazy smile touched his thin lips. "What, Reyna, have you nothing to say to your King?"

The emerald eyes locked defiantly onto his pale blue ones. "I see no king, only a murderer."

Jozef ignored the slur. She was tired. He could see it in the pinched look around the beautiful eyes, and the set of her full mouth. It took considerable power to activate and then destroy a portal in such short succession. Even for the Emerald Sorceress. Jozef began to relax. She was weak. He hid a satisfied smirk. He had waited a long time for this opportunity. Let Maya go. The child she carried no longer mattered. He had the Emerald Sorceress, herself. Without Reyna to teach her, the child was just another child. She was no threat to him. And, with Reyna under his power, he would soon have the Dragon Sword with its coveted ruby.

Old anger flared momentarily. It had been so easy to rip the Power from the Raven Wizard, leaving nothing behind of his mentor except a shriveled shell. But, Mykal had suspected him. Jozef ground his teeth.

With the help of the Emerald Sorceress, the old wizard exchanged the ruby of power from the Raven's signet ring with the inert ruby in the Dragon Sword of Medora. By the time Jozef realized the

8

deception, Mykal was a lifeless heap and the sword was nowhere to be found. The Emerald Sorceress had hidden the sword denying him the full adaptation of his usurped Raven magic. But now, Reyna stood before him, vulnerable. Jozef almost laughed.

Yes, with the Emerald Sorceress under his control it would be a simple matter to strip her power and retrieve the Dragon Sword from its hiding place. Jozef's cold, ice blue eyes glittered with visions of unlimited power.

Never taking his eyes from hers, the man eased himself in the saddle, sliding a gloved hand under his cloak, and into the pouch hidden at his waist. With a lightening quick movement, he pulled his hand from the pouch and threw a handful of crystalline powder at the woman, murmuring the words of a spell.

Too late, Reyna realized her danger. Even as she threw up her arms to protect herself, she was crumpling to the ground.

The Raven wizard slid to the ground and easily lifted the Lady onto his horse. "All too easy."

****

Kacie woke sweating, her heart pounding - again. Groaning, she sat up in bed. "This is getting to be a habit. A bad one," she groused, pushing her dark hair out of her face. "Oh No!" She froze then smashed her pillow into her face as she realized this dream continued where the first one left off.

"I'm trapped in a 'B' movie and I can't get out!" she wailed into the pillow,

"Well," she put down the pillow and drummed her fingers on the blankets. "At least it was different. Hummm. . . Maybe I should go back to sleep and see what happens next." Kacie pounded her pillow into shape, snuggled back into the bed and closed her eyes. "Then again, do I really want to know what happens next?" She threw off the covers and sat up.

"No."

Kacie waved a hand at the light. The room stayed dark. She dropped her head to her chest and sighed. "Maybe someday.... if I live long enough." She slipped her feet into her slippers, mooing along with them as she shuffled her way into the kitchen, to make herself a cup of hot blackberry spice tea.

Teacup in hand, Kacie curled up on the couch under a warm afghan and flipped on the TV, surfing through the channels until she found an old black and white Tyrone Power movie. Half way through Tyrone's swashbuckling she drifted into an uneasy sleep.

****

Kacie .... From the depths of darkness, she heard her name being called. Kacie threw an arm over her face, trying to ignore the voice, but the summons came again and again, each time more urgent than the one before.

Kacie opened her eyes and found herself standing in a void engulfed in a blinding fog. She stretched her arms as wide as she could and felt nothing around her.

Kacie.... The disembodied summons drew her forward, deeper into the mist. Kacie spun in a tight, unseeing circle. "I can't see. Where are you?" *Why on earth did I ask that? How about asking how you get out of here, Miller?* Her hands groped, trying to feel her way through the swirling white vapor. Pushing down the panic growing inside her, she took a deep breath, wiped her sweaty palms on her over-sized T-shirt and then shook her arms loose.

Kacie.... The faint voice called again. Kacie tuned everything else out and focused on the sound. It seemed to be coming from all around her. As hard as she tried, she couldn't zero in on the point of origin. *This is getting me nowhere.* She squinted into the fog and concentrated on willing it away. Maybe then the fog in her brain would piffle away too. Several moments later, she realized she could just make out a dark silhouette through the thinning mist.

That's more like it.

Kacie inched forward until she stood in front of a massive wooden door. Heavy iron hinges held it securely to a stone wall. She placed a hand on the door to push it open and a flash of blue fire sparked along her arm, shocking her. Kacie yelped and jerked back, cradling her numb arm as she watched the blue fire crackle over the door's surface before it faded away. "Oh, don't even go there with me." She set her jaw and stretched her hands toward the door, being careful not to touch it. "I want on the other side of this door."

Kacie shook her tingling arm. "And no little blue whatsit is gonna stop me. So, open up." She closed her eyes and pictured the door

10

opening. As she concentrated, in her mind's eye, she saw a deep emerald green aura gather around her, growing ever stronger in the stark haze. Kacie swayed, her hands hit the protected door. A brilliant flash erupted in front of her. The blue and green energies clashed and the door swung open under her touch.

Kacie opened her eyes and found herself in a musty stone room. She shivered and rubbed her arms, wishing she had on more than just the hockey T-shirt she slept in. *Okay, so where exactly am I?* She looked around and noticed a faint blue glow radiating through the shadows in the room. Searching for the source, Kacie took a step forward and saw the woman, Reyna, lying on a bed of white satin, in the middle of the room. Her chestnut hair spilled over a gown of deep gold velvet. Her slender white hands lay across her stomach. A dome of clear crystal encased her body and the now vary familiar blue aura of power crackled along the glass. Kacie absently rubbed her arm.

"So that's what he did with her. Is she dead?" Kacie inched closer.

The woman's eyes flew open. *Help me.* The mental plea reverberated in Kacie's mind. She tried to scream. She wanted to run, but the emerald eyes rooted her and held her silent. *Help me.*

"How?" Kacie heard herself ask. *Why do I keep asking questions?* She mentally kicked herself.

Use your crest.

"My what?"

The Trion crest. Use it to free me. Hurry, girl, before Jozef catches us.

Kacie took another step closer to the crystal dome. "I'm sorry," She shook her head. "I don't understand. What crest?"

Kacie felt, rather than heard the woman's sigh of desperation. *Just do as I say. Quickly. Around your neck, you wear a small medallion of a phoenix -*

"How did you know that?"

The woman ignored her. *Take it off and place it on the seal in the crystal. Then strike the dome with your fist.*

Reaching inside her T-shirt, Kacie pulled out the golden phoenix, rising displayed from a crown of flames. Delicate scroll work framed the piece, forming it into a miniature shield. She hesitated for just a moment before removing the necklace from around her neck. It was the only inheritance she had from the mother she never knew, and she was reluctant to part with it even for a second.

Holding the pendent tightly to her, Kacie took a closer look at the crystal dome, and for the first time, noticed a tiny circle of gold with a raven etched in the center. Remembering her last bout with the jumping blue energy, Kacie took a deep breath for courage and plunged her hand into the blue aura. To her surprise, it only felt cold and a little tingly as her arm passed through it. She laid the necklace on the seal and watched in fascination as a green glow began to radiate around the pendent, pushing the blue away. Soon, only the green aura remained.

Hurry Girl! Reyna's emerald eyes blazed, urging her to move.

The words brought Kacie out of her reverie. She made a fist and struck the crystal with all her might. A burst of Emerald power flashed around the dome shattering it into a thousand glowing pieces that vanished into nothingness.

Out of nowhere, a ball of blue fire appeared in the far corner of the room. Before the Emerald Sorceress could move to protect her, it slammed into Kacie's solar plexus, hurtling her through the air. She crashed against the stone wall and slid, un-moving, to the floor.

****

Reyna swore. Jozef knew the girl was there. He couldn't have missed the raw power she unleashed to counter his magic spells. The child would be a formidable sorceress – if she lived.

The Emerald Sorceress compressed her lips into a thin, determined line and forced herself to stand. How many years did she lie captive in Jozef's crystal coffin? It seemed like a lifetime. It was a lifetime. Maya's unborn babe was now a young woman. Reyna moved unsteadily to the unconscious girl and felt her neck for a pulse. It was strong and steady. Thank goodness. Reyna let out a sigh of relief and looked nervously around the room, expecting Jozef to appear any second. The girl must be sent back before Jozef could reach her. Without training, Kacie was vulnerable and Reyna was too weak to protect her.

"You must go back, my child. It isn't safe for you here within the Raven Wizard's reach. You are not ready to face him." Reyna took one last quick look around, gathered her long dormant powers about her like a cloak and spoke the words of the spell that would send Kacie back.

"Return to your world of protection and light, beyond the mists of darkness that await you here." On the last word, she touched Kacie's forehead. A brilliant green aura surrounded the girl and then she was gone. Reyna took a ragged breath and wearily stood.

Now it was time for her to leave. She turned toward the far wall and spied the tiny golden Trion crest lying on the floor beside the bed. Reyna slipped it around her neck and moved to stand at the center of the wall. She counted six stones over and three up. Running her hand over the rough surface, she felt the familiar, almost imperceptible swell of power radiate from the tiny depression in the bottom corner of the stone. "How convenient." Reyna smiled. "A secret Jozef hasn't found yet." She pressed and a small section of the wall slid open revealing a tiny closet sized room that held a dusty, standing mirror. As the wall slid back in place, Reyna stepped through the mirror and vanished.

CHAPTER TWO

The blaring radio in the bedroom jarred Kacie awake. She squeezed her eyes shut and flung her arm over her head trying to block out the noise as she flopped onto her stomach for a few more minutes sleep.

"Ooh," she grimaced and lifted her sore stomach off the cushions and gingerly rolled onto her side. Running a hand over the area, she bit her lip against the pain. "What the …?" A perplexed frown creased Kacie's forehead as she lifted herself off the couch and hobbled almost bent in half to the bathroom.

Kacie flipped on the bathroom light and pulled up her T-shirt for a look. "Crimeny," she gaped at the deep purple bruise that covered her entire mid-section. "Where on earth…?" She eased herself onto the side of the bathtub and wracked her brain trying to recall what she could have done to herself to cause such a bruise. Suddenly she recalled the ball of blue energy slamming into her stomach, hurtling her across the room.

No way. Kacie refused to believe it. *That was a dream. That's all. Period. Just a dream. I ran into something yesterday and I just don't remember it.* She fingered the ragged green edges of the massive bruise, knowing full well she couldn't forget doing something like that to herself. She reached for her necklace.

It wasn't there.

"Oh no." Kacie stiffened, pulling her tender stomach muscles. She groaned and abruptly collapsed in on herself, losing her balance. Her arms shot out, grasping air as she slid backwards into the tub and hit the back of her head on the tiled wall. She cried out and in one fluid movement, grabbed the back of her head with one hand, clutched her tortured stomach with the other one and swung her legs into the tub. She curled into tight a ball of pain and hit her forehead on the edge of the tub. Kacie burst into peals of hysterical laughter mixed with tears of pain as she tried to figure out which part of her battered body to tend to first. "Good Lord, what next?" She reached for her necklace again.

Her necklace . . .

The laughter died and Kacie fought back more tears as she felt her bare neck. She crawled out of the tub and made her way into the bedroom. Gritting her teeth against the pain every movement caused her, she stripped her bed and prayed the chain just got tangled in the sheets. It didn't. With grim determination, she systematically searched her room. Nothing. Kacie ransacked the living room and kitchen next, even looking in the veggie crisper. The necklace was nowhere to be found.

Think Kacie. She turned in a tight circle surveying her tiny living room. "What did you do with it?" It was around her neck when she went to bed. So what could have happened to it? It wasn't like her little garage apartment was the Taj Mahal. It had to be there somewhere. Kacie refused to let her thoughts go anywhere near the only other explanation. That wasn't an option.

In the bedroom, the DJ on the radio announced the time. "Rats." She glanced at the clock on the VCR for confirmation. She couldn't afford to spend any more time looking for her necklace. Friend or no friend, Loren wouldn't ignore her coming in late two days in a row.

Battered and mentally spinning with thoughts she didn't want, Kacie dressed and headed for work.

Unerringly, her feet led her to the crystal room and the dragon mirror. She leaned her bruised forehead against the cool glass and stroked the smooth dragon's head. "I think I'm going crazy, Gueran. Things are happening to me lately that I can't even begin to explain." Kacie drew a ragged breath and let it out slowly. "How 'bout it, do you have any answers for me?" She waited for his reply, but the dragon remained silent. "I didn't think so." Kacie patted his head and waved a hand at the lights.

"They work better if you use the switch."

Startled, Kacie turned her head and watched Mr. Weatherby demonstrate how to use a light switch, before he disappeared around the corner. She sagged against the mirror and heaved an explosive sigh. "I can't take much more of this, Gueran."

"What did you say?"

This time, Kacie yelped. "Mr. W., please don't sneak up on me like that." Kacie pleaded. "My poor heart can't take it."

"Mr. W.?" A puzzled expression crossed his features and then he smiled. "No one's ever called me that before. I think I like it. Mr. W." He chuckled and then apologized. "I'm sorry, Kacie I didn't mean to startle you, but I thought I heard you say something." He took a long look at her pale face and a concerned frown creased his brow. "Are you all right?" His eyes rested on her bruised forehead.

I'm not even close to alright. "I'm okay. I had a little argument with my bathtub this morning and lost, that's all." She touched her forehead and rolled her eyes. "It's a long story. Don't ask."

Mr. Weatherby still looked concerned, but nodded, letting her explanation stand. "Who were you talking to?" He looked around the empty room.

Kacie blushed a little. "The dragon mirror."

"The mirror? You call the mirror Gueran?" Mr. Weatherby became very still, waiting for her answer.

A chill went down Kacie's spine. She swallowed her sudden nervousness, and gave him a weak grin. "No, I call the dragon on the mirror Gueran. He doesn't seem to mind." Kacie regarded the dragon for a couple of seconds then shrugged. "Gueran's a good name for such a regal looking dragon, don't you think?"

Mr. Weatherby opened and shut his mouth a couple of times, never quite finding his voice. He settled for looking her over very carefully. After a long moment, he shook his head and gave a short rueful laugh. "You have brown eyes," he said at last. "You call the dragon, Gueran, and you have brown eyes." He shook his head again and left the room mumbling to himself.

Kacie stood there dumbly staring at the spot where he had been. Collecting herself, she grabbed her stomach and shuffled after him. "Mr. W., wait!"

He was sitting at his desk in the back room, by the time Kacie caught up with him. *I guess we had his desk, after all.* She swallowed hard to keep down the laughter that threatened to bubble up. With as much dignity as she could muster, Kacie assumed a straight face and cleared her throat. "What did you mean just now, Mr. Weatherby? What's wrong with the color of my eyes? Do you know where the

16

mirror came from? It's yours, isn't it?" The words tumbled over themselves in a rush to spill out.

Slowly, Mr. Weatherby swiveled his chair around to face her. And once again, he searched her face, looking long and hard into her eyes, trying to see . . . what? Kacie thought he looked disappointed by what he saw, or maybe didn't see. His scrutiny unnerved her, but she wouldn't look away from him. For some reason she couldn't explain, it was very important not to waver under his inspection. At length, he sighed and looked away, releasing her to breathe again.

"Brown eyes...." He stopped and started over. "The Dragon mirror was given to me over twenty years ago by a very dear friend, but no, it isn't mine. I hold it in trust for someone else. You're very attracted to it, aren't you?"

"I love it." Kacie gushed and grinned at her own enthusiasm. "You're gonna think I'm crazy, but it feels.... well .... magical to me. Is that crazy?"

Mr. Weatherby dropped his head into his hands.

"Mr. W., what's so important about my eyes? Because...."

"Hey all!" Loren burst into the back room. "Good to see you here early today... Good grief, Kacie. How on earth did you get that nasty bruise on your forehead? What'd you do, run into a wall again?" He laughed at his own joke. Kacie didn't bother to answer and Loren turned to Mr. Weatherby. "I need to go over the month end reports with you, Mr. Weatherby, before I seal them up. If you've got a couple of minutes, we could do it now before the store opens." He pulled a small stack of papers from the middle drawer of the desk and plopped them in front of her boss.

Suppressing her irritation at the interruption, Kacie listened for a moment, as Loren captured Mr. Weatherby's attention, before leaving them alone. At the door, Kacie glanced back and saw Mr. Weatherby twist slightly and watch her retreat, a thoughtful frown creased his forehead.

By the time Kacie limped to the front, it was time to open the store. She unlocked the door, wincing as she pulled it open. Then, her professional smile sprang to life. "Good morning," she greeted the handful of people waiting to get in. As she flipped down the doorstop with her toe, a brilliant rainbow reflected in the glass door. Kacie scanned the room, trying to see where it came from, but she couldn't find anything. She was about to shrug it off when the entire crystal room was bathed in a deep emerald glow. "What the...." Kacie headed over and cautiously poked her head around the corner.

A tall, slender woman stood with her back to Kacie admiring the dragon mirror. Kacie took in the loose chestnut hair waving down her back and the long red dress and decided she must be part of the local Wicca society. The green flash was probably just a reflection from the woman's jewelry. Kacie frowned slightly, she didn't remember letting her in the store. "Can I help you find something?" Kacie moved into the room and the woman turned to face her.

Kacie's mouth dropped open.

"I've found what I was looking for." The woman's intense emerald eyes bore into her.

"You." Kacie remembered to close her mouth. "Who are you? No, scratch that. What are you?"

"My name is Reyna. I am the Emerald Sorceress."

"Right. The Emerald Sorceress." *And I'll bet you're married to Merlin the Enchanter.*

"I'm not married, actually. But I did have a close friend at one time," Reyna smiled as if recalling fond memories.

I don't believe this. Kacie looked around for the hidden cameras.

"Believe it, Kacie."

"You can hear my thoughts?" She was still looking for those cameras.

"The Emerald Sorceress can do many things. Things you need to learn."

"Why would I.... No," Kacie held up her hands. "I don't want to know."

"Because you are the next Emerald Sorceress." Reyna answered her anyway.

"Me? Uh-Huh. Of course I am." Kacie would have laughed at the absurdity of the whole situation if her stomach muscles didn't hurt so much.

Reyna waited patiently. "It's true," she said at last. "You are the next Emerald Sorceress." She took a step toward Kacie. "It was decreed before you were born. I have waited a long time for you to be

18

ready to claim your birthright."

Kacie took two steps back. "Let me get this straight. You want me to believe I'm some sort of witch?" Kacie did laugh this time, arms tightly supporting screaming muscles.

"Not a witch. A sorceress. The Emerald Sorceress."

"A sorceress. Oh yeah, I see that now. Silly of me to have missed it before." She scanned the room again for cameras. "Look, I don't...."

"What happened to your eyes?"

Here we go again. Kacie peered past Reyna to look at herself in the dragon mirror. "What's wrong with my eyes?"

"They're brown. The Emerald Sorceress has emerald eyes. It's our mark." Reyna indicated her own vivid green eyes.

Kacie shrugged. "I guess that kinda shoots a couple holes in your theory, doesn't it?"

"Never mind," Reyna brushed it aside. "You must return with me."

Kacie's eyebrows shot up almost to her hairline. "Excuse me? Return with you? Return where, exactly?" *There I go asking questions again.*

"Medora, of course."

"Of course." *Jon, if this is one of your jokes, you're dead meat.*

"This is no joke, Kacie. There is much for you to learn before you face Jozef again."

"Jozef?" Kacie searched her memory and her jaw dropped. "You mean Jozef, the bad guy from my dream? The one with the big horse and the raven plastered all over his chest? That Jozef?" *Of course! Now I get it. I'm dreaming again. Any minute now, I'm gonna wake up.... I hope.* "This is nuts."

Reyna pulled something out of her pocket and handed it to Kacie. "You left this behind last night."

Kacie stared at the necklace lying in Reyna's open palm. "How ?" she whispered and closed her hand around her most treasured possession.

"Do you remember freeing me from the binding spell?"

"Remember?" Kacie almost shrieked. "I remember slamming into a wall. Look!" She pulled up her shirt to expose her purple mid-section.

Reyna surprised Kacie by smiling. "This proves my point. Only an Emerald Sorceress could have withstood an attack like that from the

19

Raven Wizard. That blow would have killed anybody else. Instead, you came away with only a little bruise."

"A little bruise?" Kacie looked at the deep purple and blue mess that was supposed to be her skin. "A little bruise?" She shook her head, incredulous. "Is that supposed to make me feel better? Hey! What are you doing?" Kacie tried to jump away from Reyna's out stretched hand. But, the woman caught her wrist and held her steady as she covered Kacie's mid-section with her free hand. The sorceress closed her eyes and took a deep breath. Warmth flooded into Kacie's body. She looked down and saw a light green aura radiate from Reyna's hand and spread across the bruised area. A second later, Reyna took another breath and opened her eyes. The green glow faded from Kacie's skin and with it, the bruise.

"How did you do that?"

Reyna shrugged and placed a hand on the dragon mirror. "The Emerald Sorceress can do many things. Are you ready to come with me now?" Reyna indicated the mirror.

"Through the mirror?" Kacie took a long step back. "Kacie doesn't sound anything like Alice, thank you very much." She shook her head. "Look, I appreciate the hocus pocus you did just now on my stomach and all but, I think I'll just stay here, if it's all the same to you."

Reyna shook her head. "Please don't fight me." She sighed wearily.

Kacie took a good look at the woman standing before her. The elegant hand resting so casually on the dragon's head was white-knuckled. Kacie looked into Reyna's face and for the first time, noticed the dark circles around the beautiful eyes, and the pinched mouth trembling with fatigue.

"Are you OK? You don't look very good. Why don't you sit down over here and I'll go get my boss." Kacie turned to leave.

"No." Reyna swayed precariously, precious energy was slipping away. "Come with me now, Kacie." She pleaded, her voice barley more than a whisper as she slid nervelessly to the ground. Reyna grabbed Kacie's hand and pulled her closer. "I'm sorry. There is so much to tell you...." she whispered.

Kacie began to panic. "Shhhh, don't talk. I'll go get help." She started to rise, but Reyna held her down.

"There's no time." Reyna said, placing something in Kacie's hand.

"You are The Emerald Sorceress now. Find the brooch. It will lead you to the sword. You must restore the King."

Kacie watched Reyna's eyes close and her body go limp. "Please, Lady - Reyna. C'mon, don't do this." Kacie pleaded. "Help!" She jumped to her feet and yelled again, frantically searching for someone who could help. "Somebody help me!"

Jon and Loren arrived at the same time. "Kacie, what's the matter?" Loren asked. "You're white as a ghost, girl."

"That lady's had a heart attack or something."

"What lady?" Jon wanted to know.

Kacie glared at him. This was no time for jokes. "That lady." She pointed, then looked at the empty spot on the floor where Reyna had been. Kacie staggered back into Mr. Weatherby's arms. "She was there. She was dead, right there." Kacie knew she sounded hysterical, but she had to make them believe her. "She was there." Kacie insisted one last time.

"It's all right, Kacie." Mr. Weatherby soothed her as he shooed Loren and Jon back to work. "Come into the back room and tell me about it."

"You've got to believe me, Mr. Weatherby. There was a dead woman right there." Kacie began to shake uncontrollably.

Mr. Weatherby guided her past the knot of curious customers and into the back and sat her in the chair next to his desk. He opened the bottom drawer and produced a bottle of Jack Daniel's and a glass. Filling the glass with the amber liquid, he handed it to Kacie. "Drink. It's whiskey, it'll help. Come, come, drink up." he urged, guiding the glass to her lips.

Kacie took a swallow and choked as the whiskey burned its way down her throat. Mr. Weatherby took the glass from her hand and set it on the desk. When Kacie slowly stopped shaking, he sat back. "Now, tell me what happened."

Feeling warm and relaxed, Kacie could think a little clearer and decided that there was no way she could ever explain what really happened. So, she took a deep breath and lied. "There was a lady in the crystal room. She asked me for a book, and a second later she collapsed." Kacie raised haunted eyes to him. "I watched her die, Mr. W. I called for help, but when everybody got there, she was gone."

Kacie spread her hands in bewilderment. "She just vanished. You believe me, don't you?" She looked down at her lap. "Of course you don't. I was there and I don't believe me."

Mr. Weatherby patted her hand. "Something certainly has you worked up and it's been my experience that people generally don't become hysterical for no reason. Although, I can't honestly say that I've heard of dead people vanishing into thin air." he told her. "Maybe there's another explanation. Maybe she just fainted and when you turned she came-to and slipped out behind you.

Kacie nodded. *She fainted. Yeah, that's it. She just fainted.*

In a pig's eye.

****

Alone in her apartment, Kacie sat watching the sunset, trying to make sense of everything. The day's events kept running through her mind like a constant video loop, over and over again. But, no matter how she looked at it, Kacie just couldn't make sense of it. It was like trying to make sense of monkey gibberish. "Find the brooch; it'll lead you to the sword and restore the King? What brooch? What sword? What King?" she scoffed. It was right out of a King Arthur novel.

Kacie took a sip of hot tea and rotated her neck. She didn't like the idea of people popping out of her dreams and into her life as if they belonged there. Things like that just didn't happen in real life. Mystery movies and dreams, Okay, but not real life.

And what about the dreams? What the devil were they all about

First, there was the same one over and over again, making her crazy, night after night, like an old record needle stuck in a groove. Then, as if that wasn't bad enough, they started panning out like some afternoon Alfred Hitchcock serial. Kacie snapped her fingers. "That's it! I'm living an Alfred Hitchcock movie. It's called THE DREAM. Staring Kacie Miller." She gave a sour laugh.

And another thing . . .

What is the problem with my eyes? Kacie jumped up and ran to the bathroom. She climbed onto the vanity and sat cross-legged on the counter leaning in closer to the mirror. *I happen to like my eye color.* She examined them from several angles, then smiled at her reflection. *I think they're a lovely shade of brown.* She turned her head back and forth, admiring the way the light reflected in their warm depths. Her smile slowly faded and with deliberate movements, Kacie reached up and removed her contacts. Motionless, she stared into the emerald eyes looking back at her, so startling against her black hair and pale skin.

For several moments she was lost in their depths remembering once again, the taunts of the kids at school. "Witch, witch, Kacie's a green eyed witch." Remembering the startled looks on the faces of adults when they saw her for the first time. Remembering the day a nun had crossed herself and hurried away from her. Remembering running home and begging Aunt Mary and Uncle John to let her get contacts to hide those hated witch eyes.

Kacie shook her head to dispel the memories and shifted her weight, grimacing as something hard pressed into her hip. "What the - Oh lord, I forgot!" Kacie dug into her pocket and pulled out a small object, and stared open mouthed at it for a long time.

She wasn't sure what she expected, but this wasn't it. She gaped at the emerald ring lying in the palm of her hand. The one-inch square cut stone was set into a heavy gold band. Carved into the face of the stone, a tiny dragon curled protectively around a sword.

Kacie caught her breath and let it out in a low whistle. "Wow!" She shifted the ring, causing it to flash in the bathroom light and shook her head. "This can't be real. Nobody in their right mind would give away something like this to a total stranger. I don't care if they were dying. Unless it was fake or...." Kacie thoughtfully tapped the ring against her teeth then frowned when she realized what she was doing, and put it down. "Maybe it was stolen. Yeah, that's it. It was stolen.

"Okay, Miller, and if it was? What then? Do you turn it over to the police? And how do you explain how you got it? Try explaining a dead person when there's no body." She gazed at the floor for a second. "Ah-hah!" She snapped her fingers. "Did anybody really die? There's no body.... And if there's no body, then maybe there's no woman.... And if there's no woman, then there's no ring.... And if there's no ring, then this whole thing is just another dream, and I'll wake up and laugh about all this some time real soon."

To test her theory, Kacie twisted around and grabbed a safety pin from her odds and ends dish and pricked her finger. "Ouch." She stuck the bleeding finger in her mouth. "Okay, so maybe this is real after all.

Now what?" Kacie thought for a minute, turning the ring over in her hand. "This thing could be worth a small fortune. Maybe I should turn it over to the police." She tipped her head and looked at herself in the mirror. "On second thought, I don't think so. They'd still want to know how I got it, and I'd still have to explain things and about half way through my story, they'd lock me in the loony bin or toss me in jail. Either way they'd throw away the key. I'd be outta luck and they'd keep the ring." Kacie leaned into the mirror and shook her injured finger at her reflection. "Kacie Miller, crazy, you may be. A fool, you are not." She gave herself a smile for her logical thinking and left the bathroom singing, "I think I'd better think it out again - Hey!" She reached a hand out behind her to wave the lights out.

Kacie yawned, completely drained. Grabbing a book off the coffee table in the living room she headed for bed, flipping the bathroom light off as she passed. Before sliding under the covers, Kacie sat on the edge of her bed and unclasped the necklace from around her neck and slipped the ring onto the chain and replaced them both around her neck. Fingering the ring one last time, she fluffed up her pillows and settled down for a little light reading.

Somewhere in the middle of the third page, she fell asleep.

****

Kacie stood before a massive set of double doors. A thin shaft of light struggled through the bleak winter's gray to puddle at her feet. A gust of wind swept past her thrusting open the huge doors. She shivered with more than the cold as she was drawn into the dark room by a force stronger than herself.

Twin flames burned in the ornate sconces on the far wall. Their flickering light cast eerie shadows across the gilded throne standing between them. Her footsteps echoed in the long, empty room as she advanced closer to the throne. When, at last, she stood before the forsaken throne, Reyna stepped from behind it. In her hands, she held a broadsword. The large ruby in the hilt winked its baleful eye at her. Reyna's sad voice rang hallow in the long hall. The Dragon is defiled by blood.

Kacie's gaze riveted to the banner hanging above the throne; a blood-red dragon, rampant reguardant, emblazoned on a white field. Horrified, she watched blood run from the creature's claws staining the white field of the banner a deep crimson before it spilled onto the golden throne tainting it with dark, sticky blood. Overhead, a raven screeched as his inky specter fell across the stained throne etching its likeness into the brown-red stain.

"Only the Emerald Sorceress can cleanse this infamy and restore the Dragon to his rightful place." Reyna's blazing emerald eyes locked onto Kacie compelling her forward. "Take the sword."

Kacie did as she was bid. She lifted the sword from Reyna's outstretched palms and felt raw power course through her body and flood into the sword causing it to pulse with Emerald fire. Kacie turned to her right and held out her hand. From within the darkness it was clasped by a warm answering hand. Between the shadows Kacie glimpsed a tall, lean figure clad in a loose white shirt, coarse, home spun pants and sturdy boots that rose to muscular thighs. She looked down at the strong, callused fingers clasped in hers and smiled. "It's time," she said, drawing him from obscurity.

He nodded once sending his sun-streaked hair flowing about his broad shoulders. Kacie led him up the dais steps to his rightful place. As he sat, he reached for the Dragon Sword and when his hand encased the jeweled hilt a blinding flash of white light erupted bathing the throne room in its cleansing radiance. Kacie shaded her eyes and stared around her in disbelief. The golden throne of Medora once again gleamed untainted and the rampant Dragon shimmered a pure white on its crimson field.

"The crimson is a reminder of the Dragon blood that was spilled on Medoran soil." Reyna answered Kacie's unspoken query.

Kacie nodded understanding and took her place behind the throne at the right hand of the Dragon King.

****

Once again the alarm dragged Kacie back to welcome reality. The radio continued to blare at her as she crawled out of bed and into the bathroom. "I feel like moose pooh. I don't look so great either." She snorted at her reflection and blinked hard several times trying to force moisture into her bloodshot eyes.

With one last look and a groan, Kacie retraced her steps into the bedroom. Shedding her LA Kings nightshirt she stuffed her head and arms through a white T-shirt, covering it with a black vest and then pulled baggy black shorts over black tights. A leather pouch slid onto the belt at her waist. There was no way she'd go into work without her brown contacts in, but her eyes bothered her enough that she slipped her contact case and a travel size bottle of solution and eye drops into her pouch. If worse came to worse, she could hide at lunch and give her eyes a rest.

As usual, Kacie went straight to the dragon mirror when she got to work. "Gueran, this is getting out of hand." She told the dragon. "My dreams are taking over my life. Waking or sleeping all I can think about is this crazy stuff with wizards and witches and swords. I can't take it any more. I'm exhausted." Kacie dropped her head onto the dragon's head trying to draw comfort from the warm wood under her skin. "But, I did get a great ring out of the deal. Although, I really don't want to think about how I got it." She pulled the ring from beneath her shirt and held it out for the dragon to see. "Wow, would you look at that." Kacie took a closer look at the etching in the stone. "Gueran, the sword in this ring is just like yours! How weird is that?"

Before she could contemplate her discovery further Mr. Weatherby popped his head around the door. "Kacie, Loren is looking for you."

Kacie let the ring drop to her chest and turned with a smile. "I'm on my way," she said and slipped past him.

****

Mr. Weatherby looked from the girl to the mirror she had formed such an attachment to. A puzzled furrow creased his brows when he saw the swirling clouds within the mirror. As he watched, the mist slowly dissipated, returning the mirror's surface to its normally clear state. "What do you know that I don't, my friend?" he asked the dragon.

****

Late that afternoon, Kacie was back in the crystal room sorting a new shipment of crystals when Jon invaded her sanctuary.

"Hey, Miller, Loren says ....What happened to your eyes?"

"Oh, for the love of...." Kacie looked away, trying to resist the urge to scream as she silently pleaded for patience. "What is the big deal about my eyes?"

Jon took her by the shoulders and turned her around to face the mirror. "I hate to break it to you, but you've got one brown eye and one very green eye."

Kacie stared into the mirror. "Oh, no. I've lost a contact." She covered her green eye and turned on Jon. "Don't just stand there. Help me find it."

Mr. Weatherby found them on their hands and knees. "Do I dare ask what you two children are doing?"

"Kacie lost a contact." Jon mumbled, not looking up.

"Oh dear." Mr. Weatherby dropped down to join the search and crawled over to Kacie. "Can you see without it?" he asked, searching the carpet with fingers as well as eyes.

Kacie nodded. "Yeah, I just wear them for looks."

"Eureka!" Mr. Weatherby proudly held up his find and froze as he stared wide-eyed at the pendant that had worked its way out of her T-shirt as she crawled around on the floor. "The Trion crest," he mouthed. "Where did you get . . ." He stopped mid-sentence and gaped at her. "You have green eyes. You have green eyes!"

Before Kacie knew what was happening, she was hauled to her feet. Gone was the laughing Fijian gnome. In his place, stood an ancient Merlin, with blazing gray eyes. Mr. Weatherby took her hand and started to pull her away, then stopped and turned on Jon. "You." He pointed to the boy. "Out. And I don't want to be disturbed."

While Mr. Weatherby's attention was on Jon, Kacie backed away from him, closer to the mirror. She froze when he looked her way again, her heart racing with fear, not knowing what to expect. But he only stared at her.

"You," he said. "All this time, searching. And you were here all along." He smiled and then began to laugh. "Right under my nose. Please Kacie; please take out your other contact. Let me see your eyes." He handed her the contact in his hand and started to laugh again, shaking his head. "Contacts. Who would have thought?"

Kacie was certain he had gone over the edge, but decided it would be better to humor him until help came. Her hands shook as she removed her other contact and placed them both in their case. Trying to give herself time to think, she made a show of returning the case to her pouch and zipping the top flap closed. She fumbled with the snap and Mr. Weatherby took a hold of her hand ceasing her nervous movements. Kacie jumped at the touch.

"You don't need to be afraid, Child. I won't hurt you." he reassured her.

Oh sure. That's what they all say just before they break out the chain saw or ice pick.

Mr. Weatherby was staring intently into her emerald eyes. "I've been searching for you for the last twenty-two years."

"Uh – huh."

He dropped her hand and turned to look into the mirror, lightly stroking the dragon's head. "You don't understand."

"No kidding."

He ignored her. "How could you? Kacie," He turned back to her so fast she yelped. "I'm going to tell you a story."

"A story? Ah, Mr. W . . ."

"No, no, it's all right," Mr. Weatherby tried to soothe her, but then he got a good look at the ring hanging behind the golden crest around her neck. "Where did you get that?" he demanded.

"What?"

"That ring. Where did you get it?"

"Yesterday, that woman I told you about," Kacie stammered, "She gave it to me just before she died."

"Let me see it."

Reluctantly, Kacie removed the chain and placed it into his outstretched hand.

Mr. Weatherby examined the ring. "The Emerald seal," he said, searching her face. "The Emerald Sorceress was here? You said the woman was looking for a book," he reproached her.

"I couldn't tell you the truth. You'd think I was crazy." *Like it matters a whole lot now.*

Mr. Weatherby waved that aside. "What did she say to you?"

"I-I don't know."

He gently shook her. "Think, Kacie. This is important. What did she

28

say to you?"

"S-she said I-I was the Emerald Sorceress now. She didn't like my eyes either." Kacie had no idea why she added that. But, Mr. Weatherby laughed.

"No, she wouldn't." He took a deep breath and let it out slowly. "So, Reyna is gone now. And a new Emerald Sorceress stands, not quite ready to take her place." He stared into the dark emerald stone before shaking himself out of his thoughts. "Poor Kacie. I've scared you half to death, haven't I?"

"Just a little."

"Let me try to explain."

"That would be nice."

Mr. Weatherby sat cross-legged beside the mirror, and patted the carpet next to him. With her heart still racing, Kacie looked longingly at the door. This was her chance to escape.

"Don't you want to know about your dreams?"

Her head snapped back to him. "What do you know about my dreams?"

"I know a lot of things."

"Right." Kacie took a step away.

The Emerald Sorceress and the Raven Wizard? A woman running in a storm? A prince in obscurity?"

"How did you...."

He patted the carpet again. This time, she reluctantly sat. "They are images of another place and time sifted through the dragon mirror you love so much. The mirror was designed to recognize you and release these images within your subconscious when the time was right."

"Right." *I should have gotten outta here while I had the chance.*

"We," he pointed at the two of them, "come from a place called Medora. I was sent here to prepare you for your return, only things didn't go as planned and I've been searching for you ever since."

"I was born right here in Santa Monica."

"Yes, you were born here, but you belong to Medora. Knowing that the child her niece carried would be the next Emerald Sorceress, Reyna sent your mother, Maya to this world where she could bear you and raise you protected from the Raven Wizard and his evil. But as I said, things didn't go as planned. Before I could be sent to help Maya,

THE EMERALD SORCERESS

Jozef captured Reyna and without the Emerald Sorceress to guide me I had no way to locate you or your mother. So, I took a deep breath and with the Dragon mirror in tow, stepped through the mirror in the Emerald Palace, hoping that your pull as the next Emerald Sorceress would land us close enough to you that you would be easy to find. Neither Reyna or I dreamed this world was so big." he laughed at their naiveté. "For twenty-two years I've searched for you. And now you're here. Reyna is gone and you are the Emerald Sorceress. It is time for you to return and fulfill your destiny. In your hands alone the future of Medora rests." He held the emerald ring out to her.

Kacie stared at him and then at the ring for a long moment. "This is way too much. I'm outta here." *I've heard some BS stories before, but this one....* Kacie snatched the chain and jumped to her feet, holding the necklace away from him and closer to the mirror.

"Kacie! No!" He reached for her and she jumped back.

The mirror flashed. She was gone.

Mr. Weatherby dropped his head into his hands. "No. She isn't ready," he whispered. "May the power protect you, Child."

CHAPTER THREE

Kacie's senses returned in a nauseating rush. The world spun at dizzying speeds, tilting sharply, trying to slide her off into the black void of nothingness. Desperately clinging to the edges, she fought to remain conscious. She swallowed hard and squeezed her eyes shut tight, willing her churning stomach to settle. She had no idea what just happened to her, but whatever it was sure packed a wallop. Through the spinning, Kacie tried to coax tenuous memories to the surface, but the gates of memory were being guarded by a mallet wielding gargoyle only too happy to defend his territory on the inside of her skull. Kacie groaned inwardly. *Never mind, I think I'm just gonna lie here and concentrate on not being sick.*

Gradually the world began to right itself and the whirling slowed. She became aware of rough hands roaming her body poking and prodding. Her temper flared and she tried to defend herself, but for some reason, she couldn't find her hands. She knew they were attached to her arms, but those errant limbs seemed to have gone missing as well. The only thing Kacie felt was the continuous churning of her stomach and the rocky ground beneath her. Little by little the roaring in her ears was replaced by the sound of fuzzy voices above her. She concentrated on them, willing the gargoyle to stop his infernal pounding.

"Nothing worth anything. Just this stuff," A female voice said, giving Kacie a final nudge with her foot. Kacie didn't have the courage to open her eyes, so she imagined the woman going through the pouch at her belt and coming up with her contact case and the two small plastic bottles of solution and eye drops trying to determine their worth.

"Put them back, Tia," A light baritone male voice said.

The girl grunted with disgust and stuffed everything back into the pouch. "We could always sell her to the slavers. At least she'd be worth something then." She gave Kacie another small kick.

Slavers? SLAVERS?! Where am I?

31

"Maybe we should bring her with us," the man said.

"Are you crazy, Derian?" Tia interrupted. "Look at her. She's obviously drunk and a whore. Who else would go around dressed like that? If we take her back to the Boar's Head they'll charge us for her room. Who's gonna pay? She doesn't have any money, do you?"

Whore? This was getting worse by the second.

"She looks like she needs help, Tia. Maybe she's hurt."

Way to go, Derian.

"She's not hurt, Derian. She...."

"Enough." A second, velvety male voice spoke up. "She probably is drunk, and we can't very well take her with us, Derian. You know that. We'll have to leave her here. She'll sober up soon enough, and go home on her own."

"I don't believe you two." There was Derian again, and he sounded ticked. Kacie would have smiled as she mentally urged him on, but she suddenly realized she couldn't find her lips, either. Besides, Derian was on a roll.

"You're all heart, Kerric," Derian continued, "the least we can do is move her out of the middle of the alley so she doesn't get trampled to death before she comes to."

My hero. Kacie tried to say thanks a lot, but all that came out was a moan. And that made her head throb. She couldn't just lie there; they'd kill her. Or worse. She had to try again. "Om nm drm" *Crimony, that hurt. Maybe I won't try after all. They can leave me right here. That'll be just fine, thank you very much.*

She wanted to let go and slide into the void, but the soft, warm voice called Kerric was talking to her, making her hold onto painful consciousness. "What did you say?" He tapped her cheeks.

Kacie managed to locate her hands and pushed at him. "I'm not drunk," she croaked, then groaned and clutched her head.

"Are you hurt?"

"I'm gonna be sick." Kacie rolled onto her side, wishing she could die and get it over with.

Too sick to be embarrassed, Kacie was grateful for the comforting hand Kerric placed on her shoulder: until he pushed her over. His strong grip kept her from going face first in the dirt – and worse, but he clearly was more interested in something that was lying under her than he was her welfare. In between spasms, she felt his other hand working whatever it was from beneath her.

"What the...." he said, and through her misery, Kacie pictured him examining his find. If she wasn't otherwise engaged, she might have been curious.

At last, the heaving stopped and Kerric eased her on her back and felt her head for injuries.

"Oh great. What are you doing Kerric?"

"Be quiet, Tia." he said. "I don't feel anything. Are you hurt?" he repeated his earlier question.

"Where am I?" Kacie whispered, opening her eyes for the first time.

Kerric caught his breath and rocked back on his heels. Without taking his eyes from hers, he stood. "We're taking her with us." He pulled Kacie to her feet.

That was too much. Her head exploded in a burst of pain and she mercifully fainted.

****

King Jozef of Medora sat on the gem studded throne of state, bored beyond endurance. He shifted to a more comfortable position, propping his chin on a bejeweled fist. Before him, yet another ambassador droned on about the numerous virtues of an alliance between his pitiful monarch and the mighty state of Medora.

Jozef sighed and glanced up at the blue and gold stained glass window to his right. He sighed again, wishing he could be outside doing anything except sitting there listening to fools. He studied the dust particles as they danced in the blue light spilling from the window to the polished marble floor, squinting his eyes he followed the pirouette of one tiny speck. Suddenly the blue light changed to a deep emerald green. Jozef started, then blinked, but the light was blue once again.

"Your Majesty?" The secretary at his elbow laid a trembling hand on the King's shoulder."Sire?" the man tried again.

The King came back to the present with a rapid blinking of eyes that had been staring too long. He turned his head and raised an eyebrow at the hand on his robe. It was snatched away.

"A thousand pardons, Majesty." The secretary bowed low. "You were…." He hesitated at the lazy smile touching the King's thin lips.

"We were…. what?" Jozef challenged, holding the old man's frightened gaze. It amused him to watch the bobbing adam's apple as the secretary tried to find a diplomatic way to accuse the King of daydreaming. But, before the hapless man could say a word, Jozef's attention was once again diverted. This time the diversion was internal. The tips of his fingers began to tingle. The sensation traveled up his arms and the hairs on the back of his neck stood on end. Soon, Jozef's whole body was tingling.

The girl was back in Medora.

A serge of excitement coursed through Jozef. A feral grin flashed and died. He stood and descended the dais steps, brushing past the astounded ambassador as if he wasn't there. The bewildered secretary skipped at the King's heels, jabbering about duties and a full day's agenda. Jozef ignored him and continued across the room.

As the King reached the great wooden doors, the secretary, his round breast heaving from the effort to keep up, completely forgot himself and grabbed Jozef's arm. "Sire, I must protest."

There was a collective gasp from the crowded room at the man's temerity. Jozef stopped in his tracks and turned to the red faced official. The flash of steel in the pale blue eyes belied the smile and softly spoken words. "Lay a hand on our person again and we will have you executed." He turned and swept out of the hall.

The chaos that erupted behind him would have delighted Jozef if he had not been preoccupied. The girl was back. She escaped his attack a few days ago, but now she was back and he would have her.

Jozef strode through the corridors of the palace, waving off those that made to join him. As he reached his own apartments the two guards lounging before the doors snapped to attention. He ignored them, closing the doors behind him, and then yanked them open again a heartbeat later. "No one is to be admitted. Is that understood?" Jozef turned on his heel and re-entered the apartments, leaving the guards to close the doors.

Hurrying through the series of rooms that preceded his bedchamber, Jozef stopped before the life size portrait of his father, Gueran and gave the regal image a habitual mocking bow of his head.

Ice blue eyes stared into the older, softer gray ones. "Well, Father, things look to become interesting again." Jozef touched the ring on his left index finger to the identical image on his father's hand. The painting slid sideways to reveal a hidden stairwell leading to a tower room.

At the top of the stairs, a raven was carved into a heavy oak door, wings spread, ready to strike. Jozef touched his ring to one ruby eye. There was a soft click and he pushed the door open and entered his private sanctuary. Ignoring the books lining the rounded walls and the shelves cluttered with potions and powders used in his magic, Jozef went to the far side of the room and stopped beside a marble bowl perched atop a matching pedestal. He placed his hands on either side of the bowl and took a deep, calming breath. Relaxing the muscles of his neck and shoulders, he passed an open palm over the bowl. The clear water began to swirl and cloud.

Jozef stared into the cloudy water, waiting for it to clear. He spoke an impatient incantation and the water stilled and became inky. From the depths, a vision of Reyna rose to the surface, floating on a funeral pyre. Her rose-gold hair spilled over a blanket of fresh flowers that covered her lifeless body. The pyre burst into flame engulfing the sorceress. Jozef threw back his head and gave a short bark of triumphant laughter as the vision sank once again into the blackness.

Show me the girl." His cold eyes glittered as he peered into the scrying bowl. Long moments passed and still nothing appeared within the murky depths. Annoyed, Jozef took a leather pouch off a shelf beside him and sprinkled a pinch of powder into the water.

Show me the girl," he commanded again. A billow of blue smoke exploded into the air. When the haze cleared, instead of being a window, the water turned a deep emerald green showing him nothing.

Jozef swore. The girl was being protected. "Not for long," he promised. "Not for long. You're in my world now, my little sorceress. Reyna is dead. She can't protect you any longer. Soon I'll have you."

****

When Kacie opened her eyes again, it was dark and she was in a bed. Not a very comfortable one, but still, it beat the hard ground. Sounds of laughter and colorful cursing drifted up to her from below to pierce the blackness of her room. She wrinkled her nose at the smell of stale beer and sneezed as she got a good whiff of cheap cigar smoke.

35

"This must be the famous Boar's Head," she said, then realized her head wasn't throbbing. Cautiously, Kacie moved it from side to side, and smiled. The dizziness was gone too. "Cool." She grinned in the darkness.

What she did feel, though, was a very real need for a bathroom.

"Okay, Kacie, girl, here's the real test," she warned herself before swinging her legs over the side of the bed. When the world didn't tilt, she stood. "Very good. Now all I have to do is find the bathroom. Of course, I have to find the door first."

She made a tight circle where she stood, looking for –Ah hah! There it was, to her right a sliver of light ran along the floor. "The door!" she laughed.

Kacie yanked it open and was accosted by faded red and gold flocked wallpaper. "Aaaakk!" She threw her arm up to shield her eyes. "Who decorated this place?" An ornate mirror hanging on the wall across from her caught her attention. She crossed to it, and had to wipe away several layers of oily grime before she could see herself in its faded surface. "Crimeny!" Making a cross with her index fingers, Kacie shrank back from her own reflection. No wonder they wanted to leave me where they found me. She made a face at herself as she finger-combed the worst of the tangles out of her hair and threw it in a rough braid in a vain attempt to make herself more presentable. She couldn't do anything about the dark circles around her eyes, but those brilliant green eyes - the source of all her troubles – had to go.

Kacie reached to her belt pouch and pulled out her contact case and the bottle of solution. "How about that? They left my things where they found them. Amazing." She shook her head and put a couple drops of solution into each plastic well moisturizing the tiny lenses, then popped in her contacts and smiled at her brown-eyed reflection. "Much better." She turned and made her way down the dimly lit corridor.

Who in their right mind would put smoking oil lamps in a hotel? I'm surprised the fire department hasn't closed this place down. She shook her head at the flagrant safety violations.

Kacie reached the narrow wooden stairs, just as a tall man climbed the last step. She stared up into laughing brown eyes and a wide, lopsided grin. "Well, if it isn't our mystery lady out for an evening stroll. Feeling better?"

Kacie identified Derian's light baritone voice. *So that's what he looks like.* "Much better, thank you." She looked him up and down, from his tall, slender build, to his curly brown hair and angular, friendly face. *Cute.* She smiled up at him and tried to slip past.

"Whoa." Derian grabbed her arm. "Where are you going?"

"I'm looking for the bathroom."

"The what?"

"The bathroom." Kacie bobbed up and down a little. "You know, nature calls."

"Oh." Derian nodded understanding. "You mean the outhouse."

"Yeah, the outhouse." *Outhouse?* "This place doesn't have indoor plumbing? Never mind. Just show me where the - outhouse is."

"It's out back." Kacie tried to push past him, but Derian took a firmer hold on her arm. "You can't go down there like that."

"Like what?"

"Like that." He indicated her clothing. "Undressed." He grinned and raised an eyebrow. "It isn't decent."

"Undressed?" Kacie looked down at the black vest covering her dirty white T-shirt, her shorts, torn black tights and scuffed bright green Doc Martin's. "What do you mean, undressed? I'm dressed. I'm a little worse for wear, but I'm dressed."

Just then a young woman made her way up the stairs. She was wearing a long, faded brown skirt and a tight fitting bodice over a burnt orange shirt. Giving Derian a seductive smile, the girl pushed her billowy sleeves above her elbows and Kacie stared open mouthed when the girl winked at Derian as she squeezed between them.

Derian grinned and trailed a long finger down the girl's cheek then placed a light kiss on her up-turned lips. "Later," he promised. The girl pouted, looking from Derian to Kacie then shrugged and sauntered on down the hall.

Kacie rolled her eyes . *I've died and gone to Ren Faire hell. Please tell me this is a movie set.* She took a good look around her; at Derian's course spun cotton pants and shirt, and his knee-high boots. She noticed the stag horn knife thrust in his waistband and the sword swinging at his side. This time, she really saw the smoking lamps in their wall sconces. It was like something out of a romance novel.

Kacie's stomach twisted and she slumped against the wall. "I don't think we're in Kansas any more, Toto," she whispered.

"Excuse me?" Derian was clearly confused.

Well, that made two of them. Kacie pushed away the sick feeling in her gut. "Never mind. Just show me where your outhouse is." She yanked her arm free and started down the stairs, only to find her path blocked – again.

Derian stepped around her cutting off her escape.

Kacie's wanted to scream. Instead, she took a deep breath and surprised herself by holding onto her patience. "I really need to use the bathroom or outhouse or whatever. Okay?"

Derian laughed. "As charming as you look in your state of undress." His roaming eyes were frankly appreciative. "You'd never make it past the tap room."

Now, Kacie knew she was going to scream. "Look, I don't have anything else to wear and I have to go. Now."

Derian thought a minute. "I know." He snapped his fingers.

"My eyes are turning yellow, here...."

He took her by the arm and dragged her, protesting, all the way back to the room. Ignoring her comments about his parental heritage, Derian scooped up a cloak from the room's only chair and draped it around her shoulders, covering her from neck to floor. In a grand gesture, he extended his arm. "Shall we?"

Kacie glared at him. She wadded the cape up around her knees and raced down the stairs with Derian following behind her, laughing at his great joke. At the bottom, he turned her in the right direction, calling over his shoulder, to someone she couldn't see. "She needs some clothes."

A small, slender girl about her own age, sprawled in the rickety chair beside the bed when Kacie was returned to the room. She was examining the end of her long auburn braid. The girl glanced up when they entered and looked Kacie up and down before she pointedly looked away. "I found her some pants and a shirt." She told Derian, waving a negligent hand at the pile of clothes on the bed, ignoring Kacie.

My, aren't we friendly.

"I had to steal something off someone's line. I knew my things would be much too small for her."

"Thank you, Tia," Derian began.

"I'm sure they'll be fine." Kacie cut him off, pulling Tia's attention to her and smiled sweetly. "Thank you. I know how much trouble it must have been for you to find these for me. I appreciate it. Really."

Tia made a sound in the back of her throat and rose, heading for the door. "I'll be in the tap room."

"Get dressed and meet us downstairs." Derian swept her a deep bow. His expression was sober, but Kacie didn't miss the gleam of mischief dancing in his eyes.

Pig.

As soon as Derian shut the door, Kacie went to the small mirror on the wall opposite the foot of the bed and inspected herself again. *Okay, so my braid isn't waist length or titan red. It's still a pretty cool jet black. It's thicker than hers too.*

"Oh, that's pathetic, Miller." She turned her back on her reflection, giving her attention to the clothes on the bed.

With a resigned sigh, Kacie pulled the plain brown pants over her shorts, securing them with her belt and was surprised to find how well they fit. Tia might be a snob, but she had a good eye. She took off her vest and slipped the course, billowy shirt over her head, tucking it into the pants, then pulled her vest back on. Kacie held out her arms and watched the huge sleeves swing back and forth. "I look like Tyrone Power."She looked down at her feet. "Except for the Doc. Martins." She twisted an ankle back and forth, admiring her clunky footwear and for some reason, that struck her as very funny.

Before long, the laughter turned to tears and she sank to the bed. Burying her face in the covers, Kacie sobbed. What was happening to her? Where was she and how did she get here? The questions chased themselves round and round until she gave herself a mental shake and sat up. "Get a grip, Miller. Feeling sorry for yourself won't get you anywhere." She sniffed and wiped her eyes. "But, I tell you what; if this is another dream, now would be a great time to wake up." Kacie searched the room for hidden signs of reassurance and found none. She sighed. "Well, who knows, maybe someone in my trio of saviors will have some answers." She snorted at that unlikelihood and waved the lamp out as she left the room.

Kacie stuck her head back into the totally dark room. "Wow, it worked." She grinned.

****

"Kerric, you've had some wild ideas before." Derian shook his head. "But this is crazy."

"Look at her eyes, Derian. She has to be The Emerald Sorceress. No one else has eyes like that." Kerric flipped his shoulder length, sandy brown hair back in a gesture of annoyance. This debate was getting old.

"Like what? I've seen her eyes, Kerric. There's nothing special about them," Derian insisted.

Kerric opened his mouth to argue, but Tia leaned across the table and laid a hand on his arm. "Why would the Emerald Sorceress be laying drunk and half naked in an alley in Alorn, three hundred miles from Kiramer and the Emerald Palace? Besides, everybody knows King Jozef has the Emerald Sorceress locked up in Desar Castle under one of his spells. And, even if she did escape somehow, this girl can't be the Emerald Sorceress, she's too young."

Kerric jerked his arm away, his hazel eyes snapping and pulled something from his boot. He carefully laid it on the table. "How do you explain this?" He sat back and ran a long fingered hand through his hair. A satisfied smile touched the corners of his wide mouth as both of them stared bug eyed at the emerald ring rocking gently in front of them. "She had this too." He tossed the phoenix crest next to the ring.

"Where did those come from?" Derian asked in a hushed voice.

"They were lying under her."

"That doesn't mean anything, "Tia said, her cobalt eyes glued to the ring. "She probably stole them." She shrugged. "The girl's a thief as well as a whore." Tia reached a hand toward the ring, and looked up sharply as it was snatched away before she could touch it.

Kacie stood there, ring in hand, glaring at them. "Where did you get this?" She pinned each of them with a cold stare, as she reached down, picked up her necklace. Sliding the ring back on the chain, she hung it around her neck and tucked it inside her shirt away from prying eyes.

When no one answered, Kacie swiveled to Tia, and in a voice dripping with icicles, said, "Never call me a whore again."

Tia gave her a contemptuous laugh and looked around Kacie to Derian. "Did you get your horse shod today, Derian?"

Derian looked between the two girls and Tia tapped his arm, claiming his attention. "Yes, this morning," he answered.

Kacie flushed at the insult. She was so furious she couldn't speak. *I would kill to see that little witch fall flat on her butt.* Smiling a tiny smile, she pictured the legs of Tia's chair braking.

A loud crash, followed by an even louder string of oaths, startled Kacie into opening the eyes she wasn't aware of closing. Her hand flew to her mouth, almost in time to stifle the burst of laughter that escaped. Before her, Tia sat on the floor amidst a pile of kindling that was her chair a moment ago. She was dripping with ale and the barmaid stood over her, hands on hips, looking disgusted at the mess she'd have to clean up.

"Oh dear, how did that happen?" Kacie asked. Tia glared at her and Kacie bit the insides of her cheeks to keep from grinning.

The man sitting beside her rose. "If I'm not mistaken, you did that," he said in the soft velvety tones she recognized as Kerric's.

Kacie whirled on him. "Me?" she squeaked. "Are you crazy? I couldn't do that. No way. I was thinking about it, but...." Her voice trailed away.

Kerric took her by the arm. "Come on." He led her out of the room.

Kacie followed in silence as he herded her back upstairs to the room. She waved on the light, and jumped when the lamp sprang to life, producing a soft glow. Kacie sank onto the bed and picked at the hem of her vest, a frown of confusion on her brow.

Kerric leaned against the wall, his arms folded across his muscular chest, and watched her. "So, my Lady Emerald, would you care to tell me what you're doing here?"

"What?" Kacie looked up, bewildered

"What are you doing in Alorn, Lady Emerald?"

"My name is Kacie," she corrected. "Where did you say I was?"

Kerric pushed his lean frame away from the wall and crossed the room to sit in the chair next to her. "You don't have to pretend. I know who you are, my Lady. If you're in some kind of trouble maybe I can help."

41

"Trouble? Hah! I'm not in any trouble. I'm in Oz. I just melted the wicked witch of the west, and you're the bleedin' Tin Man! Oh nooooo, I'm not in trouble."

She peered into his light hazel eyes and plunged into her story. "Look, my name is Kacie Miller. I'm from Santa Monica, California and I work for Mr. Weatherby at a bookstore called The Dreaming Tree. Mr. W. owns this great dragon mirror. Anyway, some old lady came into the store the other day and gave me this ring." Kacie fished it out from under her shirt and held it up for him to see. "Then, right before my eyes, she slid to the floor and died. And if that wasn't bad enough, she vanished into thin air. Poof." Kacie threw up her hands. "She was a figment before anybody else saw her. Let me tell you, I went bazonkers and everybody thought I'd lost my mind. Then, to make matters worse, Mr. W. sees the ring and my pendent and freaks. I panic, fall into the mirror, get knocked out and wind up here. Only I don't have a clue where here is. The only thing I do know is; that witch downstairs hates me, and things that shouldn't work do."

She drew in a deep breath and let it out in a long sigh. "And I really want to wake up now." She dropped her head into her hands and groaned. "That was the most ridiculous story I ever heard," she mumbled to no one in particular.

Kerric chuckled. "That is quite a story." Kacie's head snapped up. "Be easy. I'm not mocking you, but you must admit it does sound a bit.... unusual." He stretched across the short distance separating them and took her chin in his hand and turned her head from side to side. "What happened to your eyes?"

Not here too. "What's wrong with my eyes?" Kacie jerked her head from his grasp. "Everybody has a problem with my eyes." She slid to the floor at the far end of the bed, out of his reach.

Kerric's eyes narrowed. "They're brown."

"Yeah, and?"

"They were green when we found you."

"Were they?"

They stared at each other.

"All right, if you're not the Emerald Sorceress, how did you come by the Emerald signet?"

"The what?"

Kerric sighed. "The ring."

"I told you, a lady gave it to me. Then she died, and poof," Kacie waved her hands again. "She vanished into thin air. Weren't you listening to me?"

"Did she tell you her name? Did she say anything to you?"

"I don't remember." *Good grief. Relax, Torquemada, the Inquisition ended five hundred years ago.*

Kerric looked at her for a long, unblinking moment then let out another sigh and rose. Scrubbing at his face and neck, he paced the small room before he came back and dropped to his haunches in front of Kacie. Capturing both of her hands in his, he began again. "She must have said something to you when she gave you the ring. Think." He gently shook her. "This is important."

Deja vu. Where have I played this scene before?

Kacie leaned her head back and closed her eyes, she was trying to get another headache, and the way her luck was running, this place wouldn't have aspirin. Then, she gave a soft chuckle.

"What?" Kerric shook her back to the present.

"She didn't like my contacts, either. Come to think about it, nobody's liked my contacts lately."

It was obvious he had no idea what she was talking about. "What else?"

"Well, she said I had a lot to learn and she was sorry she wouldn't be around to teach me."

"Is that all?" Irritation tinged his tone.

"No." Kacie dropped her eyes and watched her hands finger the hem of her vest a second before she looked up at Kerric again. "She also told me that I was the Emerald now."

Kerric stared at her bland expression. "I knew it." He stood and looked down at her, his cheek dimpling as the corner of his mouth raised in a half smile. "I knew you had to be the Emerald."

"Okay, I'll bite. What's an emerald - besides a green rock?"

"Not what - who. The Emerald Sorceress is Medora's most revered mage. She is the keeper of Medoran knowledge and protector of the Dragon Throne."

"Yep, that's me all right." Kacie stood and moved closer to him. "I hate to rain on your parade, Kerric." She looked up into his open, square face with the light stubble on his strong chin and the tiny dimples in his cheeks. *Nice.* She swallowed hard before continuing. "I am no sorceress, wise person, protector, whatever. I'm just Kacie, lost in Oz. And like Dorothy, I wanna go home. So, if you don't have any ruby slippers, take me to the wizard."

"NO!" Kerric yelled and grabbed her by the arms, scaring her half to death. "You must never go to him. The Raven Wizard is evil."

Whoa, easy Kerric." She pushed him away from her. "It was a joke."

"Emerald...." he began

"Kacie," she corrected

"The wizard, Jozef is no joking matter."

"From where I stand, it's all a joke. A sick one, but still...." she shrugged. "I want to go home. Can you help me? If not, take me to someone who can."

"The Emerald Palace."

"The what?" *I know I'm gonna be sorry I asked.*

"We have to go to the Emerald Palace.

"Of course we do. It's in the Emerald City, right?"

"No. It's in Kiramer. So, I suggest you get a good night's sleep. It's a long journey and we'll start early tomorrow."

"Wonderful." Kacie said to the room at large, when Kerric had gone. She stretched out on the lumpy bed and folded her arms behind her head. "I know I always said I wanted to travel and have a good adventure, but this is ridiculous." She yawned, suddenly exhausted.

****

Kerric found Derian and Tia in the common room where he left them. He snagged a tankard of ale from the tray of a passing serving girl and flipped a coin onto the tray. The woman frowned at the theft then smiled at the small silver piece resting next to her hand. With a nod, Kerric took a long pull off the ale and threaded his way across the crowded room.

"We leave for Kiramer before first light," Kerric announced, hooking a chair from a neighboring table with a foot and dragging it over so he could sit.

"Kiramer?" Derian and Tia chorused.

"What the devil are we going to do in Kiramer?" Tia demanded

"What about Duke Raefield and your position as sword master to his court?" Derian asked.

"What about the money he was going to pay us?" Tia wanted to know.

Kerric sipped his ale until their questions stopped. "We have to take the girl to the Emerald Palace," he said, and waited for the next storm to erupt.

Tia's mouth dropped open. Derian reached out and pushed her chin up, closing it for her. She swatted his hand away. "Have you lost your mind, Kerric?"

"Maybe." Kerric nodded once. "But, that doesn't change anything. This girl is the Emerald Sorceress. I don't know how or why, but she is."

"Didn't we have this conversation earlier?" Tia asked Derian

Derian nodded. "Kerric, the girl has brown eyes."

Kerric sighed and ran a hand through his hair then leaned forward and rested his arms on the table. "When she opened her eyes in the alley today they were a clear emerald green. I have no idea how she changed them to brown tonight."

"That's easy." Tia threw a casual arm over the back of her chair and slumped sideways in a more comfortable position. "Her eyes always were brown. They only reflected green in the sunlight."

"Brown eyes don't reflect emerald green, Tia. Besides, the girl said she was with Reyna when she died. Reyna gave her the signet ring and told her she was now the Emerald Sorceress."

"The girl said this? And you believe her? Well, if she said so I guess it has to be true." She laughed outright, ignoring Kerric's growing anger. "If," Tia stressed the word. "If that girl was with the Emerald she probably murdered Reyna and stole the ring then concocted this ridiculous story. I can't believe you bought it, Kerric."

Kerric went very still while Tia spoke. Only the tick in his clenched jaw gave evidence to his tightly controlled anger. When he spoke, his voice was low and cold. "Do you honestly think she could have murdered the Emerald Sorceress, Tia?" Scorn dripped from his voice. He stared at her until she looked away from him and then his gaze swung to Derian for a long moment before he took a deep breath and began again.

"If this girl's story is true and Reyna is dead and she is the new Emerald Sorceress, she's obviously in some sort of trouble. And if she doesn't get help all of Medora will suffer more than it has already under Jozef's rule. That's a chance I can't afford to take. She could very well be our last hope." He ran both hands through his hair as he eyed each of them in turn. "I leave for Kiramer with the girl tomorrow. If the two of you think I'm wasting my time you're free to go on to Duke Raefield and take the jobs he offered you. I'll do this alone."

Stunned silence followed his words as Tia and Derian looked from each other back to Kerric's immobile face.

"Kerric, be reasonable." Tia began then stopped, unable to meet his hard hazel eyes. She dropped her gaze and drew patterns in the spilled ale on the table.

Derian cleared his throat and the cold stare turned to him. "I don't know that I agree with you on this, Kerric. Hear me out." He held up a hand and Kerric closed his mouth. "I don't know if I believe this girl is the Emerald Sorceress or not, but you obviously do. And if you feel this strongly about it that's good enough for me."

"You're both a couple of fools."

Kerric and Derian turned as one toward her. "Well Tia?" A crooked smile tugged at the corners of Derian's wide mouth. "Are you a fool with us?"

"The first paying job we get in six months that doesn't involve risking our hides and you two want to give it to give it up just like that." She snapped her fingers at them.

"You can still go ahead." Kerric told her.

"And leave you two village idiots to get yourselves killed over some murdering, thieving, whoring chit? Not a chance. Someone has to be around with a level head. Do you realize that if she is the Emerald Sorceress, and I'm not saying she is, but if she is Jozef will be hot on her trail – and ours? Do you really want to tangle with the Raven Wizard? Don't even think about the fact that the man is also the King of Medora."

"All the more reason to get the girl to the safety of the Emerald Palace as quickly as possible," Kerric said and drained his tankard.

"The Emerald Palace is sealed, Kerric. What if the girl can't get in?" Derian asked.

"We'll deal with that when the time comes."

"Unbelievable." Tia rose and strode away from the table and out of the Boar's Head, disappearing into the night.

Derian chuckled to himself and followed after her leaving Kerric alone with his thoughts.

CHAPTER FOUR

"Get up. We ride before day break."

Through the slits in her eyelids, Kacie saw Tia's hostile face hovering above her. She groaned and covered her head with the scratchy lump that passed for a pillow at The Boar's Head. "It wasn't a dream," she whined before flinging the smelly thing onto the floor and scowling around the dark room. "Have a heart, will ya? It's still dark out."

Tia snorted. "It's almost dawn."

"Like I said, it's the middle of the night."

Tia hovered above her, hands on her hips. "Just get up. Kerric won't wait."

"Ask me if I care," Kacie mumbled as Tia swept out of the room. "Hey! I don't know where the stables are!" She yelled at the closed door as she threw back the rough woolen blanket and slid out of bed.

Kacie waved a hand at the lamp on the table and jumped when it came on. "Hah! It worked!" She waved at it again, and the light went out. Another wave and it came on again. Kacie giggled. Delighted with her new talent, she regarded the small oil lamp with a tilt of her head. "You know, this tiny lamp really doesn't put out enough light for this room." She raised her hand a few inches. The light brightened. Kacie burst out laughing. The higher she raised her hand, the brighter the room became. She pushed it down and the room dimmed. "This is great!" Kacie danced around the room raising and lowering the light, while she sang, "If they could see me now, that little gang of mine."

"You were supposed to meet us at the stables." Kerric leaned against the doorway, arms folded across his chest as he watched her play.

Kacie jumped and whirled to face him and she knew he saw her scarlet cheeks before the light went out. They stood in the dark for several long moments.

"Could we have some light, please?"

"Sorry." Kacie wiggled her fingers and a tiny flame flickered in the lamp.

"A bit more."

Kacie gave him a sheepish grin and raised the light. "This is all new to me. I guess I got a little carried away."

Kerric gave a short bark of laughter. "A little? Every lamp in Alorn has been flickering on and off for the past half-hour."

"Oh dear." Kacie buried her face in her hands. "I'm sorry. I had no idea," she snickered. "This really is new to me. Can everybody do this here?"

"Let's go." He turned and headed down the hall. Kacie had to skip a few steps to catch up with him.

"Where exactly, are we going?" She flicked her fingers at a wall lamp as she passed, and grinned when the flame flared.

"Emerald...." Kerric gave her a warning glance.

"Kacie," she corrected.

Tia met them at the stable door and threw Kacie a contemptuous glare. "Everything's ready," she told Kerric, holding the door open for him to pass. "We've got provisions to last us a couple of weeks," she said, closing the door behind him.

Kacie stood outside, looking at the closed door. "I don't think she likes me."

The door swung open again just as Kacie reached for it. Kerric grabbed her shirtfront and propelled her inside. "Quit stalling. We're late as it is."

"Forgive me, I'm sure. But I didn't...." Kacie trailed off as Derian placed a set of reins in her hands. She looked along the reins to the biggest reddest horse she'd ever seen. "What am I supposed to do with this?"

"That's your horse." Derian said and swung himself into his own saddle.

"And?" Kacie realized they were all sitting on horses packed for a long trip. "You don't really expect me to ride this thing, do you? Why can't we just take a four-by, or something?"

"What's a four-by?" Derian asked

"You know, a Jeep, a truck, a car? Something with four wheels and an engine. You put gas in it, step on the pedal and VAROOM, off you go down the road...."

49

Derian just shook his head.

"No?" Kacie mirrored the movement. "I didn't think so."

"Just mount up so we can go," Tia broke in.

"Mount up?" Kacie looked from the huge animal to Tia, and Derian, and back to the horse, knowing she'd never be able to drag herself up that far. "How?" She looked around for something to stand on.

"I don't believe this." Tia jerked her horse's head around and urged him out of the stable. "I'll be on the road," she called over her shoulder.

Derian slid to the ground. "I'll take care of this." He told Kerric. "You go after Tia."

Kerric nodded and nudged his mount gently in the ribs and trotted after Tia. "Don't be long."

Derian leaned against her mount, stroking the animal's neck. "Kerric says you're the Emerald Sorceress. Are you?"

"Don't beat around the bush, Derian. Speak right up. Just say what's on your mind."

He studied her for a long moment and she could tell he was assessing what he saw against what he thought The Emerald Sorceress of Medora should be. "Kerric isn't usually wrong." He shook his head, clearly torn between loyalty to his friend and leader and his own doubts.

"Trust me, I'm not a sorceress. I'm just Kacie."

"We'll see." Derian pushed himself away from the horse's shoulder and bent forward, lacing his fingers together. "Okay, now step into my hands and I'll boost you up. Then swing your leg over and sit in the saddle.

Kacie's eyes narrowed and her lips pursed. "I'm not a total idiot. I know what a boost is."

"No one said you were." He jiggled his laced hands. "Shall we?"

Kacie glared at him as she stepped into his hands and he heaved her up. She swung her leg over with such force that she almost toppled off the other side. Only Derian's quick reactions steadied her in the saddle. "If you laugh, I'll hurt you."

"I wouldn't dream of it." He flashed her a lopsided grin, but his eyes were watering as he turned away and mounted his own horse.

"Don't worry; in a week you'll think you've done this all your life."

Kacie paled. *A week? How far are we going?* She decided she didn't have the courage to ask. Instead, she said, "How do you make it go?"

Derian cleared his throat, and Kacie swore his shoulders shook for a second before he answered. "Nudge her with your heels."

Kacie kicked the mare hard in the ribs and the startled animal bolted out of the stable at a dead run. Kacie let out a frightened squeal and squeezed her eyes shut. *I'm gonna die.*

Derian cursed and chased after her.

Kacie bounced uncontrollably, wildly kicking the galloping mare's sides. The creature responded with more speed. Derian cursed again and raced after the runaway pair heading straight for the forest.

"Help!" Kacie screamed. "Derian, how do you make this thing stop?" She pulled on the reins, but the animal only sprinted faster.

Ahead of her, Kerric turned in the saddle. His mouth dropped open and he spun his horse around. Racing from the outer edge of the forest, he cut across the open road to intercept the mare's flight. "What do you think you're doing?"

"Don't yell at me, just make it stop!"

Kerric circled around Kacie, pacing beside the frightened horse. "Let go of the reins," he ordered.

"I can't." Kacie turned wide, terrified eyes on him, pleading for help.

Kerric edged his stallion into the mare, turning her away from the trees, while he slowed his own speed, slowing the mare with him. Controlling the stallion with his knees, he reached over and pried the reins out of Kacie's vice-like grip. Once he had the lead, it was an easy matter to stop the horse.

As soon as she stopped, Kacie slid off the trembling animal onto legs turned to water. She sank to the ground and shook. Dashing the tears away with the back of her hand she saw Derian charging down on her and gulped.

"I said nudge her!" Derian shouted, skidding to a halt and dropping to the ground in one fluid movement. "Are you crazy, kicking her like that?" he grabbed Kacie's arms and shook her. "You could have been killed." He folded her into a fierce hug. Then he was shaking her again. "Don't ever scare me like that again," he said, hugging her once more.

In spite of her fright, Kacie began to laugh and color returned to her pale cheeks.

Kerric watched from above, an amused smile twitching at his mouth. "Give Derian a lady in trouble," he snorted. "All right, the danger's over. Get back on your horses and let's go."

Kacie pulled away from Derian. "Not on your life. I am not getting back on that thing ever again."

Derian stood and stretched down a hand to help her up. She ignored it. "You have to," he urged rather than ordered.

Kacie crossed her arms and folded her legs. "No." She looked between them daring either of them to do something about it.

Derian raised an eyebrow at Kerric.

"Throw her across here." Kerric indicated the space between himself and the packs behind him.

Derian grinned and lifted Kacie easily into his arms, perfectly willing to comply.

"Okay, Okay, I'll ride. I'm not happy about it, but I guess I don't have much choice." She threw Kerric a dirty look. "Bully."

"Good girl." Derian switched directions and settled her into her own saddle.

Kerric leaned over and took her reins. "Don't sulk." He clicked his tongue and they calmly walked back to the impatiently waiting, Tia.

"I can steer my own horse."

Kerric gave Kacie a look that left no doubt in her mind what he thought about that, as he led them into the forest.

On and on they rode. Day in and day out, they rode. Weeks past, and still they rode. Kacie began to shiver. She looked up at what could be seen of the gray sky through the trees and a drop of rain landed in her eye. *Of course.* She blinked, wiping the moisture away and grumbling to herself. *What's one more inconvenience?* She was sore in places that had no business being sore, and she wanted off the bouncing, bone jarring, teeth rattling, fly bait of a forsaken creature she was being forced to ride. But, the last time she asked if they could stop and rest for a while, Kerric laughed at her.

"We have only been riding for a couple of hours," he said.

Liar. Kacie knew for a fact that they had been in the saddle for weeks. It wasn't in her nature to complain, but she was tired, cold, hungry, sore and her butt was asleep. Now, on top of it all, it was going to rain. Some adventure.

As if in answer to her complaints, thunder rumbled in the distance, and rain began to pour. In two minutes flat, everything was soaked. Her hair was plastered to her head and her clothes clung to her. She shivered and sneezed. *Terrific.* She sneezed again. *Now, I'm gonna catch cold and die of pneumonia.*

"Kerric," she called ahead to him. "Can we please stop for a while and get out of this rain?"

"Lady Emerald," he began with exaggerated patience,

"Kacie," she corrected.

"If you can find a place where we can get out of the rain, I will be happy to stop. Otherwise, there's no point. We might as well be wet and moving, as wet and sitting."

"What about food. Are we ever going to eat, or don't you believe in that either?"

"There's jerky in your saddlebag. Chew on that until we make camp."

"Jerky? Oh yum. Just what I've always wanted." She rummaged through her pack until she found a small bundle wrapped in white cloth. Kacie opened it and pulled off a hunk. Sinking her teeth into the thready meat, she ripped away a small piece and growled as she exaggerated chewing the tough mouthful. "Mmmmmm, this is good. Thank you."

Kerric rolled his eyes and turned away.

Just when Kacie realized that every part of her body was numb beyond the point of ever feeling anything again, Kerric called a halt. *Thank you, Lord.* She tried to pull her leg back so that she could get down and found, to her horror that she couldn't move. A second try fared no better. *Oh, this is lovely. I'm gonna be stuck up here all night.* Kacie looked around for help and sighed when the only person she saw was Tia coming toward her, saddle in hand. *Just my luck. Oh well, at this point any help is better than no help.* "Ah, excuse me."

Tia glared up at her. "What?"

"I can't get down."

"Oh, for heaven's sake." Tia rolled her eyes and dropped the saddle. She reached up and grabbed Kacie's arm with surprising strength, and pulled her off the horse. "There, you're down." She picked up her things and strode away.

Kacie cried out at the pain caused by her sudden forced movement, and would have fallen if Derian hadn't steadied her. "Walk it off, it'll help," he told her as he led her over to Kerric. "She's saddle sore."

"I can't feel anything from my waist down." She complained with a rub in the appropriate place.

Kerric took her arm and supported her as she limped around the clearing a couple of times. "The soreness will go away soon," he assured her. "And look, it's quit raining. What more could you want?"

"A fire?"

She sounded so pitiful, Kerric chuckled. "A fire would be nice," he agreed. "But with all the rain today...." He spread his hands.

"You're supposed to be the all powerful sorceress," Tia began.

"I never said I was a sorceress," Kacie interrupted.

Tia ignored her. "Use your magic, Lady Emerald. Make us a fire," she sneered.

Kacie narrowed her eyes and glared at Tia. "What would you like me to do Tia, call down fire form the air? Fine. You got it." She pulled away from Kerric and made a big show of pushing up her sleeves, then pointed to the ground a couple of inches from Tia's feet. "BURN!" She commanded in her best TV wizard's voice.

Tia let out a curse and jumped back when a roaring fire sprang to life inches from her. It died just as quickly, as Kacie yelped at the same time and stuck the offending finger in her mouth. Tia made a very wide, very quiet circle around Kacie to the far side of the clearing.

Kerric shot a startled Derian an 'I told you so' look. "Do that again." He pounced on Kacie, making her yelp a second time.

She shook her head. "I - I can't. I don't know how." She sagged against him and looked up bewildered. "What's happening to me?"

"You are the Emerald Sorceress." Kerric grinned down at her, making his dimples sink into his cheeks, an expression of jubilation on his face. He stood her squarely on her own two feet. "Now, do that again." He shook his head at the protest in her eyes. "We need the warmth and something to cook on."

Always ready to be helpful, Derian collected a hand full of semi-dry leaves and twigs and put them in the recently chard spot and winked encouragement at her.

"Guys." Kacie looked between them. "You're not listening to me. I don't have the faintest idea how I did that. I couldn't do it again even if I wanted to."

Kerric held her at arm's length and looked deeply into her brown eyes. A perplexed frown flitted across his features. He shook his head, then said, "You want to. Do it."

"C'mon, Emerald," Derian cajoled.

"Kacie," she corrected

"Kacie, then," he agreed with a slight nod, coming to stand next to Kerric. "Please try. What did you do a minute ago?"

"I pointed to the ground and said burn."

"But, what were you thinking? What did you see in your mind?" Derian coaxed.

Kacie bit her lower lip and thought for a minute, and a slow, mischievous smile spread across her face. "I pictured Tia going up in flames."

Derian roared with laughter. Tia shot him a look that should have killed him. Kerric cleared his throat and looked away.

"You asked." Kacie defended herself.

With watering eyes, Kerric coughed and looked back at her. "Yes we did, but you can't burn Tia, we need her." He ignored Kacie's snort and threw a quelling stare at Derian who continued to laugh. Realizing it was wasted effort, Kerric turned back to Kacie, giving her a little shake to make sure he had her attention. "Picture the leaves burning, this time."

Why not. She shrugged and closed her eyes and pictured the pile of leaves consumed by fire. In her mind's eye, she saw the flames becoming stronger and warmer as Derian added bigger and bigger pieces of wood to the blaze.

"Open your eyes," Kerric whispered in her ear.

Kacie did, and gasped in disbelief. Before her, danced the most beautiful fire she had ever seen. It was warm and cheery without the smoke or sizzle and spit that should have accompanied wet wood.

"Did I do that?" she asked Kerric. "No way, you guys had matches, didn't you? Come on, you can tell me. Where'd you hide them?" She held out Derian's shirt looking for hidden pockets.

Darien batted her hands and grinned. "That was your doing, M'Lady." He gave her a little bow, then frowned, puzzled. "What are matches? No, don't tell me." He shook his head and headed into the trees. "I don't want to know."

Kacie turned to find Kerric staring at her. "What?"

He smiled a lazy half smile at her, one cheek dimpling. "I was just wondering if the Lady Emerald would charm us some dinner out of the woods."

Kacie stared at him.

"I guess not. It was just a thought." He turned and followed Derian out of camp.

****

The next morning, Kacie was amazed her muscles weren't screaming. After a full day of trying to not to fall out of the saddle, walking shouldn't have been an option. Oh, she was sore, no doubt about it, but a few minutes of stretching reduced the soreness to bearable twinging. Chalk one up to the daily training required for playing league roller hockey. Kacie gave herself a mental pat on the back.

"Mount up." Kerric interrupted her congratulations. And then, miracle of miracles, he handed her CJ's - she named her horse after the jeep she wished she was riding - reins with only a "nudge her gently," before he mounted his own horse.

This might be a good day after all. Kacie forced herself not to think about the long ride ahead or the reasons why she was riding a horse in the middle of a seventeenth century forest instead of her jeep on the Los Angeles freeway. Until she had some answers, continuous questions hamstering around her mind wouldn't do her any good. So, she relaxed, determined to enjoy the beauty around her.

The first thing she noticed was that the pungent, musty smell of rain-washed earth and rotting leaves tickled her nose. And, the variety of lush green trees and other plants fascinated her. It was amazing that so many plants could flourish in the dark forest without much sun. Kacie never would have believed it. And the noise; compared to the rain soaked silence of the day before, there was a full blown riot of noise in the forest now. To help pass the time, Kacie tried to count the different animal and bird sounds she heard. Of course, she didn't have a clue what sort of animals made most of the sounds, but it was fun to guess.

Wrapped up in her own world of discovery, Kacie was surprised when Kerric called a halt and she discovered it was late afternoon. Her stomach rumbled, but she ignored it as they emerged from the trees onto a lush meadow carpeted with dainty bluebells. A gentle slope led down to an inviting lake. A swim at that moment sounded like the best thing she'd heard of in a long time. Eagerly, she swung off CJ and shook out her stiff legs. *Wow, would you look at that, Kacie Miller gets off her horse without help!*

"I told you the soreness would go away," Kerric commented as he passed, saddle in hand.

"Who said anything about not being sore?" Kacie grunted and looked longingly at the lake, but first, she led the mare down to the water's edge for a drink as she saw Tia doing with the other horses.

"Take her saddle off," Tia told her. "You can let her wander loose; she'll stay with the others."

Kacie watched, and imitated Tia's movements, and to her surprise, managed to get the saddle off with only a little fumbling. She lugged it and the packs back to camp and dropped them off with the others. Turning back to the water, she fancied she heard it calling to her, inviting her in for a refreshing swim.

A second later, Kacie was sprinting down the sloping meadow, shucking clothes as she went. Hopping on one foot at a time, she managed to untie her shoes and let them drop where they would. Pared down to her shorts and T-shirt, Kacie ran about twenty paces into the lake before she fell face first, with a loud splash. An instant later, she erupted from the water, yelling. "Cold! Crimeny, that's cold!"

From his spot on the bank, Derian laughed at her. "See those mountains?" He pointed to the large mountain range to the north of them, just beyond the tree line. "This lake is fed by them. It's too early in the season for it to be warmed up yet." He watched Kacie leisurely backstroke past him. "Come out before you turn blue."

Kacie splashed water in his direction, lightly spraying him. "Come in. It's wonderful."

"No thank you." He shook his head at her and walked back to camp.

Kacie floated letting the water support her tired, sore muscles until the ringing of metal against metal caught her attention. She stopped swimming and watched the three friends spar while she floated in the cool water. Fascinated by the swordplay, Kacie waded out of the lake for a better look. She sloshed up the hill, and found a puddle of sun a safe distance from the fighting. Shivering, Kacie stretched out on the grass to let the sun warm her and dry her off while she watched.

At least it was a safe distance, until Kerric slipped dodging a well-aimed thrust and had to roll away from Derian's two-handed attack. Kacie jumped to her feet and over Kerric's rolling body, narrowly avoiding a collision.

"You're quick." Kerric grinned at her.

"Grass slippery?" Kacie extended a hand to help him up.

"Your turn." He held his sword out to her.

"Me?" Kacie squeaked, shaking her head. "I can't fight."

"Then it's time you learned."

Kacie looked from the sword to Kerric's expectant face and it occurred to her to wonder if anyone ever said no to him. For a heartbeat she was about to test her theory when he thrust the sword into her hand and let go. Kacie yelped as the weight of the broadsword painfully pulled at her arm and the point promptly dropped to the ground. With two hands, she managed to get it waist high before it fell again. She looked accusingly at Kerric. "What's this thing made of – lead?"

"Take it easy with that." He took it from her with one hand and easily swung it to his shoulder.

"You're a creep. Do you know that?"

Kerric threw an authoritative arm around her shoulder and guided her into the fighting circle. "Tia, let's see your sword, the Lady Emerald . . ."

"Kacie." She stuck her elbow in his ribs for emphasis.

Kerric sidestepped out of harm's way. ". . . is ready for her first lesson."

Kacie made a face at him and took the sword Tia offered. "OK, boss, now what?" She concentrated on Kerric, ignoring the look that shot between Derian and Tia.

"Now we begin."

"Right." Kacie assumed her best Tyrone Power en guard position and started lunging back and forth, slashing furiously at the air. Kerric leaned on his sword and watched her, his face a mask. Kacie glanced at his granite posture and her wild gesturing slowed. "What?" She gave one last, weak lunge and let the sword drop to her side. "Oh, C'mon Kerric, you act as if my life depends on this stuff."

"It does." Kerric slowly circled her.

Her smile vanished. She tracked him, mirroring his movements. "Isn't that what I have you for; to protect me?"

Tia snorted.

Kacie turned, throwing her a dirty look and out of the corner of her eye caught a blur of movement. She whirled back to see Kerric's broadsword arcing toward her head. In the blink of an eye Kacie's natural instincts took over. She dropped her sword, covered her head with her arms and ran, screaming, for the trees. "What are you doing?" She yelled, peeking from behind a tree.

Ignoring their hysterical laughter, Kacie mustered all the dignity she could summon and strolled down to the lake with every intention of drowning herself.

A few minutes later Kerric joined her on the shore. "Come out," he ordered.

Still embarrassed, Kacie trudged out of the water. Kerric patted the ground beside him and she sat. He draped a blanket around her shoulders and she huddled into it. "Your instincts are very good."

Kacie's head snapped up. She didn't need his needling now, she was too mortified, but the look on his face was serious.

Kerric smiled at her confusion and explained. "When faced with an enemy in an unfamiliar situation the best thing you can do is run. Confronted like you were, by someone bigger, stronger and more experienced than yourself; if you had tried to defend yourself knowing nothing about swords or how to use them you would have died." He patted her leg reassuringly. "By screaming and running away you startled your opponent and saved your skin. If only because it was the funniest thing I've ever seen," he laughed again and ran a hand through his hair.

"Great. My enemies are going to laugh themselves to death."

Kerric sobered. "The point is, you are alive. Alive to learn the skills you need to fight an enemy that's bigger, stronger, more skilled." He held up a finger. "But maybe not more deadly."

"Can you teach me?"

Kerric nodded. "That is the idea." He stood and reached down to help her up.

Kacie took his hand and he led her back up to the fighting circle. He handed her Tia's sword and this time she stood waiting for his instructions. Kerric nodded satisfaction and began teaching her the fundamentals of sword fighting, gradually taking her into a few basic moves. She was a quick study. Kerric whirled in a tight circle and brought his sword arcing down toward her head once again. This time she answered by swinging her sword up in time to block the stroke. Kerric smiled and sidestepped. Her overextended reach left her flat on her face in the dirt. Kerric gave a nasty chuckle as he slashed downward. Kacie waited until the last possible moment before she flipped over and thrust her feet between his legs and pulled up with all her might while she rolled away from the sword point. Kerric went down in a heap, his sword thrown from his hand by the force of her unexpected move. Before he knew what happened, she was sitting on his chest with her blade against his throat. On the sidelines, Derian whooped. Kacie grinned down at Kerric.

"Give?"

"Never." Kerric heaved himself over, rolling Kacie with him, pinning her, his sword now at her throat. He leered down at her. "Never give an opponent a chance to reverse the situation." He stood and pulled her to her feet. "That was a very good move, by the way. We'll continue tomorrow."

Kacie gave a weak nod, too tired to answer. She was dripping with sweat and felt like she'd been pulled through a wringer. *I don't think I can do much more of this.* She trudged back down to the water and sat on the edge. She didn't have enough energy to do more than dip her hands in and wash her face off. Exhausted, she lay back and closed her eyes. *This is worse than any exercise program I've ever been in. A couple months of this and they won't recognize me back home.*

Home.

Suddenly, Kacie's chest hurt. She sat up and hugged her knees, staring blindly across the lake's placid surface. On the hill above her Tia and Kerric laughed. Kacie felt sick. *I've been pretending this was all some fancy vacation, but it's not.* She dropped her forehead to her knees. *This is real. All of it.* She swallowed hard, blinking back the tears swimming in her eyes. "What if I'm stuck here forever? What am I gonna do if I can't get back home?" Kacie clenched her jaw, dashing the tears from her cheeks. "That's not an option."

"Kacie." Derian's light touch on her shoulder startled her out of her thoughts. "Come eat."

She glanced up at him, wondering if he had heard her outburst. But, he gave no indication as he led the way back to camp.

Kacie found a big maple tree a little apart from the others and sat, absently fingering the hem of her vest.

"Derian and Tia made the stew tonight." Kerric informed her, handing her a large tin plate.

"Thank you." She took the plate without looking up, making a point of ignoring him when he continued to stand over her, staring.

Kerric watched her push her food around for a bit before squatting down on his haunches beside her. "Lady Emerald?" he spoke softly.

"Kacie," she said, through clenched teeth

"Are you all right?"

"Just peachy." She glared at him, daring him to say something about the tears in her eyes.

"Can I help?"

"Can you help me get home?" Kerric didn't say anything. "I didn't think so. She leaned her head back and closed her eyes, willing him away.

A moment later, a gentle finger wiped away the tear that slid from the corner of her eye. "You are home," Kerric whispered.

Kacie opened her eyes and watched him turn away and join Derian and Tia by the fire. She did her best to tune them out, but their easy banter was hard to ignore.

"We need to find you a sword." Kerric tossed a pebble at Kacie.

"What ever for?" She wanted to know.

"You need your own blade. You didn't think you'd be able to use Tia's all the time, did you?"

"I don't see why I need one at all."

"I'm not going to be your body guard. I don't care who you claim to be." Tia squinted her cobalt eyes in a disgusted look.

"No body asked you to." Kacie glared back.

"How about this?" Derian produced a branch that was just about the right size and length.

In spite of herself, Kacie was drawn into his game. "What am I supposed to do with it?"

"Turn it into a sword, Lady Emerald," Tia suggested.

Kacie eyed her for a long second and then smiled. "Hummm," She took the limb from Derian and got to her feet, holding it above her head. "Behold, the mighty sword of – what country did you say this was?"

"Medora," they chorused.

"Medora. Right." Kacie cleared her throat dramatically and struck her pose again, drawing all eyes upward to her oak branch. "Behold, the mighty sword of Medora!" At her words, a pale green light began to swirl around her and the pretend sword. All at once the limb was gone. In its place, Kacie held aloft a great shinning sword of polished steel. A blood red jewel flashed in the golden hilt, a dragon etched in gold, danced among the runes down the length of the blade.

Tia gasped. "It's the Dragon Sword. How'd she...."

Kacie stared, unseeing. Her brown eyes blazing emerald fire from deep within. "The Emerald Sorceress shall awaken the sleeping one! Together, they shall claim the blade and restore the Dragon to his Throne!" The forest rang with the power in her voice.

****

The stunned trio watched in disbelief as the aura around her dissolved, along with the vision of the sword. Slowly, the echo of her words faded back into the night, and once again, she was only a girl holding a branch. Kacie sighed and slid to the ground.

Derian lifted her wrist, to feel for a pulse. It was strong and steady. "She's only fainted," he sighed with relief.

"How did she do that?" Tia whispered.

Kerric slid himself under Kacie, cradling her head in his lap while Derian tried to rub the circulation back into her arms. Kerric caught his wrist and stared up at him. "Do you still doubt?"

"Her eyes...." Derian whispered, lightly touching Kacie's closed lids. He chose to ignore Kerric's smug expression.

"What happened?" Kacie asked, drawing everyone's attention back to her. Realizing she was in Kerric's lap, she tried to sit up. "What am I.... ooh." She put a hand to her head as a wave of dizziness swept over her.

Kerric gently eased her back against him. "Just relax. You fainted."

"I what?" She eyed them suspiciously. "I never faint."

"You don't remember anything?"

"I remember playing around with that silly stick, then waking up in your arms."

Kerric noticed the color in her cheeks and thought she was regaining her strength. He cautiously sat her up ready to catch her if he was wrong.

"Do you remember the sword?" Tia asked her.

"What sword? I remember thinking about...." She trailed off, looking at each of their shocked expressions and groaned. "What did I do this time?"

"Well, My Lady Emerald...." Derian began.

"Kacie," she corrected.

Kerric turned her face to him to with a light finger on her chin. Slowly, he shook his head back and forth. "Emerald," he insisted.

Kacie bit her lip. "Please, Kerric, what? Tell me."

"You conjured up the Medoran Sword of State. That's what."

CHAPTER FIVE

Alone in his tower sanctuary, Jozef stared, unseeing into the cold hearth before him, the half empty glass of wine all but forgotten in his slack fingers. For three days he'd relentlessly pursued Medora's new Emerald Sorceress with no success. Every time she used her talents, cold fire shocked his body with the raw power of her untrained magic. It should have been an easy task to follow that wild energy back to its source. But, the girl was being protected. Jozef ground his teeth. An impenetrable emerald fog obscured her from him. He couldn't even get a glimpse of her or where she was. Jozef cursed. Not for long. Not even Emerald magic was strong enough to protect her forever. The sharp jaw set in a determined line. He would have her soon, and then the Dragon Sword with its stolen Raven's eye would be his.

After twenty-six years, entrance into the Brotherhood of the Raven would be his. The full scope of the Raven Wizard's powers would be his. Vindication would be his! Jozef allowed himself a tight smile. How easy it would be then to control this young girl, guide her, and mold her, train her and bring her Emerald Powers into full bloom just before he ripped them from her. His cold eyes glittered and a shiver rippled over him. Briskly rubbing his arms, already feeling the Emerald Power coursing through his body, making every hair stand on end.

That wasn't his imagination. The girl was using magic again. He sprang to his feet, dropping the forgotten wineglass. Stepping on the spreading stain, Jozef hurried across the room to the scrying bowl. This was the strongest magic she'd used so far. Now he would have her.

Jozef dropped a pinch of sulfuric powder into the water and leaned in expectantly. "Show yourself my little sorceress." Through the swirling water, he caught sight of the dense forest and narrow riding track that could only be the road from Alorn to Trion and Kiramer.

Kiramer!

"Of course." Jozef gave a bark of laughter for his own shortsightedness. The girl was headed to the Emerald Palace. "More. Show me more." He passed a hand over the water and his attention riveted to the image of the Dragon Sword held aloft. "More," Jozef commanded, trying to see through the green fog. Slowly, ever so slowly, the edges of the thick mist shredded showing him long, straight black hair spilling over a well-shaped arm that tapered into the fine-boned hand holding the Medoran Sword of State. The prized ruby in the hilt flashed in the firelight and then two wide, emerald eyes, framed by long, black lashes, locked onto his; reaching across time and space binding him entranced as the forest echoed with her prophecy.

The emerald eyes closed, releasing him. Jozef gasped and staggered back a couple of steps. Gripping the cold edges of the marble, he pulled himself back to the scrying bowl. Jozef took a deep breath and blew it out, rotating his neck. "Show me the girl," he said in a raw whisper, willing the reformed cloud to dissolve. Again it obeyed and the water cleared. This time Jozef peered down at four young travelers lounging around a campfire, talking in hushed tones. He had a clear view of a petite young woman with a long auburn braid draped over one shoulder and cobalt blue eyes. "How did she do that, Derian?" The girl's voice echoed through the bowl. "I don't know, Tia." The man swiveled.

"Well, well, Derian Dahlen." A dark smile of recognition parted his lips as Jozef filed the information before turning his attention to the other two members of the group. He leaned forward, straining for a clearer look, but they remained shadows against the fire.

Jozef blew across the watery vision, willing the flames to part, but instead, the fire blazed into the night sky. He threw an arm up and snapped his head away. Blinded, Jozef tried to rub away the spots dancing before his eyes. When he could see again the water was only water. The images were gone.

Jozef left his tower almost satisfied. True, he hadn't seen the girl, but he knew her companions and through them he would control her. The results were the same.

Jozef descended the narrow stairwell to his bedchamber and pulled open the ornate doors to the outer sitting room. Lounging servants jumped to their feet. "Send for the Earl of Amsden," he ordered and withdrew.

Several minutes later there was a discreet knock and the tall, whip-like Amsden strode in. Sweeping off his black velvet hat the man bowed low, brushing the ebony ostrich plume across the plush carpet. "Sire?" he spoke in a deep, sandpaper voice.

"Come here," Jozef ordered. "Look into the fire and tell me what you see."

Amsden went as bidden, tossing the hat onto a chair. Jozef threw a pinch of powder into the flames and Amsden gaped. "The Dragon Sword?" He turned to the King. "What does it mean?"

Jozef let the image die and crossed to the two overstuffed chairs in front of the fireplace. "It means," he said, sinking into one. "That you are going to Trion."

Amsden stared at him. "Sire?"

Jozef stretched out his legs admiring the shine of his boots. "The Emerald Sorceress travels to Kiramer. You will intercept her at Trion."

Amsden didn't follow the King's logic. "How do you know she'll go to Trion?"

"She'll go."

"But,"

"Leave it to me. She'll have no choice. That is why you must be there to intercept her and bring her to the castle."

"Trion castle? Sire, you would take the girl to her own home?

"My home." Jozef snapped to his feet. "The Aideny titles and lands were forfeit for treason to the crown." He paced the length of the hearth, then stopped and rested a casual hand on the mantle. The tense body relaxed and a gentle smile touched Jozef's lips when he turned. "The child should be in her own home, surrounded by the comforting images and possessions of her family during this difficult time of adjustment and discovery for her. As her parents' childhood friend, I'm certain it would be their wish for me to guide their only child in the daunting task of mastering her considerable gifts." Jozef inclined his head humbly. Cold eyes focused on Amsden from below blond lashes. "You leave at once."

Amsden bowed and turned to leave.

"One more thing," Jozef began. "She travels with Derian Dahlen."

Amsden stiffened, his already pale face blanched as the King's arrow hit its mark.

"Ah, so you do remember. I thought you might." Jozef turned back to the fireplace. "Be in Trion before the girl," he said, stirring the coals with a booted toe.

Without a word, Amsden bowed himself out of the room and Jozef was confidant that his orders would be carried out.

****

All day Kacie rode in silence. They were almost to Trion - wherever that was. And, from there, it was another four days or so to Kiramer and the mystical, magical Emerald Palace, where Kerric assured her everything would be put right. But, Kacie suspected that their perceptions of 'right' were worlds apart - no pun intended.

Kerric was sure the Emerald Palace would somehow zap her memory and make her the sorceress everyone expected and loved. Kacie just hoped it had a pair of ruby slippers.

This place was too weird for her. She wanted to go home where things were normal and she could wave her hand at stuff all day long and nothing happened. She wanted to go home where a stick had the good sense to stay a stick. Never mind that she had spent her whole life believing that she should be able to do these things, and never could. Now that she was doing them it was scaring the jellybeans out of her.

Way back in the deepest, darkest, dustiest corner of her mind a glimmer of thought struggled to life. Maybe Kerric was right and she really was this Emerald Sorceress. She squashed the idea like a stinkbug. She was Kacie Miller from Santa Monica. Period. End of story.

"We'll stop here for the night." Kerric broke through her thoughts.

Kacie sighed with relief. *Good. Maybe now I can give my squirrels a rest.* She rubbed her temples. *They're getting dizzy.* She dismounted and hauled her gear off C.J. and dropped it beside the others. She smiled at Derian standing beside a freshly gathered pile of kindling, and slowed to a halt when she saw the mischievous glint in his warm brown eyes.

"What?"

"Care to do the honors?" He nodded to the wood.

"No, no." She held up her hands and backed away. "You go right ahead. I'm perfectly happy to share the honors with you." She turned and fled into the woods, his laughter chasing after her.

Kacie walked until she couldn't hear him any longer and found herself on a moss-covered path. Kneeling to unlace her Doc Martins, she slipped her feet out of her shoes and wiggled her toes, luxuriating in the cool ground cover. Not far away, the music of water cascading over polished rocks reached her ears. She headed for it, sinking to her ankles in the lush carpet of moss with every step. Above her, a bird warbled. Kacie cocked her head to listen and smiled.

Moments later, she was looking down at a narrow brook bubbling and splashing its way through a small ravine. Kacie slithered down the slippery grass covered bank and splashed in the water until she spied a huge tree close by. Its branches were laden with fragrant purple flowers; one massive root had worked its way above ground and now snaked around the base of the tree. Kacie ducked through the thick canopy of leaves and sank to the ground with a sigh. Using the moss covered root for a pillow, she plucked a bluebell stock growing beside her and twirled it between her fingers. She stretched out and closed her eyes allowing the soothing sounds of the water to calm her and still the million questions running rampant in her mind.

"Here you are." She jumped at Kerric's soft voice beside her. "Sorry," he apologized and held up the two freshly skinned rabbits for inspection. "Dinner. What are you doing out here?"

"Relaxing."

Kerric shook his head. "Don't wander by yourself, you'll get lost." He held out his right hand and pulled her to her feet. Draping an arm across her shoulders he herded her back to camp. She went with a small sigh, looking back only once.

Derian and Tia were no where in sight when they returned. Kerric didn't seem to notice as he immediately skewered the rabbits and propped them over the fire before settling down on a convenient rock. Kacie watched him for a bit then made a couple of slow circuits around the small clearing. She pulled a leaf off a low hanging branch and shredded it as she went. When she noticed Kerric's eyes following her, she let the leaf flutter to the ground and brushed her hands on her pants. Circling the fire, she sat next to him and began to draw pictures in the dirt. "Tell me about the sword."

"The Dragon Sword? What do you want to know?"

Kacie shrugged and looked up. "Everything I guess. What's so special about it? Is it magical or something?"

"Or something. Legend has it that the sword was forged high on Mount Danua beside the waters of Lake Zegari at the beginning of time by the Emerald Sorceress."

"But how did the Kings of Medora get it? And, why is it called the Dragon Sword?"

Kerric leaned forward and rested his arms on his legs, lacing his fingers together. "The Dragon Sword is the symbol of the Medoran throne. "Legend says that the Emerald Sorceress, Lara, gave it to the first King of Medora. Medora was nothing more than a collection of warring tribes then."

"Hold on a sec." Kacie interrupted and jumped up to nab the wine skin from Tia's pack. She knew the beginning of a long story when she heard one.

"Help yourself." Sarcasm dripped from Tia's voice as she and Derian wandered back into camp.

"Thanks, I will." Kacie took long swig. Here, have some." She handed Tia's wine to her and sat back down, wiggling herself into a more comfortable position in the dirt across from Kerric and looked up. "Okay, go ahead."

Kerric frowned at her. "From her tower at the top of Mount Danua, the Emerald Sorceress watched the tribes fight their endless wars, each minor chieftain claiming that he was the true ruler of Medora. The Emerald hated this never ending fighting and decided to put a stop to it. One night, as she sat wondering how to proceed, she fell into a fitful sleep and dreamed of the great sword flashing through the sky to land in the heart of Medora. In her dream, she watched as one man stepped from the shadows to take up the sword. At once, the fighting stopped, as the lords and chieftains laid down their arms and gathered around this man and the sword as one nation. And, the land that once ran red with blood turned green and flourished.

"When the Emerald Sorceress woke, she left her mountain home, taking the sword with her and traveled to Medora. She called the tribes together and showed them the sword saying that enough blood had been shed. The people watched in astonishment as she sank the sword into the heart of a large stone, and told them that the true king of

Medora would be the one that could extract the sword form the stone."

"OH! AAHGGH!" Kacie clutched at her throat and threw herself to the ground thrashing back and forth in agony. "No, No, No!" She pounded her fists in the dirt then pushed herself up, holding out her hands to stop his narrative. "Let me guess, everybody tried. All the rich and powerful lords, all the knights and all the mighty warriors." She threw her arms wide. "Everybody. But, nobody could budge it until a fourteen year old squire named Arthur just happened by and needed a sword for his foster brother."

"No, that isn't how it happened at all." Tia gave her a sour look.

"Harvey was a thirty year old baker," Derian interjected with a perfectly straight face as he sat next to Tia.

Kacie blinked once and gaped, open mouthed, before falling over again. She pulled her vest over her head and howled until tears streamed down her face.

"No, he wasn't." Kerric frowned at Derian who raised a challenging eyebrow. "Alright," Kerric conceded. "Harvey was posing as the baker's nephew in Desar at the time, but it was a disguise," he said, and threw a disgusted look at Kacie whose raucous laughter was now punctuated with hick-ups. "Do you want to hear the rest of this story, or not?" He prodded her with the toe of his boot.

Kacie sat up and wiped her face dry, sniffing loudly. "Sorry," she hick-upped. "Please continue. I wouldn't miss this for all the world." She hick-upped again and gulped in a deep breath, holding it while she did a quick count to ten. "So, was Harvey a baker or not?"

"Harvey Renberg was a northern chieftain, known as The Dragon." Kerric stressed the title.

"Ah-hah! Sword of the Dragon; the Dragon Sword. I get it!" Kacie hick-upped again, frowned and held out a hand for the wine.

"Can't put anything past you." Tia handed the wine skin over.

Kacie squinched her face at Tia before gulping three big swallows. When she was sure her hick-ups were gone, she said, "Okay, I'll bite. Why was Harvey pretending to be the baker's nephew?" She passed the wine back.

"To get a feel for the conditions in the south." Kerric intercepted the wine skin and took a drink before continuing. "Harvey had already unified the north and he wanted to do the same for the south. Posing as the baker's nephew left him free to move about without suspicion and people weren't afraid to talk to him."

"Smart man," Kacie observed.

Kerric nodded. "Very," he said, securing a tilting spit more firmly in the dirt before it fell into the fire.

"So, let me get this straight: Harvey's in Desar scoping out things for a southern coup and the Emerald Sorceress just happens to show up spouting this nonsense about Medora needing to be unified by a trial with this sword thing." She refused to go anywhere near the sword and the stone bit. Crinkling her forehead, she nodded. "Convenient. So, how'd they pull it off?"

"She might not be as dumb as I thought," Tia said, in a stage whisper to Derian.

Kacie ignored her.

"You were right about no one being able to move the sword."

"Surprise, surprise," Kacie deadpanned.

"All day, the gathered Lords and Chieftains tried and not one of them could draw the sword. Angrily, they shouted at the Emerald Sorceress, who continued to watch passively as they argued and fought amongst themselves.

"Late that night, Harvey, still posing as the baker, brought food and wine to the Emerald Sorceress who had not moved all day from her spot beside the sword in the stone." Kerric pretended not to hear Kacie's groan. "The Emerald smiled her thanks and he bowed to her and tried to back away. But, he was seized and roughly pushed forward again. Someone yelled that since none of the lords or knights were acceptable, they should let the baker try. Instantly, the cry was taken up.

"The Emerald Sorceress held up her hand for silence, then asked if it was truly their wish to let the baker try. They shouted their agreement and Lara beckoned Harvey forward. The instant he grabbed the jeweled hilt, he was bathed in a radiant light as a rampant dragon seemed to claw the air above him. Lara pointed to the sky and cried: "Behold! The Dragon of Medora!"

In stunned silence, the crowd watched the sword slide easily from the stone. Harvey knelt before the assembled Lords and offered himself and the sword to them and the land. Lara placed one hand on the blade and one hand on Harvey's bowed head, accepting both in the name of Medora. She raised Harvey and stepped behind him at his right shoulder, showing the world her support. And, the Emerald Sorceress has supported and protected the throne of Medora from that day forward," Kerric finished, running a hand through his hair.

"I gotta hand it to them," Kacie mused. "The plan was brilliant. They unified the country and not a drop of blood was shed. Brilliant." Growing thoughtful, she drew abstract designs in the dirt for a moment. At length, she looked up again. "So why did I conjure up this Medoran icon?"

"The Dragon Sword disappeared twenty-five years ago," Derian said.

"Sooo?" She turned and motioned for him to elaborate.

"So, maybe you're going to find the sword and put our rightful king back on the throne," Derian continued.

"Excuse me?" Kacie looked from Derian to Kerric. "What's this about a rightful king? Nobody said anything about a rightful king." *Find the sword. Restore the king.* The words echoed in her mind. Kacie pushed them away. "I thought Jozef was the king?"

"Jozef holds the throne because he murdered his father and older brothers. And because of his powers as the Raven Wizard, the great Lords of Medora fear to oppose him," Tia supplied for her.

"But," Derian added. "It's said that Jozef missed someone and there's a lost prince out there somewhere." He waved his hand to indicate the vast world. "They say Reyna spirited the prince and the Dragon Sword out of Desar on the night of the attack and hid them someplace where Jozef wouldn't be able to find them."

"And, you think I'm going to find the sword and restore this lost prince?" She wrinkled her nose at him. "I don't think so."

"If you don't do it Emerald, who will?" Kerric asked her.

Kacie stood and crossed to him, planting her hands on her hips. "You don't listen very well, do you?" She locked onto his eyes and held them. "Pay close attention, Kerric. I am not your Emerald Sorceress. I don't find lost swords and I do not restore displaced kings to their thrones. Got it?" She nodded her head up and down and reached out and took Kerric's head between her hands, moving it to match hers. "Good. Now repeat after me. I, Kerric . . ."

His mouth twitched in amusement. "I, Kerric . . ." he repeated.

"Promise that my only goal in life is to help Kacie get home, where she belongs."

"What if you belong here?" Kerric asked.

Kacie pushed him roughly away, and he grinned devilishly back at her.

"I hate you."

****

The sun was at zenith when they broke through the forest at the edge of the Trion River the next day. Kacie emerged from the dark tree line blinking furiously at the sudden glare of bright sunlight. "Sunglasses! Sunglasses! My kingdom for a pair of shades!"

"What are you blabbering about?" Tia groused.

Kacie ignored her. "Wow, would you look at that." She squinted at the wide river rushing past them.

"The Trion River," Kerric informed her, reining his horse in beside her. "And that." He pointed. "Is the city of Trion."

Kacie followed his finger down stream and could just make out the outline of buildings in the distance. "Cool. Are we going there?"

"No," Derian said so sharply that Kacie snapped her head around to stare at him and Kerric chuckled softly to himself.

"I don't know." Kerric ran a hand through his hair. "It might be a good idea to stop in Trion. We could rest there a couple of days before continuing."

"I thought you were in a hurry to get The Emerald to Kiramer so she can save the world?"

Kerric shrugged. "Medora's waited this long for her. I don't think another couple of days will matter."

Kacie swiveled around and raised both eyebrows at him. Kerric's face was poker straight, but his eyes danced with devilry as he watched Derian sputter in horror. His face still a mask, Kerric focused on Kacie for a second and casually let one eyelid slide shut before he turned his horse down stream. "The more I think about it, the better I like the idea. We'll cross at the bridge."

"You're an evil man, Kerric Rouse," Tia mumbled at him as he rode past and Kerric flashed her a two dimple grin. "I don't know, Kerric," Tia said louder for Derian's benefit. "Derian's got a point. Do you really think we should take the extra time? "

Kerric pretended to consider this for a bit. "You could be right, Tia. Maybe we should just push on through to Kiramer. Let's cross at the bridge and skip Trion this time. We can always stop on our way back."

"If you two are through. . ." Derian glared at them. "And I'm not crossing that bridge either."

"Did I miss something?" Kacie asked everyone in general.

"There's a warrant out for Derian's arrest in Trion," Tia told her.

"Thank you, for bringing that up, Tia," Derian grumbled, not budging an inch toward the bridge.

"Why?" Kacie followed after Tia and Kerric.

"Lady Rebecca," Kerric interjected.

"Ooooh." Kacie nodded sagely. "Now I understand." She shook her head. "No, I don't. Who's Lady Rebecca? Oh, crimeny." She made a face. "What is that smell?"

Beside her, Tia sniffed the air and shrugged. "I don't smell anything."

Kacie wrinkled her nose and fanned her face in a vain attempt to dispel the acrid stench of sulfur burning her nostrils. She scanned the area around her for the source and noticed a small puff of blue smoke hovering just above the shallow water lapping at the gravely shore. As she stretched forward for a better look, a slight breeze blew the smoke away and the tiny ripples settled themselves into the image of a black raven on a field of purple. Kacie frowned. This was too weird.

She took a breath to call Kerric when the raven shimmered and dissolved, reforming itself into the face of a man. Kacie gasped and covered her mouth, eyes wide, as she found herself looking at the short, dark blond hair, close-cropped goatee, and pale blue eyes of the man she knew as the Raven Wizard from her nightmares. *What is going on?* As if in answer, the eyes of ice focused on her, and ever so slowly, the thin lips parted in a feral smile. Kacie shuddered, bumping her mare with her knee causing the horse to step into the water obliterating the vision.

Gradually, she became aware of her fingers being pried loose one by one from their death grip on her reins. Confused, she looked blankly at the hands Kerric was trying to rub circulation into, then up into his face.

"Emerald?" Kerric peered into her ashen face as he continued to rub warmth into her icy hands. His stallion nervously sidestepped, brushing against her leg and Kacie blinked, focusing on Kerric at last.

"What happened?"

"I wish I knew." Her eyes were still haunted by the vision. "I saw a face in the water. It was weird." Kacie shook off the feeling of unease and shrugged with a nonchalance she was far from feeling. "It was probably nothing." She silently pleaded with him not to press her for details she didn't have.

Kerric held her gaze for a long moment. At length he nodded once, not understanding, but accepting her need. Kacie breathed again.

"Okay, so give. What's the deal with Derian and this warrant in Trion?" She tried to direct his attention away from herself.

"I told you. Lady Rebecca lives there."

"So what's Lady Rebecca got to do with the price of tea?"

"Lady Rebecca Howard is the Countess of Amsden and the Queen's closest friend and constant companion," Kerric explained. "As part of the Queen's guard Derian and the Lady Rebecca were," he paused to clear his throat. "Together often."

Kacie's jaw dropped. "Derian?" She twisted around in the saddle. "You had an affair with the Countess? That's why there's a warrant out for you? Was the lady that upset with the service?"

Kerric blinked at her then roared with laughter. "As I understand it, she was well pleased."

"Then what....?"

"Her fiancé paid an unexpected visit," Tia chimed in.

"Oh no!" Kacie chortled. "They got caught? You got caught?" She shot Derian an amazed look.

Ignoring Derian's warning glare, Kerric warmed to his story. "He was lucky to get away with all his parts. As it was, that's all he did get away with."

"What happened?"

"Don't mind me." Derian dismounted and squatted by the river bank and picked up a handful of rocks. "Go ahead and tell the world my business. I'll just sit here until you're finished." He threw a small stone as hard as he could across the river.

"The Earl of Amsden was furious."

"He wasn't the Earl of Amsden then," Derian interrupted, sourly. "If you're going to tell the story, tell it right. They weren't married. He had no right being there."

"And you did?" Tia shot at him as she tossed her own rock into the water after his.

"And the title is her's not his."

"Anyway," Kerric continued. "James Howard burst in on them with sword drawn and Derian, always quick on his feet, jumped out of bed and pulled the canopy down around the man's ears. He blew out the light and in the confusion, slipped through the secret door in the Lady's chamber and high tailed it through the palace with every soldier in the place hard on his heels. They chased him through every hall and room in the palace, from cellar to attic."

"So, how'd he get away?" Kacie stole a look at Derian who was pointedly ignoring them.

"He used a secret tunnel and slipped into the forest behind the palace. I found him the next morning up a tree naked and half frozen." Kerric shook his head and chuckled. "That afternoon the warrant for his arrest went out. I think the good Earl would like to have Derian castrated."

Kacie began to laugh. Picturing Derian's adventure in vivid detail, she rocked back and forth and almost slid out of the saddle. Only Kerric's quick steadying hand saved her.

"Whenever you're finished." Derian stood and climbed back into the saddle. "I'd like to get across the river before that storm breaks." He pointed to the black clouds gathering on the horizon. "I don't like the look of them. They're moving too fast for a regular spring storm."

Kerric looked up at the sky and frowned at the black clouds swarming above them blocking out the sun that had shown brightly a moment before. "This isn't right. No storm moves that fast." He looked over at Kacie. "Are you alright?"

Kacie put a hand to her forehead. "I don't feel so good." She tilted sideways.

Kerric caught her before she toppled from her horse. "Lady Emerald? What's wrong?"

"I don't know." Kacie shook her head. "I feel so weird, all hot and cold at the same time." She gathered her strength and pushed herself away from Kerric, gritting her teeth in an effort to stay upright without his support.

Kacie squinted trying to clear her vision, but everything around her was tinged a deep blue, and every nerve in her body tingled as if electrically charged. "Magic," she whispered. "We've got to get out of here."

As if on cue, a spear of lightening crackled through the air and a huge elm at the water's edge exploded. The crash of thunder that followed almost deafened them as the black sky unleashed a torrent of freezing rain. The horses screamed in terror, and as the riders fought to control their wild mounts, a gale wind whipped up giant waves.

Too late, Kacie screamed a warning that was swept away by the roaring wind, choking her with a mouthful of water. She watched helplessly as Tia was swept from her horse and disappeared under the seething river. Disregarding his own safety, Derian dove in after Tia and was sucked under too. Panic stricken, Kacie tried to get to Kerric, but before she could move, a wall of water crashed over her slamming her into the river.

End over end she tumbled, held under and dragged along the river bottom by the savage current. A sharp pain shot through her arm where raked across the edge of a submerged rock. Kacie grabbed for it and held on for dear life while she battled to pull her legs under her. Using the boulder for leverage, she pushed against it with all her might, propelling herself to the surface. Coughing and vomiting water, Kacie gulped air into her lungs. Half blinded, she squinted against the stinging rain and tried to swim toward the riverbank rushing past at an alarming rate. Struggling against the current, she fought to keep her head above water as the churning river tossed and tumbled her along like a rag doll. Again and again she was sucked under and spit out, swallowing water with every breath.

Terrified, Kacie struggled until she was too exhausted to fight anymore. Letting her body go limp she quit struggling and concentrated on just breathing as the water swept her along. She soon realized that the river was pushing her toward the shore. Kacie relaxed then and let the current do the work for her.

The force of the raging water pushed her hard into the gravely bank and with her last ounce of strength, Kacie pulled herself up past the water line and collapsed. Her arms and legs stung where she scraped them against the sharp rocks, but she couldn't have cared less. She patted the dry earth with numb, thankful fingers. Her last conscious thought was for the others.

The freak storm passed as suddenly as it came upon them and the warm sun on her face woke Kacie. She was dog-tired and her body felt like lead, but she was alive. And that wasn't something she would have booked on earlier. Saying a silent prayer that the others were safe as well, Kacie forced her weary body to sit up, and dared to pry her welded eyes open. A blurred kaleidoscope of shapes and colors greeted her. In spite of her fatigue, she laughed. "Now that's a miracle." She cupped a hand under her eyes and popped out first one contact, then the other. "I can't believe they stayed in." She blew on them before opening her soggy pouch and tipping them into their case.

Every muscle in her body pleaded with her to stay where she was and sleep for at least a week, but Kacie knew she had to get up and look for the others. She rolled over onto her hands and knees and was gathering the courage for the final push to her feet, when a man-sized shadow fell across her. Kacie lifted her head and stared up at Derian through the curtain of her matted, hair.

He was as bedraggled as she felt, with his torn clothes, and scratched face. "Derian!" Kacie was never so glad to see anyone in her life. "You made it!" she grinned up at him without moving. "Tia, did you get Tia?"

Before he could answer, Tia stepped into her line of vision. She was immaculate. Not a wrinkle. Not a hair out of place.

Kacie dropped her head to the ground and shook it slowly back and forth. *I hate her.*

Derian shocked her out of her commiserating by grabbing her around the waist and lifting her to her feet. She yelped and glared at him. "I could have done.... it.... What?" Derian and Tia were both staring at her. "What?" Neither of them said a word.

A crunch of booted feet on gravel distracted them and Kacie followed their gaze. *Kerric! Thank goodness.* She sighed with relief and trotted behind them as they hurried to meet him. Looking tired but in good shape, Kerric led all four horses up the beach. He dropped their reins and gripped Derian's shoulder and lightly stroked Tia's cheek. He turned to wink at Kacie and went dead still, staring at her.

Kacie held his gaze and waited for the inevitable; refusing to fidget while Kerric studied her from under his thick lashes. She raised her chin a fraction and he gave her a smug, half smile before deliberately looking away from her.

"Our supplies are gone," he told them. "We'll have to go into Trion for more."

Derian swore - colorfully.

CHAPTER SIX

Jozef waved a bejeweled hand over the water, allowing the images to dissolve and turned to the bookcase beside the scrying bowl. Running the same hand along the underside of the third shelf, his fingers searched for and found an almost imperceptible knot in the hard wood and pressed. The bookcase inched forward, hesitated then slid silently sideways. In the center of the hidden chamber a tall mirror stood waiting. "Trion. My sitting room," Jozef commanded and stepped into the black framed mirror, emerging a second later in Trion castle. The swirling images within the mirror bathed the closet-sized alcove in a rainbow of colors allowing Jozef to see the door only a step away. He lifted the peep-hole cover and peered into the room beyond. Assured that it was empty, Jozef slid the door open and as he crossed to the elegant white and lapis sideboard against the far wall, the decorative wall panel whispered back into place, concealing the mirror room.

Jozef poured himself a glass of wine from a crystal decanter and drained it in one quick swallow. Setting the goblet down with a sharp clink of glass striking stone, he reached up and tugged on the blue velvet sash hanging beside the server. In another room a bell tinkled. Almost instantly the door opened.

"Send for the Earl of Amsden," Jozef ordered, not bothering to turn around.

When the door clicked shut again, Jozef placed his hands flat on the cool, blue surface, and took a deep breath. Letting it out in a long thin hiss, he poured himself another drink.

Goblet in hand, he crossed to a window and drew back the light blue gauze curtain, and as his gaze wandered over the gardens below, a movement off to the side caught his attention. Jozef turned in time to see a gray cat jump at a sparrow pecking for bugs on the lawn. With a startled chirp, the bird flew into the air and landed safely on a low hanging branch. Again and again, the tabby jumped, trying to reach his quarry, his tail fuzzed and flicking in annoyance as the sparrow chittered, tauntingly just beyond the cat's reach. Jozef frowned and turned away. He took a sip from his glass and moved to the white marble fireplace just as Amsden, dressed in his usual black, entered the room.

"Sire." Amsden bowed low.

"The girl will be in Trion within the hour. Place your men," Jozef came right to the point.

"And Dahlen?"

Jozef nodded and watched Amsden's jaw harden. "The Emerald Sorceress is your first priority. I don't care what you do with Dahlen, but if you let the girl escape, his son will claim your title before the sun rises again."

A tick jumped at the corner of Amsden's left eye and Jozef could almost hear his teeth grind as the barb hit home. Amsden's dark eyes turned black with suppressed anger as he gave the King a stiff bow of his head, acknowledging the order and swept out of the room.

Jozef set the unfinished glass of wine on the fireplace mantle and followed Amsden out. He had his own preparations to make before welcoming the new Emerald Sorceress to Trion castle.

****

"I just think it would be safer for Kacie if I stayed with her in the forest," Derian continued the argument he'd started the minute they left the river bank and set out on the main rode into Trion. "You said yourself, Kerric that she could be in danger. What if Jozef is here waiting for her? If that storm was caused by magic then we're being lured here so that he can capture her."

Kerric raised an eyebrow and shook his head. "We're all safer if we stay together," he said as they approached the city walls.

"That's easy for you to say," Derian grumbled under his breath. "It's not your head on the block."

Kacie couldn't quite make out what else Derian mumbled as he dropped behind them in a last ditch effort to hold off the inevitable for as long as possible. "Good try though," she told him and followed Kerric through Trion's north passage. "Crimeny." Kacie stared at the massive iron gates that sat open on either side of the arched portal. "People actually move those things by hand?" she asked, just before they were plunged into darkness. "Jeeze, is this a gate or the Brooklyn tunnel? Hello. Hello. Helloooo...." she made her voice smaller and smaller, gradually fading away in a mock echo. "How big is this puppy, anyway?"

"Trion's walls are twenty feet thick," Kerric said over his shoulder.

"Why?"

"The King likes to be secure when he's here," he told her as they passed under a portcullis suspended above them.

"Can you say paranoid?" Kacie ducked away from the rusted points hanging way too close to her head, wishing they were secured in place by more than a thick rope.

"Jiminy Christmas. Would you look at that." She pointed to the busy city beyond the gate.

"Hey! Watch where you're going." Tia jerked her mount to the right, just missing Kacie's motionless horse.

Oblivious, Kacie stared at the wide cobblestone boulevard stretching out before her. Less than a mile long, the bustling street opened onto a large square, centered by a round fountain shooting cascades of water high into the air. On either side of the fountain, cookie cutter buildings of red brick, lined the boulevard and circled the square. Kacie's mouth twitched. "Looks like Main Street at Disneyland," she said, as an ornate carriage, pulled by a pair of jet black horses, clattered past, claiming her attention. And then, she was staring at a gilded sedan chair being carried by two men in bright red and orange velvet livery. "Crimeny."

Toto, this for sure ain't Kansas anymore.

"I hate to spoil this moment of discovery for you, but can we get off this street?" Derian urged, hunkering deeper into the folds of his cloak.

Ahead, Kerric chuckled and turned down a side street crowded with vendors hawking their wares to the throngs of people milling from brightly colored stalls to weathered carts over flowing with market day necessities.

"Don't stop and gawk," Tia ordered

Kacie made a face at her, but kept going, ogling at everything so slowly that Tia reached over in disgust and grabbed the reins out of Kacie's hands. Kacie snatched them back. "Do you mind?"

"Yes, I do mind," Tia snapped. "Move it a little faster. You'd think you'd never seen a city before."

"I've never seen anything like this before," Kacie rotated her head, trying to see everything all at once.

"That's obvious."

Behind them a butcher shouted to the crowd, his deep voice booming above the other vendors vying for customers. Derian whirled, his sword half drawn.

"Will you relax?" Tia shook her head at Derian. "It's been six years."

Kacie's ears perked up and she turned to look at Derian. "Your affair was six years ago? What are you worried about?"

"Nothing." He looked pointedly at Tia. "Nothing."

Tia shrugged and followed Kerric down an alley until they stopped behind a rambling public house.

"We'll stop here and eat. Then we can get our supplies and be out of town before night fall," Kerric said.

Kacie glanced up and read the bold lettering on the brightly painted wooden sign hanging over the door and almost fell off her horse. "The Lame Swan?" Her mouth dropped open and she clamped a hand over it. She looked from the teetering one-legged swan on the sign to Kerric who raised an eyebrow at her, then at Tia who looked at her like she was mindless. She bit her cheeks and soberly climbed down from her horse.

There's a bad movie somewhere in all of this.

As they dismounted, a boy ran from the shadows to take their horses. Kerric tossed him a coin. "See to their care."

The boy plucked the coin out of the air and bit into it - testing. A second later, his teeth flashed and he began to whistle as he led the horses off to the tavern's rickety stables.

Ignoring the curious glances of the scullery, they tramped through the busy kitchen and into the smoke filled common room. Derian led them to the darkest corner of the room and angled his chair so that he sat with his back to the wall. Tia straddled the chair to his right, and Kacie took the chair directly opposite him. Wordlessly, Derian motioned for her to move out of his line of vision.

Kerric signaled to a serving girl as he made himself comfortable between Derian and Kacie. "Four ales and four bowls of stew," he told the girl.

83

THE EMERALD SORCERESS

Kacie watched the girl smile and give her hips an extra swish as she walked away. *Oh brother.* She rolled her eyes. "How long were you guys in Trion?"

"Long enough," Derian grumbled.

Kerric let out a bark of laughter, drawing attention to them. He quieted to soft chuckles. "Two years. I studied swordsmanship with the master at arms and Derian served in the Queen's guard. He studied . . . other things." Kerric winked at Kacie, his dimples teasing at his cheeks.

I so wish he wouldn't do that. Kacie swallowed hard and became absorbed in the wood grain of the table.

"So, Kacie," Derian seized the momentary silence to direct their attention away from himself. "Your eyes have acquired a unique shade of emerald since our swim earlier. How is that?"

Kacie's eyes went round. "Rats! I forgot to put in my contacts."

"I tried to tell you they were green." Kerric's grin was pure smug evil.

"Dimples or no dimples, he's gonna die a slow, nasty, horrible death," Kacie muttered under her breath.

Derian nodded. "I stand corrected. With eyes like that she could only be the Emerald Sorceress," he teased.

Kacie looked to heaven for support, and then glared at both of them. "Yeah, well I'm a pretty poor sorceress. And I'm not admitting I am," she hurried to add. "You know, you guys keep telling me I have all these powers and I don't have a clue what they are or even how to use them."

"You'll learn," Kerric assured her. "That's why we're going to the Emerald Palace. I'm sure that once you get inside everything will become clear to you."

"I guess. You won't mind if I hold onto my reservations until then?"

"Of course not, my Lady Emerald." Kerric bowed his head to her.

"And, while we're on the subject." Kacie pinned him with a long stare. "Can't you just call me Kacie?"

Kerric was thoughtful for a minute and then nodded. "Every Emerald Sorceress has had a name. From Lara all the way down to Reyna," he conceded.

"Yours is Kacie Miller," Derian chimed in. "Kacie Miller, the

84

Emerald Sorceress from Santa Monica," he teased her.

Kacie sighed. She knew a losing battle when she saw one. "You're hopeless. Both of you."

"Who ever heard of a sorceress named Kacie," Tia cut in.

Any retort was cut off when the serving girl returned with a loaded tray.

Kacie scanned the smoky room while the girl set the ale on the table. A man at the next table met her eye and raised his mug to her before draining the tankard. Not looking away, he wiped his mouth and stood, bumping the sword at his hip against the table. He steadied the weapon in its worn scabbard with one hand and put his hat on with the other one. Tossing a few coins onto the table, he nodded to Kacie and left the tavern.

Bemused, Kacie watched him disappear through the door, then dismissed him and turned back to look at the ale sitting in front of her and sighed. "I'd kill for a soda right about now. You don't happen to have one hiding in the back, do you?" She looked plaintively up at the girl.

"Soda? What's a soda?" The girl turned to question Kacie. "Oh!" she exclaimed, almost dropping the tray.

Only Kerric's lightening reflexes saved him from being christened with their dinner. "Whoa, girl. Watch what you're doing." He snatched the tray from her slack fingers and set it on the table. When she didn't respond, Kerric twisted around to see what had her so enraptured and groaned. The girl was staring dumbfounded into Kacie's emerald eyes. "Of all the times for her to choose to make them emerald," he muttered.

"The Emerald Sorceress," the girl mouthed in a hushed whisper, mesmerized by Kacie's eyes.

Kacie shook her head. "This isn't what you think. It's a trick of the light."

"What light?" Derian and Tia said at once.

"Don't help," Kacie shot back.

"The Emerald Sorceress," the girl repeated, searching Kacie's face. "But, you're so young." She frowned slightly, then nodded once. "It's true then; Reyna's dead." She looked down a moment, then raised her eyes once more to Kacie's, hope stamped plainly on her expectant face. "And, now you're here. You'll set things right."

"Kerric, we don't need the attention," Derian urgently interjected.

Kerric nodded agreement and took the girl's hands, forcing her to turn away from Kacie and face him. "What's your name?" he asked, softly.

"B-Bridget, sir." She turned her head around to look back at Kacie.

"Bridget." Kerric released one hand to reach up, gently returning her attention back to him. "Bridget," he repeated. "We need your help. You're right, this is the Emerald Sorceress. . ."

Kacie gasped. "Kerric. . ."

"Not now." Kerric threw her a quick quelling look and she clamped her mouth shut. "Bridget." He rubbed his thumbs across the back of the girl's hands and Bridget turned from Kacie and looked down at her hands and then at Kerric. The corners of her mouth tilted up. He had her full attention. Kerric smiled, dimpling.

Oh please.

"Bridget, I need your help," Kerric continued. The girl nodded and Kacie snorted. Kerric kicked her under the table, never taking his eyes off Bridget's face. "We're on secret business for the Emerald Sorceress. That's why we're traveling like this." He indicated their tattered appearance. "No one can know that the she is here in Trion. She'll be leaving soon, but until then her identity must be kept a secret."

"Do you protect her?" Bridget managed to ask.

Kerric nodded. "I do, but her safety depends on secrecy. Will you help me protect her? Will you keep our secret and tell no one you've seen her?"

Bridget nodded. "I won't tell anybody," she said and faced Kacie. "Your secret's safe with me, my Lady."

"Thank you," Kacie said with solemn dignity.

"That's my girl." Kerric squeezed Bridget's hands then brought them to his lips and feathered a kiss on each of them.

Kacie watched the girl blush and move away with a sigh. "You're good," she told him. "And that hurt, by the way." She punched him in the arm.

"It was meant to."

"Brute." Kacie reached for her ale and as she drank, slid a glance at the girl and found herself under scrutiny. Bridget turned away, embarrassed at being caught, but Kacie again saw the hope registered there.

All of a sudden the mug in her hand was too heavy to hold. She set it down with a thud, splashing a bit of ale over the edge. Kacie stared at the golden liquid trickling down the side of the pewter mug as if it was the most important thing in the world. But, her attention persisted in wandering where she didn't want it to go. It was one thing to have Kerric spouting this sorceress nonsense at her. She could tell him he was delusional and believe it. But this.... Kacie slid another look at Bridget.... this was totally different. She couldn't escape the truth she saw on Bridget's face.

Kacie squeezed her eyes shut tight. *This is crazy. It's just plain crazy. I can't even get myself home. How am I supposed to save the world? How can I be a powerful sorceress? I don't even make a good pixy.* She scrubbed her face. *I just want to go home where I belong.*

Kacie opened her eyes to find Kerric studying her closely. Their eyes met and he seemed to be reading her thoughts. A soft encouraging smile touched the corners of his mouth.

"To the Emerald Sorceress." He saluted her with his mug.

"Not funny, Kerric."

"It wasn't meant to be."

Kacie deliberately looked away from him. "I thought we were going to get supplies and get out of here?"

"Amen to that," Derian agreed and it was a toss up as to whether he or Kacie was on their feet first.

****

Following behind the others, Kerric sighed as he stepped out of the tavern. Would she ever believe? If she didn't accept her destiny soon it could be too late. How long would Medora have to suffer until another Emerald Sorceress came to power? If Kacie failed, would there even be another Emerald Sorceress? The thought stopped Kerric in his tracks. An icy chill ran down his spine and he shuddered. No. He pushed the fear aside. He'd make her believe and accept her destiny. There was no other choice.

Kerric watched Kacie follow after Derian. Apparently deep in thought, she stopped at a tailor's stall to finger a length bright pink

87

satin, but it was obvious that she wasn't paying much attention to the expensive material.

"We have to talk," Kerric said, behind her.

Kacie let the material drop. "No." She moved away from him. "We don't."

"Yes, we do." Kerric took her by the shoulders and turned her around to face him. "This isn't a game. Medora's future depends on you."

Kacie's eyes flashed in the bright sunlight. She opened her mouth and then shut it again, taking a deep breath instead. "Kerric, what if someone came up to you one day and said: 'Surprise, you're Medora's long lost Prince. And, as its true ruler it's up to you to save the world.' What would you do? How would you feel?"

"That isn't possible."

"Why?" Kacie asked, strolling to the next stand.

"Because I'm not royal. I'm a farmer's son. I was raised growing this." He held up an ear of corn. "Now, I'm a soldier for hire." Kerric shook his head in denial. "I'm not a prince. I'm Kerric Rouse from Kiramer."

"Exactly."

Kerric stopped short, surprised to hear himself echo Kacie's well used phrase. "It's not the same."

"Of course it is. I was just a girl working at a book store. I didn't even know your world existed until I woke up in that alley three days ago. Now, suddenly, I'm in this weird adventure and you're telling me I'm something I thought only lived in books. Forgive me if it's taking me a while to adjust."

Kacie was searching his face for some sign of understanding and he did understand that she was confused, but he also knew how important her acceptance was.

"Kacie," he began as he took her hands in his. "I don't know where you've been or why you don't remember who you are, but you have the mark." He touched the corner of one emerald eye. "And, you have power. We've all seen you use it," he chuckled and Kacie blushed. Kerric's smile deepened then faded. "You are the Emerald Sorceress." Kacie took a breath and Kerric shook his head to forestall her protest. "Trust me until you can believe." He traced her cheek with one light knuckle. "Can you do that?"

Kerric held his breath as her emerald eyes locked onto his, seeming to read his soul, knowing that Medora's fate rested with what she saw there.

At last Kacie nodded. "Okay."

Kerric breathed again. "Good girl." He hugged her tight.

Kacie pushed him away and shook her finger at him. "But, if we don't find anything at the Emerald Palace you have to promise to help me get home. Deal?"

A shadow of a frown crossed Kerric's face.

"Kerric."

Kerric threw up his hands in surrender. "Alright. Deal."

As they shook on their pact, Kerric scanned the market and swore. "Amsden. Stay here," he ordered over his shoulder as he took off running.

****

"Not likely." Kacie was a half step behind him, craning her neck, as she ran, to see what was going on. "Oh no." She blanched.

Two dozen uniformed guards, led by a tall man dressed from head to toe in black, marched purposely to where Derian stood haggling over a loaf of bread.

Ahead of her, Kerric stopped and whirled so fast that Kacie would have plowed into him if he hadn't grabbed her shoulders. "Hide under there." He hauled her to a tinker's stall. "And, whatever you do, don't let Amsden," he pointed to the man in black, "see your eyes."

"Why?"

"He works for the King. Now hide." Kerric pushed her under the table then turned on his heel and was gone. "Derian!"

At Kerric's shout, Derian looked up from bargaining and saw Kerric sprinting toward him with sword drawn. Derian dropped the bread, instantly searching the area for danger.

Before Derian could move, Amsden, flanked by the palace guards stepped around the baker's cart. "Derian Dahlen, I arrest you in the name of the King." His deep, gravely voice carried clearly to Kacie's hiding place.

Derian whirled and took a step backward. "I don't think so." He ducked behind the baker's stall, intending to sprint away.

Amsden reacted instantly and cut him off. "There's nowhere to go, Dahlen."

Derian eyed the sword pointed at his throat and grinned. "If you insist." He rolled under the booth and drew his sword in one smooth movement. Springing to his feet, Derian jumped onto a table and slashed down at Amsden's head. Amsden blocked the blow with the loud clang of metal meeting metal, and then thrust at Derian's gut. Derian sprang back, slipping on a tray of pastries. He caught his balance with only a slight bobble and heaved a vicious kick at Amsden's face. Amsden twisted away and Derian leaped off the table, up-turning it and ran.

Sprinting past a butcher's store, Derian knocked over a tall stack of wooden chicken coops hoping to buy a few seconds. With a loud crash the crates broke sending frightened chickens into the air and into the faces of the pursuing soldiers.

"After him, you fools," Amsden shouted, kicking a chicken coop out of his way.

"Go, Derian!" Kacie edged out a little for a better view and saw Tia step into the street just as Derian bounded past. Blocking the soldiers' path, she momentarily shielded his escape.

At Amsden's signal four guards broke off to take care of Tia as he and the others streamed around her after Derian.

Hardly seeming to notice that she was out numbered, Tia's sword flashed. She kicked a man twice her size in the chest and he went down hard. Whirling, the heel of her hand connected with another guard's throat, almost crushing his wind pipe.

"Two down," Tia smirked, blocking a downward slash with her sword as she pulled a knife out of her boot.

Her opponent parried her block and advanced. Avoiding both sword and knife, he rained down a cascade of two handed blows, forcing her steadily backward as she struggled to protect herself.

A second later, Kerric flashed into view behind the guard, smashing the hilt of his sword against the man's head. The guard dropped like a stone.

"Behind you," Tia warned as several more guards joined the fight.

Kerric whirled and sidestepped. The hacking sword slid harmlessly along the length of his blade, but the man's momentum took him within Kerric's reach. Fast as lightening, fist connected with nose. There was a loud crunch of bone. Blood poured and Kerric's attacker fell to his knees howling in pain.

Out of the corner of her eye, Kacie saw Derian stop in the middle of the street not far from her hiding place and wheel around to face Amsden again.

They circled each other, measuring. "You shouldn't have come back," Amsden said and attacked.

"What can I say? I have a soft spot for Trion." Derian set up a blinding net of steel, blocking each of Amsden's thrusts. "How is Rebecca, by the way?"

"My wife," Amsden stressed the word. "Is not your concern." He threw himself headlong into the attack with renewed force.

"Rebecca will always be my concern," Derian taunted as he paced himself, waiting for an opening in Amsden's defense.

Kacie scooted out a little farther and watched Derian play cat and mouse with Amsden. She shook her head. "How did I manage to get myself in the middle of a sword fight? I don't even have a sword. Not that I'd know how to use one even if I did have one." She looked at the rotting wood above her head. "Which would be why I'm hiding under a tinker's cart."

Kacie made a face at herself and looked past Derian in time to see a soldier rush Kerric from the side. Kerric spun and sliced open his opponent's sword arm. "Man, he's good," she mused in awe as the man grunted and dropped the sword, his hand useless.

Kerric hooked a toe under the fallen sword and flipped it up into his left hand. The wounded man ran away and Kerric twisted to block another opponent's jab with one sword and gave a quick thrust to the man's unprotected side with the other one. Preoccupied, he didn't notice a second guard rushing up behind him.

"Kerric, look out!" Kacie jumped from her hiding place and sprinted for Kerric. Without thinking, she whipped her arm back and then forward again in a throwing motion. A ball of emerald fire shot out from the center of her palm and slammed into the back of Kerric's assailant just as the man thrust his sword toward Kerric's ribs. The soldier screamed as the sphere exploded.

Kerric jumped back and stared as the man fell unconscious at his feet, green energy still crackling along his inert body.

Kacie skidded to a stop in front of Kerric and placed a hand on his shoulder. "Are you okay?"

Kerric jerked away from the jolt that coursed through him at her touch and looked up, a tiny dimple teased at one cheek. "You're glowing, my Lady Emerald."

Startled, Kacie held up her arm. A thin emerald aura undulated just above her skin. She shook her arms sharply and the glow faded. "That was interesting."

"Very." Kerric rubbed his tingling shoulder as he looked around them, alert for another attack. "I think we need to go."

Kacie followed his gaze and saw that Amsden was watching her. Their eyes met. Amsden directed a curse at her as he parried a low jab from Derian and stepped in close, shoving Derian hard away from him. "This isn't over, Dahlen," he growled.

As Derian stumbled backwards, Amsden gave him a half bow. "The King thanks you for delivering his prize right to the palace steps." He turned on his heel and raced toward Kacie, thrusting his hand deep in his pocket as he ran.

"Kerric! Get her out of here!" Derian yelled after Amsden.

"Come on," Kerric urged and Kacie didn't resist when he put his hand in the small of her back and hurried her down the street, giving three short whistles at the same time.

Ahead of them, Tia's head came up, searching. She saw Kerric and nodded; quickly dispatching the guard she was toying with and ran to join them.

"Get the girl! The one with the black hair!" Amsden shouted and Kacie slowed for a quick look behind her just as they rounded a corner. Amsden was hard on their heels and gaining.

"Oopsey. Feet don't fail me now!" She whipped around and picked up the pace; her head down and her arms pumping.

Kacie didn't see the human mountain step in front of her until she ran into his granite chest. A rock hard arm went around her waist and Kacie was lifted off her feet and held tight to the guard's side like so many potatoes in a sack. Her scream was cut short by the vice-like grip around her throat. Her vision feathered gray around the edges as Amsden appeared in front of her.

SHERRY BESSETTE

"Kacie!"

She heard Kerric shout from inside the tunnel she was fast spiraling down. Kacie squeezed her eyes shut for an instant and then opened them again, trying to focus on Kerric's fuzzy form as he headed back for her. "Kerric," she croaked.

Amsden's head snapped around and Kerric stopped. They stared at each other for a moment before a mocking sneer lifted Amsden's upper lip. "Oh yes, be a hero, Kerric Rouse. Please," he encouraged with a beckoning wave of his fingers. "I'd love to kill you too."

At Amsden's signal the guard holding Kacie tightened his hold around her neck. Kacie gasped and clawed at the man's arm trying to get air into her lungs. Through the ringing in her ears, Kacie heard Kerric snarl and saw his fists clench as he edged forward, but his path was cut off as guards closed around Kacie and Amsden, forming a human barricade.

Amsden dismissed Kerric with a snort and turned back to Kacie. Helpless, she watched him take his hand out of his pocket, open his fist and blow a fine crystalline powder into her face.

"Kerric," she raised an entreating arm out to him.

As the world spun black around her, she saw Derian forcing Kerric away from her. "You can't help her if you're captured too." Derian's words followed her into unconsciousness.

CHAPTER SEVEN

Kerric shook off Derian's hold on his arm and helplessly watched Amsden throw the unconscious Kacie over his shoulder and disappear around the corner.

"We have to go." Derian pointed to the knot of guards rapidly closing on them.

Kerric still hesitated. His whole body screamed to go after Kacie. Every fiber of his being strained to charge past the oncoming soldiers and give chase. He'd follow Amsden through the main gates and into Trion Palace itself, if that's what it took to get the Emerald Sorceress away from the Raven Wizard's corrupted influence.

"Now, Kerric."

Kerric threw back his head and let out a blood-curdling cry of impotent frustration as he spun and raced back toward the Lame Swan. Scanning the area around them, he frowned. "Where's Tia?"

"She went ahead to get the horses."

Kerric nodded, as they ducked into an alley and charged up a back street leading to the tavern. Seconds later, they burst into the Lame Swan's courtyard with their pursuers hard on their heels. "Good girl," Kerric muttered, seeing Tia waiting for them, already astride and leading their horses. Without breaking speed, Kerric and Derian vaulted into the saddle and the three of them galloped for the city's main gate.

As they clattered into the central square, Tia cocked her head at the troop of mounted soldiers rounding the fountain from the opposite direction. "Horses."

Kerric and Derian spared a quick look. "They didn't waste any time getting here," Derian grumbled, kicking his horse's sides. Kerric didn't bother to answer as he followed suit and put heels to ribs.

The trio reached the gate just steps ahead of the soldiers. They had one chance at escape. "Get through the gate." Kerric drew his sword and wheeled around behind Derian and Tia. As soon as they were clear, he swung the sword over his head and slashed down with all his strength, severing the thick rope holding the gate in place. Lying flat against his horse's back, Kerric ducked under the free-wheeling iron gate, narrowly escaping the rusted portcullis before they slammed home with a loud, ringing clang.

Angry cursing and the screams of horses sharply pulled up against the iron barricade, followed Kerric, Derian and Tia down the dusty road leading away from Trion, toward the river and relative safety of the forest beyond.

Galloping flat out, they clattered across the wooden bridge that spanned the Trion River, slowing only as they plunged into the dense woodlands north of the city.

Kerric never thought he'd be grateful for the endless forest patrols he pulled during his time as a palace guard, but he found himself blessing every one of them as Tia and Derian fell in behind him and they wove their way deep into the dark, leafy sanctuary. As soon as he was sure they were out of sight, Kerric turned north, away from the city for a long while and then edged his way south again, criss-crossing and doubling back on his path so that if their pursuers did pick up their trail they'd have a difficult time distinguishing which one was the correct one.

Derian threw a quick glance over his shoulder. "I think we've lost them." He slowed to an easy canter as Tia came along side.

Kerric pulled on the reins, and pressed his left knee into his horse's side, slowing and turning at the same time. The big war horse flicked his ears back and danced sideways. "Easy boy." Kerric stroked the bay neck and scanned the area, listening and looking for anything out of the normal. At length, he nodded and swung his mount around again as he eased the pull on the bit and gave a little nudge with his heels. The stallion shook his head and bolted after Derian and Tia. "I think you're right," Kerric agreed and fell in step with them.

"Did that seem a little too easy to anybody else?" Derian looked behind him again.

"That's because they already have what they want and it isn't us." Tia told him.

Kerric shook his head. "They're still back there. Jozef wanted the

Emerald Sorceress, yes, but Amsden still wants Derian. He wouldn't give up that easily. My guess is there are three or four men canvassing the woods for us, but the main force is posted along the outer edges of the forest with orders to keep us out of Trion." Kerric pointed to a partially hidden path. "That way."

Derian nodded and turned off the road, leading them single-file until the path opened onto a small clearing. Reining in, he called back. "Stop here?"

"Looks like a good spot to me." Tia stood in the stirrups, stretching. "It's about as good as we're gonna get." She swung down and led her horse off to the side, secured the lead around a tree trunk and then moved out of the way as Derian eased his horse in beside hers.

He began tying off the reins and then paused and glanced back at Kerric. "You don't think Jozef will kill her, do you?"

Kerric dismounted and leaned his arms across his saddle. Dropping his head into his arms for a moment, he took a deep breath and shook his head. "I don't think so." He straightened and turned. "At least not right away. ozef is all about power and there's no-one more powerful than the Emerald Sorceress. He wants her power not her life. Not yet." Kerric wasn't sure if he was trying to convince Derian or himself.

"A lot of good all that power did Reyna." Tia settled on her haunches and stabbed the earth with her boot knife.

Kerric acknowledged that truth with a nod. "Which is exactly why we have to get Kacie away from Jozef as soon as possible. If he's able to strip her powers." Kerric spread his hands wide and let the thought hang between them.

Derian whistled. "Jozef Renberg with the Emerald Sorceress' powers as well as the Raven Wizard's." He shook his head as he sprawled out on a convenient patch of soft moss.

"He'd be unstoppable," Tia agreed. "So what do we do?" She looked from Derian to Kerric.

Derian shrugged and leaned back to grab a small twig.

Kerric watched him pull a knife from his boot top and begin to strip the bark away. "I'm going back for her," Kerric said at last, crossing the clearing to perch on a tree stump.

Derian's hands froze and he looked sharply up at Kerric, but before he could say anything, Tia jumped in.

"You're going back for her?" Tia's eyebrows rose almost to her hairline. "You mean we're going back for her," she stressed the plural.

"No, I have to go alone." Kerric held up a hand to forestall her retort. "The three of us would be too conspicuous. Alone, I can slip past the guards." He waved a hand in the direction of the forest edge. "And get into the palace unnoticed."

Tia was up and pacing. She made a full circuit of the small clearing, before planting herself in front of Kerric. With her hands fisted on her hips, she cocked her head. "I suppose it would be useless to point out how dangerous that is?"

Kerric nodded. "Completely."

"Or that Jozef single-handedly over-threw the crown of Medora, murdering his own family to do it?"

"Uh-huh." Kerric nodded again, watching her pace back and forth in front of him.

"Are you going to help me?" Tia rounded on Derian.

Derian looked over at Kerric, calculated the stubborn set of his jaw and declined. "No." He motioned for her to continue.

Tia threw her hands up in disgust and whirled back to Kerric. "He's a wizard, Kerric."

"I think that fact has been firmly established."

"Well, you obviously weren't paying attention or you wouldn't be going off alone to fight him."

"Who said anything about fighting him?" Kerric got to his feet and put his hands on her shoulders. Circling around, he turned Tia with him and forced her down on the tree stump. "The plan, Tia." Kerric leaned forward until their foreheads touched. "Is to get in and get Kacie out before Jozef knows what's happening."

"And, how exactly, are you going to do that?"

"You know," Derian began, not looking up from the long piece of bark he was worrying off a stick. "I know a secret way into the palace." He dropped the stick and slid his knife back into his boot and grinned over at Tia and Kerric.

"You do?" Kerric and Tia chorused.

Derian nodded once. "Of course. How do you think I got out of there the last time? It puts you in the family chapel, beside the quire."

"I didn't know there was a secret passage in the family chapel."

97

Kerric leaned forward.

Derian winked at Tia. "That's why it's a *secret*."

"Okay, so how do we find out where Jozef's holding Kacie? We can't very well go knocking on doors." Tia pretended to knock on an invisible door. "Sorry to disturb, but is the Emerald Sorceress being held prisoner in here?" She shook her head. "I don't think so, Derian. Besides, she could be in the dungeon. We can't go poking around Trion Palace like this." She waved a hand at her plain trousers and boots. "Someone's bound to notice."

"Which is why I need to go alone," Kerric reiterated. "Alone, I can blend in if I have to with little to no commotion."

Derian nodded apologetically to Tia. "I hate to admit it, but he's right."

Tia scowled at both men and Kerric wrapped her in a quick bear hug. "I'll be careful. I promise. And, I'll be back in three days at the latest." He released her and turned to Derian. "How do I find this secret entrance of yours?"

Derian pulled his knife again and scooted over to Kerric and began drawing diagrams in the dirt. When he was sure Kerric was secure with his instructions, Derian sat back and asked; "What are we supposed to do while you're off playing the hero?"

"Stay here and out of trouble," Kerric quipped, heading for his horse.

Tia jumped down from her perch. "You're leaving now?"

"Yes. They won't be expecting anything this soon. They'll think we're still running." Kerric swung up into the saddle, gave them a jaunty salute and turned his horse back to Trion.

"If he isn't back in two days I'm going after him," Tia told Derian.

"One," Derian countered.

****

Secluded in his room, Jozef peered into the glass-like surface of the scrying bowl and watched as Amsden rode hard for the palace. In his arms, Amsden held the Emerald Sorceress. Jozef leaned closer, trying to make out her features, but the unconscious girl's head bobbed and slid to Amsden's chest, her long black hair spilling over her face. Jozef swore. Even now she was being shielded from his sight. A small spark of satisfaction flared as he watched Amsden give a sharp shrug of his shoulder and her head fell back, bouncing unsupported as they clattered through the streets of Trion. She would have a stiff neck to accompany the headache she'd wake up with.

In the water, Jozef saw Amsden ride past the palace gates, across the parade grounds and jerk his mount to a stop at the foot of the steps. A liveried groom ran to grab the horse's bridle, holding the lathered animal steady as Amsden signaled to a footman.

"Take the girl." He dumped Kacie into the man's arms and dismounted, hurrying up the steps. "Bring her," Amsden ordered, not bothering to turn around or slow his pace as he led the way inside and up the Grand Staircase to the third floor.

Jozef obliterated the watery images with a wave of his hand. Turning on his heel, he strode through the palace, anxious to inspect his prize. He met them on the threshold of the former Duchess' suite.

"The girl, Sire." Amsden inclined his head to the king as he stood aside for the footman to precede him.

"Put her on the bed and get out," Jozef ordered.

The footman hurried through the sumptuous green and white sitting room and into the sleeping chamber. He laid Kacie on the canopied bed and bowed to the king as he made a hasty retreat.

Jozef took a deep breath and finally moved toward the bed for his first look at the girl he turned a kingdom upside down to acquire. "So much fuss for such a little thing," Jozef mused, staring down at the unconscious girl. Could this child truly be the key to his future? He lifted one eyelid with a thumb and stared at the vacant emerald iris. Satisfied, he let the lid close again. Jozef brushed a strand of midnight hair from her face and watched the even rise and fall of her chest. In her drug induced sleep she didn't look like the most powerful sorceress Medora had ever known. She looked young and vulnerable. That made him smile.

Jozef sat on the bed next to Kacie and traced her high cheek bones and oval jaw line with one light finger. "She has the best features of both her parents," he said and looked up at Amsden standing beside the bed.

"She looks like her mother," Amsden agreed.

"Yes, she does." Jozef regarded her for a moment more then stood. "She'll sleep the night through. Get her out of these clothes and find her something more appropriate to wear before you bring her to me tomorrow"

Amsden inclined his head, acknowledging the King's order as he followed Jozef into the sitting room beyond.

"I want the guards doubled at all the gates and at every entrance into the palace." Jozef turned at the far door and pinned Amsden with an icy stare. "Place guards at the ends of every corridor as well. This place," he waved his hand to encompass the entire palace, "is riddled with secret passages. I don't want her companions anywhere near the Emerald Sorceress."

"I'll put guards outside this door. They won't get to her."

Jozef shook his head. "No, don't attract any attention here. Post guards at the end of the corridors only. And, James." Jozef's mouth twitched at the corners. "Don't kill them once they've been captured. I may need them. Just put them in the dungeon."

The tick in Amsden's cheek began to twitch. This time Jozef did smile; a cold, calculating lift of his thin lips. His eyes were as hard as ever as he placed a comforting hand on Amsden's shoulder. "Cheer up. You'll get your turn – after I've done with them." Jozef chuckled and led the way into the gallery. "However, until they are captured, you will stay here and guard her."

****

With a casualness he was far from feeling, Kerric ambled up the main road leading to Trion Palace. He had left his horse at the Lame Swan and donned his long coat in an effort to blend in with the last of the stragglers trying to get inside the palace grounds before the gates closed for the night. Kerric kept his head down, giving the appearance that he was just another weary traveler at the end of a long day.

Behind him, the creak of a wooden cart grew closer and Kerric moved aside to let it pass. He nodded to the two dirty boys perched on the back of the bouncing cart, their arms wrapped protectively around sloshing tins of milk. They stared vacantly at him until a breeze lifted his coat and their eyes widened as they saw the worn leather scabbard hanging at his hip and the polished steel handle protruding out of it. Kerric frowned and gave a practiced flick of his wrist, flipping the long coat forward, concealing the sword. The boys looked at each other and then lost interest as the cart bumped and bucked along the cobble stone road and they had to concentrate on keeping their cargo from falling out.

Kerric stopped just short of the gates and knelt, pretending to inspect the heel of his boot while he took in the details around him. Four sentries stood post outside the heavy, black rot-iron gates. Beyond the gates, the garrison was going through its normal routine of preparing the palace for the evening watch, but Kerric noticed extra guards posted at the entrances of the palace as well as several of the out buildings that opened directly into the palace. Jozef was expecting company, but they were expecting three not one. That gave him the edge.

Kerric stood and continued on. He nodded to the sentries and walked through the gates and onto the parade grounds. Behind him, the heavy gates closed for the night. Kerric turned and shielded his eyes as the setting sun glinted across the golden crest of the Aideny family. His eyes traced the familiar phoenix rising displayed from its flaming crown and for the first time it occurred to him to wonder why Jozef allowed the devise to remain in place.

With another look around, Kerric veered left past the garrison barracks and ducked into the stables. He quickly traversed the labyrinth of horse stalls, stroking a curious velvety nose or two that was thrust at him as he headed for the tack rooms and the training ring beyond. A moment later, he was jogging through the paddock doors, heading for the trees beyond.

At the edge of the woods, Kerric welcomed the growing shadows of night and slowed to a walk as he threaded his way through the trees. Ahead, and still unseen, he knew was a small lake and on the other side of the lake was the bath house. Kerric found the gravel path leading to the lake and soon saw reflected light from the palace windows shimmering on the still blackness of the calm water. He skirted the lake and crossed the wide manicured lawn stretching up to the bath house.

Kerric hesitated on the threshold, allowing his eyes to adjust to the defused light filtering through the tall windows that flanked the door. After a moment, he found a lamp sitting on a small serving table against the far wall. Kerric memorized its position and pulled the rich taffeta curtains across the windows and closed the door. In complete darkness, he cautiously moved across the room to the table and felt for the lamp. With one hand on the lamp, he fumbled in the small leather bag hanging from his belt and a second later, struck flint to steel. The lamp sprang to life, its soft glow showing him the hall that would take him to the back parlor.

Kerric moved quickly into the parlor and scanned the room. Remembering Derian's instructions, he counted off three panels from the right side of the door and made a wry face as he pressed the nose of the cherub peering over the top of the decorative molding. A whisper of sound and a rush of cold air told him that something had moved, but the wall in front of him was as solid as ever.

Kerric raised the lamp and stepped back to inspect the room and his foot plunged into empty space. He clutched the lamp tighter, his free arm flailing as he tried to keep from pitching backwards into the abyss. Kerric snapped his head around and saw a three foot section of the flooring standing open beside him. He grabbed for the edge of the upright floorboard, scraping his knuckles as he steadied himself. Kerric shook his stinging hand then stuck the bleeding knuckles in his mouth.

"Ouch!" He yanked the lamp away from his thin shirt and scorching skin. "Leave it to Derian to leave out important information – like the secret passage is in the middle of the floor." He rubbed his singed chest with his splintered knuckles.

Still grousing to himself, he held the lamp higher so that he could inspect the narrow stairwell that lead nowhere as far as he could see, except into blackness. "Well, I'm not getting anywhere standing here." He gave a fatalistic shrug and descended the steep stairs. Above him, the open floor panel automatically settled back into place, sealing the secret entrance behind him.

It was a short descent to solid ground and soon Kerric found himself in a narrow tunnel. He hunched his tall frame and twisted his wide shoulders so that he fit in the cramped space without losing either skin or his head and followed the meandering tunnel the quarter of a mile back to the palace. Just when he was sure he'd be six inches shorter and have permanently scarred shoulders, the tunnel opened onto a circular room with a winding stone staircase in the center. Kerric let out a sigh of relief as he straightened and stretched his contorted body before beginning the long precarious climb up the rough-hewn steps.

The five story climb from the tunnel to the cramped landing at the top of the stairs left him winded. With his hands on his knees and his head down, Kerric sucked in several gulps of air to slow his breathing. "Whoever built this passage was a short, sadistic...." A noise in the room beyond caught his attention. Kerric located the peep hole in the wall paneling in front of him and doused the light.

He slid the cover aside and peered into the chapel. At first all he could see was the herringbone pattern of the nave floor, but by bending a little and angling his head sideways, he was able to make out the single pew of the far quire. Three small candles, evenly spaced on the flat banister of the music stands, infused the dark wood of the tiny quire with a burnished glow. A shadow of movement caught his attention and Kerric pivoted slightly to watch a lean chaplain, still dressed in rich gold and white robes from the evening devotions, cross the chancel to the High Alter.

The man tipped his thinning grey head to the wooden Crucifix standing in the center of the alter and said a quick reverence before he blew out the fat candles on either side. After rearranging the golden chalice and plate more to his liking, the man gave a final twitch to the red satin alter cloth and exited the chapel by a side door.

Kerric watched for a few more minutes to be sure that the old chaplain wasn't coming back. When he was relatively certain it was safe, Kerric pushed on the secret portal and stepped into the room and made his way down the nave to the rear entrance. Kerric grabbed hold of the ornate door handle and paused to say a quick prayer to whichever Saint held sway there. Finding the Emerald Sorceress and getting her out of the palace wasn't going to be easy and frankly, he figured he could use all the help he could get – just in case Derian left anything else out.

Kerric eased the chapel door open and emerged into the corridor. Getting his bearings, he listened for any unusual noises. Everything was quiet. Kerric pivoted and jogged along the long gallery, past the two gilded doors that shielded the suites used by the former Duke Alexei and his Duchess. Kerric ignored them. Even though Queen Alaina and Derian's Rebecca were fond of the chapel and used it often when they were here, Jozef avoided this wing. He doubted Jozef would put Kacie here.

At the corridor junction beyond, an unseen man coughed and at least two others laughed encouragement to their companion. Kerric froze and then plastered himself to the wall, easing back the way he came. He kept one eye on the corner as he felt for a door handle. At last, his hand contacted a golden lever. Kerric prayed that the door had been oiled recently as he pressed the handle down and slid through the narrow opening he made for himself.

"Well, well, if it isn't Kerric Rouse."

Kerric whipped around at the sound of the familiar gravely voice. He took one look at the long black hair and solid black clothes of the man leaning against the fireplace mantle and swore.

Amsden drew his sword. "This is too good to be true." He advanced on Kerric.

"That isn't exactly how I'd put it," Kerric muttered, side-stepping Amsden's first thrust, narrowly drawing his sword in time to block a second as he backed out of the room.

The ringing of steel echoed down the hall as Amsden launched a ferocious two handed attack aimed at Kerric's head and upper body. Kerric parried each blow in quick succession then jumped back, out of reach and pulled a dagger from his boot. Dancing in again, he slashed at Amsden's midsection.

Amsden twisted away, smashing Kerric's wrist with the hilt of his sword. The dagger flew out of Kerric's nerveless fingers and clattered across the marble floor. Kerric swore and shook his hand to get the circulation back.

Smelling victory, Amsden stepped in close, his sword circling above his head and slashing down in a killing stroke.

Kerric ducked and threw his whole body at his opponent, catching Amsden full force in the stomach with his shoulder. The air left Amsden's lungs with a grunt as he was flung back, stumbling into the wall. Gasping for breath and stunned, Amsden slid down the gilded wall paneling. Kerric stood over Amsden, the point of his sword pressing against the man's throat.

"Kill me and you won't make it to the end of the gallery alive," Amsden sneered. His glance slid up the threatening blade and came to rest on Kerric's face. "Give up and you might just live out the rest of the day."

Kerric gave a short bark of laughter. "Why would I give up?" He pressed the sword point a little harder, noting the satisfying circle of crimson swelling past the steel blade.

Amsden looked down both ends of the gallery then back to Kerric. "I can think of eight reasons why you should give up now."

Kerric froze as a sword was placed against his throat just under the chin and another slid across the back of his neck. The blade went slack in Kerric's hand. Amsden pushed the sword away and got to his feet while a palace guard relieved Kerric of it. When the weapon was safely in the soldier's hands, Amsden doubled his fist and cold cocked Kerric in the jaw. Kerric's head moved with the blow allowing most of the force to slide away.

"Is that all you've got?" Kerric's smile was contemptuous.

"No." Amsden circled Kerric. "I have you," he said when they were face to face again. "All I have to do now is wait for your friend to show up looking for you and I'll have my revenge as well."

"What makes you think Derian will come looking for me?"

Amsden signaled and a guard smashed Kerric on the back of the head with the hilt of his sword. Kerric dropped like a stone.

"Oh, he'll come,"Amsden told Kerric's unconscious form. "Put him in the dungeon," he ordered. A triumphant smirk lifted the corners of his mouth as he watched Kerric being dragged away. "And, find out how he got in."

CHAPTER EIGHT

The woman gathered her velvet dressing gown around her swollen body and lowered herself as gracefully as she could into the delicate gold satin chair placed before a white lacquered vanity. With a weary sigh, she inspected her reflection. A slender hand rose to her breast and righted the small filigreed crest that had turned itself over in the course of the day. She traced the golden phoenix with a finger, a frown of worry creased her smooth brow.

Shaking her head, she pushed away whatever worries were there and dipped her hands into the porcelain bowl resting beside her right arm. She swirled the yellow rose petals floating in the water and closed her eyes, inhaling the sweet scent before bringing her wet hands to her face. She was tired and in spite of the cold, rainy weather outside, the cool water on her face was refreshing. Opening her eyes, she dropped her hands into her lap, caressing her extended belly. A light smile touched her lips, before becoming a grimace.

"I'm as anxious for you to be out of there as you are my little one." She pressed on the spot where the unborn baby's foot continued to kick. "There's little doubt about it; you will be a spirited one," she said with an indulgent smile around gritted teeth. "You'll be a match for anyone." Her smile faded, replaced by the worried frown of a moment before. Her golden brown eyes were sad as she slid her hands protectively around the child she carried.

"Would Your Grace care for assistance in disrobing before bed this evening?" a deep, resonant male voice said from the door of the bed chamber.

"Alexei!" The woman swiveled around, her smile welcoming. "You're back!" She opened her arms wide. In an instant, he was on his knees before her being enfolded in her tight embrace. "And, you're wet." She pushed him away.

"In case you haven't noticed, wife; there's a storm raging outside." He stood and shucked his drenched cloak.

"You could have gotten rid of that." She pointed to the sodden heap of wool puddeling on her floor. "Before you came to me."

Alexei bent his tall frame in half as he swept her an apologetic bow. "A thousand pardons my lady. My only thought was to gain your side, my beloved Maya."

Maya made a face. "Your only thought was to get to the mulled wine you knew would be in my chamber."

"That also," Alexei admitted and wrapped his arms around his wife's shoulders, kissing the top of her head. He turned his face, resting his cheek against the silken tresses and inhaled the delicate lilac scent as one strong hand slid down and stroked her belly. "And how is my daughter this evening?" he asked and received a strong kick for an answer. "Oh ho! The lady is in fine form, I see."

Maya winced. "If you call making her mother very uncomfortable in fine form."

Alexei laughed as he straightened and began removing the pins from Maya's hair. "She'll be a strong, lively child," he declared, taking the gilded hair brush from the vanity and brushing long strokes through the luxuriant mass. He paused, his eyes becoming soft and distant. "We'll marry her to no less than a King. She will be the most important lady in Medora."

Maya shook her head at his father's dreams. "She's going to be the Emerald Sorceress, Alexei. From the moment of her birth she will be the most important lady in Medora."

Alexei sobered. He handed the brush to Maya and crossed to the fireplace. Maya watched through the mirror as he took the bottle of wine from its warming rack and poured himself a glass. "I want you to go to Kiramer tomorrow," he said without turning around.

"Alexei, no." Maya stood and came to him. "I can't leave you. I won't leave you." She placed a pleading hand on his arm.

"We have no choice, Maya." Hiding his pain behind a determined mask, Alexei stepped away from her influence and circled behind the white and gold chair beside the hearth. "Jozef knows about our child and her destiny. Your time is near and he'll make his move soon. Reyna told you this herself when she was here last week. You cannot delay any longer. For your safety, for our daughter's safety, you must go to Reyna. For my sake." Alexei swallowed hard and concentrated on tracing the flower pattern on the chair for a moment, then looked up again. "I couldn't live if something happened to you." Alexei saw the stubborn set of his wife's jaw and his voice and face became hard. He could not let her sway him. "You will obey me in this, Maya. You will go tomorrow."

****

Kacie woke slowly. A slight headache pulsed behind her eyes. She pushed it away so that she could bask in the warm glow of love coursing through her veins.   Like her headache, Kacie ignored the undercurrent of menace the dream held and wiggled deeper into the soft mattress. She tucked the velvet comforter around her chin, a smile tickling her lips as she replayed the dream in her mind. She sighed and snuggled further into the warm folds of velvet.

A frown crinkled Kacie's tightly closed eyes an instant before she opened them and looked down. "I don't have a velvet comforter." She trailed her fingers over the plush, gold material, and her brows furrowed as she glanced up at the canopy above her. "I don't have a canopy, either." She followed the gold and white striped pattern to where it tied off to two carved rosewood bedposts.

"What the . . ." Kacie sat up and scanned the elegant gold and white room around her. Rubbing her temples, she tried to clear the cobwebs from her mind. "Why can't I think?" She scrubbed at her face and forced herself to concentrate.

Images forced themselves through the haze in her befuddled brain. Sausage fingers pressed into her throat, choking her. Near by, a tall man with long sandy hair, his handsome face contorted with anger and fear as he fought to get to her.

Kerric

Memory flooded over her. She knew where she was and how she got there. Kacie threw back the covers and swung her feet to the floor. Gathering the voluminous folds of the red, satin nightdress around her calves, she rushed toward the door.

A wave of dizziness swept over her and Kacie stumbled. She caught the edge of the white lacquered vanity, dropped into the delicate gold chair and rested her head on her arm until the room stopped spinning.

Whew, I don't know what was in that stuff that guy blew into my face, but man....

108

Kacie raised her head and leaned closer to the guilt mirror and inspected her reflection. "Oh yeah, Miller, you'll get real far lookin' like that." She rubbed her pale cheeks, trying to put a little color in them, then pulled down the lower lid of one bleary eye and shook her head. That drew her attention to the black bird's nest that used to be her hair. "Yep, you are definitely a Miss America contender." She sighed at the hopeless reflection and flipped over the Phoenix crest hanging around her neck as she looked down at the porcelain bowl at her elbow.

Kacie swirled the yellow rose petals floating in the water and inhaled. "Mmmmmm, nice." She wiped her hands on her nightgown and picked up the gilded hair brush lying in front of her. With long, slow strokes, she pulled the brush through her tangled hair, luxuriating in the soft bristles on her tight scalp.

Mid-stroke, Kacie's eyes saucered and her hand froze. She dropped the brush, ignoring the water that splashed on her as it fell into the porcelain bowl. "It can't be." Kacie looked through the mirror at the large fireplace behind her, half expecting to see Alexei shying away from the flames of a roaring fire to retrieve the wine mulling in its rack.

Kacie stood and crossed to the white and gold chair beside the cold hearth. "This is Maya's room," she whispered and griped the back of the chair leaving dents in the soft fabric. Her hand shook as she traced the flowers just as Alexei – no, her father - had twenty-two years before. She swallowed hard and sank into the seat; her legs too weak to support her.

Kacie dropped her head between her knees and concentrated on breathing. There were truths to be faced and questions that wanted answers, but just then she had to breathe.

"I see you are back with us."

Startled, Kacie's head snapped up and she spun around. "You!" She stared at the apparition standing in the doorway. He was more shadow than man, dressed from head to toe in black. *Where did he come from?* She forced her heart to slow to normal, and unclenched her fists. "You kidnapped me. Why?"

Amsden seated himself in the floral chair on the other side of the hearth and arranged his lace cuffs. When he was satisfied he raised his small black eyes to her. "The King wished to meet our new Emerald Sorceress."

"Where are my friends?" Kacie asked. Amsden said nothing. Kacie waited and still he said nothing. "They escaped didn't they?" She slumped back as a tidal wave of relief washed over her.

Amsden rose. "I've ordered you a bath and some decent clothes."

"Excuse me?" Kacie jumped to her feet. "Just who do you think you are?"

He looked down his long hawk nose at her as if studying an insect. "You cannot wander the palace looking like a gutter rat." He pointed to her clothes still lying in the corner. "Someone might throw you away with the garbage," he said, crossing to the door again.

Gutter rat? Gutter rat! "Who are you calling a gutter rat?"

Amsden looked back the way he came and snapped his fingers. He stepped aside and three chamber maids filed in. The first one carried towels and a basket of bath oils and perfumes. The tall girl in the middle had her hands full of shoes, stockings and under garments, while the last maid held a beautiful gown of pale lavender satin and a champagne underskirt.

Instead of putting the things on the bed as Kacie expected, Amsden pushed on the edge of a wall panel and it sprang open to reveal a hidden dressing room. Everyone filed into the little room and Kacie trouped right along behind them.

As the first girl went through the door on the left, and into the bathing room, Kacie noticed the gilded edge of another door peeking over the top of a painted silk privacy screen. She threaded her way between Amsden and the maids, ducked behind the screen and stuck her head around the door. It was the privy.

"Well, at least I don't have to go outside to use the outhouse," she mumbled and peered into the bathing room in time to see the first maid put a plug in the huge marble tub. *Ooh, a bath.* Kacie sighed, suddenly feeling every speck of grit and grime accumulated on her body by a week spent in the woods on horseback. "And running water too." She grinned in delight, as the girl turned the gold handles, flooding the tub with steaming water.

Kacie elbowed Amsden out of her way so that she could get into the room for a closer look. Finally inside, she made a tight circle and whistled at the gold veined floor to ceiling mirrors lining the walls. Wow, *I feel like I'm in a palace. Oh wait. I am!* She laughed at herself.

"These are your maids." Amsden broke into her reverie, calling her back into the dressing room. "They will assist you with your bath and dressing. When you have finished, join me in the sitting room."

Toad.

Kacie made a rude gesture behind his back then started slapping at the hands trying to remove her clothes. "Excuse me. I can undress myself." She broke free and backed into a corner.

Kerric Rouse School of Fighting; lesson number one: When out numbered, find a corner.

"We are here to assist you, M'Lady." The tall maid stepped toward her again.

"I don't think so." Kacie crossed her index fingers in the sign of the cross to ward off evil, and the maids stopped. "I've been bathing myself for a long time now. Thank you, very much. I think I can handle it on my own."

"But, the Earl of Amsden has ordered us -"

"The Earl can take his orders and stick them up his . . . nose."

They giggled, and then sobered. "M'Lady, you mustn't. He'll hear you."

"Ask me if I care." Then, seeing their concern was real, Kacie relented. "Okay, look, I don't want to get you guys in trouble. So, I'll tell you what we're gonna do. You stay out here and be real quiet while I go take a quick bath - alone. Then you can help me put that get-up on." She cocked her head at the dress. "Because between you and me, I don't think I could get into all that by myself."

Before they had time to react, Kacie slipped past them and closed the door to the bathing room behind her, wedging a small table against the handle for good measure.

Kacie shed her nightgown, slid into the tub and sank to her chin in the warm water. A long sigh floated from her lips. *I've died and gone to heaven.* She closed her eyes and let herself drift with the sheer luxury of it all. For just a little while she let her fears and troubles drown in the lilac scented bubbles. They'd all be waiting when she was done. But, for now, she just soaked.

All too soon, a soft knock brought her back to reality. "Okay, okay."

She threw a skeptical look at the toiletries table barricading the door. Kacie bathed and washed her hair as fast as possible, in case her maids took it into their heads to come in and try to help her.

Pulling a towel from the basket, she got out of the tub and dried off. "I need underwear." Kacie stuck her head around the door and held out her hand.

The maids exchanged a worried look. "My Lady. . ." one of them began.

"I'm not budging until I get underwear." There was an urgent discussion and then she was handed a white linen chemise and pantaloons. "Thank you." Kacie smiled and vanished again, reemerging a minute later. "Okay, ladies, do your stuff."

Forty-five minutes later, Kacie had been transformed. "That's me?" She stared at her reflection in the full-length mirror. "Crimeny. That can't be me. I look like I belong at the French court of Louis-Something-or-Other." Kacie shook her head and the elegant lady in the mirror shook her head too, her black ringlets bouncing. "I don't believe it." She lifted her skirts to admire the low-heeled lavender slippers on her feet. "If only Kerric could see me now." She grinned and gave herself one more admiring glance.

"You do clean up rather nicely,"Amsden admitted from where he lounged against the dressing room door.

"Don't you ever knock?"

"I grew tired of waiting." Amsden strolled over and stood behind her. He picked up one black curl at her nape and twirled it around his fingers before letting it fall again.

"That's no excuse for bad manners." Kacie jerked away from him and swept out of the bed chamber and into the adjacent sitting room. Her steps faltered a fraction as she took in the opulent sea green room. *Wow.* She recovered her composure a second later and frowned at Amsden.

Kacie lowered herself into a chair and made a show of arranging her skirts. Amsden sat on the couch opposite her. She stopped and quirked an eyebrow at him. "Please, do be seated." It was easy to be snooty when you looked like a queen.

"You're a cocky little gutter rat. The King will like that. Reyna was such a bore, so stuffy, so -predictable."

Kacie leaned forward, her elbows resting on her knees. "So, what does this King of yours want with me? I'm a nobody." She spread her hands wide and slouched back crossing her left ankle over her right knee. "I'm just a girl from the beach."

"My Lady Emerald . . ." His sandpaper voice grated on her nerves.

"My name is Kacie, Kacie Miller."

"Kacie," he tried the sound and obviously found it distasteful.

Kacie bristled. "I happen to like my name."

"I'm sure you do."

I'm sure you do' . . . What a toad. I wouldn't be looking down my nose at other people if I were you; not with that Snidely Whiplash mustache and stupid little tuft of hair under your lip.

"The King will inform you of everything you need to know in his own time."

Outside, the bell in the clock tower rang ten times and Amsden got to his feet. "It's time."

"Joy." Kacie was about to say more when he grabbed her arm and hauled her to her feet. She shook off his hand and glared at him. He gave her a mocking bow and swept an arm out for her to precede him into the gallery outside her apartments.

Mustering her dignity, Kacie stepped past him. "Where exactly are we going?"

"This way." Amsden moved around her and led the way.

"Just out of curiosity, have you ever considered wearing something besides black?"

Amsden ignored her as he led the way down a long gallery, up a wide marble staircase and along another gallery. Absorbed in her incredible surroundings, Kacie almost stepped on his heels when he stopped before an ornate, gold leafed door, and knocked. A light baritone voice bid them enter.

Amsden pushed open the door and ushered Kacie into a small, sun-filled library. "The girl, Sire." He bowed low.

Kacie pulled her eyes from the book-laden mahogany shelves lining the rectangular room, to inspect the man gazing out at the courtyard below. The King was a lean, wiry man, dressed from head to toe in cream satin shot with silver thread,

He ran long fingers through his close-cropped, fair hair and slowly turned. Kacie gasped. She was staring into the face of the Raven Wizard from her nightmares. A shiver ran down her spine and she tried to look away, but his pale blue eyes captured hers holding her motionless.

Behind him, the sun flared, blazing through the tall window, blinding her. She threw up an arm to protect her eyes and squinted against the glare. A telltale blue aura surrounded him.

Kacie clicked her tongue. "Oh, for heaven's sake." She flicked her hand and the glare died. "I've seen better tricks from party clowns."

Amsden whirled on her. "Watch your tongue, Gutter Rat, before you loose it."

"Back off, Jack." Kacie glared at him.

Jozef waved him off. "She's right, it was a meager display." He moved to Kacie's side and inclined his head to her. "Nicely countered."

Kacie stared at him, unblinking. "If you say so."

"I do say so." He glared down at her for a moment. "I have been searching for you for a very long time, My Lady Sorceress,"he glowered and then his expression cleared and Jozef smiled delightedly at her. "And, here you are at last." He spread his arms wide, welcoming her.

Kacie turned her back on the King and perched on the big mahogany desk behind her. Swinging her legs back and forth, she picked up the writing quill lying beside her hand and began twirling it between her fingers. Taking her courage in hand, she looked up at Jozef and took a deep breath. "Everyone keeps telling me I'm the Emerald Sorceress. And who knows, maybe I am." She shrugged. "But, I don't believe it and right now I'm thinking I'd make a pretty pathetic sorceress – emerald, ruby or even papier-mache." Kacie gave him a weak smile, then focused on the twirling quill. "I can't imagine why a powerful wizard like you would want to waste your time with someone like me." She raised her eyes to his. "So, how about if you send me back home and we can both forget I was ever here. Okay?"

"But, you are home, my dear. ust look around you." Jozef took the pen from her hands and laid it on the desk before gripping her knee and swinging her around to face a life-size portrait of a man hanging on the wall behind the desk. "That is your father, Alexei Aideny, tenth

Duke of Trion."

Kacie looked up and her mouth went dry. He was younger than in her dream, but there was no doubt that this was the same man. Her father. She slid a covert glance at Jozef; as expected, he was watching her reaction. Kacie refused to give him any. She licked her lips and pulled herself together. Ignoring his scrutiny, she stared up at the tall, broad shouldered young man dressed in rich blue riding leathers. A large, well-shaped hand rested on the head of a great white hound. The handsome face under a shock of warm brown hair was open and friendly with just a hint of mischief in the clear blue eyes and the up-turned quirk of his full mouth. But, behind the mischief, she recognized stubbornness in the strong, square chin. An unexpected lump caught in her throat and Kacie found herself wishing that she had known him.

"This was Alexei's study," Jozef broke into her thoughts. "We spent many long hours in this room over a chess board and a bottle of brandy. Alexei used to sit in this chair," he sat and ran his hands over the polished arms, "and stare at that painting of his beloved wife." Jozef pointed across the room.

Kacie craned her neck around to the other end of the room and her heart almost stopped. Without a word, she slid off the desk and went to stand before the large fireplace where a painting of a woman about her own age hung above the mantle. Kacie swallowed hard and fought back the tears.

Maya was dressed in a gown of red brocade, standing next to a white pianoforte, her thick black hair tumbled in lose curls over one ivory shoulder. Brown eyes sparkled below delicately arched brows, and a smile danced on her sensual wine colored lips. Around her neck, she wore the crest of Trion. Kacie's hand went to her necklace.

"The family resemblance is remarkable," Jozef said, from behind her.

Resemblance, nothing! It's like looking into a mirror!

Kacie forced herself to turn away from her mother's image and pretend interest in the floor to ceiling books lining the walls. "This is a nice room."

"Yes, it is," Jozef agreed. "This has always been my favorite room at Trion. That's why I left everything exactly the way Alexei had it. It is my tribute to the memory of a good friend, and happier times." Jozef scanned the room before his gaze returned to Kacie's skeptical face.

"I'm sure he'd appreciate that."

"I promised your father, that I would watch over you until you were ready to take your rightful place, but then, Maya disappeared before you were born. You cannot know how much it distressed me that you were out there somewhere; growing up in who knew what vile conditions and there was nothing I could do about it."

Yeah, I'll just bet you were heartbroken.

"It pained me deeply that I could not keep my solemn vow as King and friend. Your father would be very pleased to know that you are at last in Trion where you belong."

Who is he trying to kid?

"When you have been here for a while and see all that Trion has to offer...." He cupped her chin with his hand and tipped her head back so that he was looking into her vibrant, emerald eyes. ". . . all that I have to offer, you will wonder how you ever lived anywhere else." Jozef looked deep into her emerald eyes, his voice low and hypnotic. "Don't fight what you are, Lady Emerald. Let me teach you; take you step by step toward your destiny.

Kacie blinked, breaking the spell. She shook her head sharply to clear away the lingering echoes of his voice. "But, I can't be that person. Why won't you believe that?"

"Because." Jozef ran his finger over her tense jaw. "If I believed that, I would kill you on the spot."

Kacie paled and swayed, backing into Amsden who grabbed her arms and held her steady as Jozef continued, his eyes hard.

"But, I know that you are the Emerald Sorceress, however much you try to deny it." Jozef leaned in closer and whispered. "And, one way or another, my dear, you will learn that I am your master. And, you will become the Emerald Sorceress I have envisioned for so many years."

CHAPTER NINE

"Never mind." King Jozef strolled to the open window and leaned against the round mahogany table beneath the sill. He drew back one of the sheer curtains covering the window and gazed out across the manicured lawn below. "Do you know what a scrying bowl is?"

Kacie shook off Amsden's hand and shot him a 'curl-up-someplace-and-die' look before she twisted around and gaped at Jozef's relaxed stance.

Kerric was right; the man's psycho. A second ago he was trying to kill me! Now look at him . . . I've got to get out of here. Her heart hammered in her chest as Kacie's gaze raked the room, but Jozef stood between her and the far door and Amsden leaned with his arms folded across his chest, beside the other one. Their eyes met and almost as if he read her thoughts, Amsden's hand dropped to the hilt of his sword and he shifted his weight, blocking the door. Kacie fought her panic.

Think, Miller. Calm down and think so you can find a way to get yourself out of here!

"Do you know what a scrying bowl is?" Jozef repeated the question.

And, whatever you do, don't antagonize him until you figure a way out of this mess. Kacie took a couple of mental deep breaths. "I," she cleared her throat and started again. "I know what they are, but I've never used one."

"Come here." Jozef motioned her to him and stepped aside. As he moved, a light breeze fluttered the curtain across a blue porcelain bowl that had been concealed by his body.

She forced herself to move toward the table as ordered and looked into the bowl that had been filled with water.

"With this bowl we can scry – see - many things," Jozef continued.

Kacie glanced from the clear water to Jozef. "Like what?"

"Like your apartments, here in the palace, for instance." He snapped his fingers and Amsden placed a black velvet pouch in the

King's palm and retreated to his post again.

Jozef opened the bag, took out a pinch of fine powder and sprinkled it across the surface. A billow of red smoke erupted from the bowl. Kacie sneezed and fanned the acrid stench from her face. When the smoke cleared, she leaned in for a better look at the roiling red water. "Now what?"

"Watch." Jozef spoke an incantation that she didn't understand, and passed his open palm over the bowl.

The swirling water stilled and the muddy color dissolved into an image of a white and gold flowered chair sitting beside a wide fireplace. "That's the room I just left."

Kacie grinned, surprised to see Maya's bed chamber. She tilted her head a little and the image panned with her, stopping as the vanity across the room came into view. "Cool." She bobbled her head back and forth and up and down, so that she could see the entire bed chamber.

Jozef watched her for a moment, and then nudged her out of the way. "If you wish to see other areas within the bowl, move your finger over the surface of the water." He drew his finger in a slow circle. The view of the room rotated like a slow moving camera displaying every inch of the room. When his finger stopped so did the images.

Kacie was impressed. "Now that could be very useful."

"Especially if you need to keep track of something or someone."

Holy Peeping Tom, Batman! Kacie froze and blushed from her hairline all the way to her toes. *This pervert can watch me take a bath if he wants to! Oh no, this is definitely not good.*

Jozef didn't seem to notice her acute embarrassment as he waved his hand over the bowl and pronounced the words of the spell a second time. The water churned, obliterating the bedroom scene, then settled into a picture of a sun dappled woodland clearing.

Kacie set aside her embarrassment for the moment, fascinated at seeing a man and woman sitting beside a small campfire with wooden plates of food in their laps and pewter mugs resting on the ground beside them. Kacie gasped as she recognized Derian and Tia and bit her lip. *He can use this to find Derian, too. Okay, now I really don't like this thing.* She cast a surreptitious look at Jozef to see if he noticed her reaction. He raised an eyebrow at her. Kacie groaned inside. *Good one, Miller. It's a good thing you aren't in charge of keeping state secrets.*

"Didn't you have three companions?"

Ice cold dread coursed through Kacie's veins. *Where's Kerric?*

"We seem to be missing one."

Jozef's right; unless he's taking a leak, he should be there with Derian and Tia.

Jozef moved his finger over the water and the scenery scrolled to the surrounding area. They saw a squirrel scamper up a tree and a family of rabbits dining on the tender spring underbrush, but no Kerric.

Okay, Kerric, what are you up to?

Jozef trailed his finger back to the clearing. "Maybe they can tell us where he went." He said something under his breath and suddenly Kacie was listening to Derian and Tia's conversation.

"I don't like it, Derian. We should never have let him go alone. What if he gets caught?" Tia tossed the dark liquid from her mug into the fire and rose to her feet. She made a couple circuits around the clearing before Derian said anything.

Please tell me he's not coming to get me. Kacie started picking at the hem of her lace sleeve as she continued to listen.

"Will you relax, Tia? Kerric is fine and he'll be back soon."

At his station by the door, Amsden gave a low snort. Kacie turned to him and Amsden slowly shook his head back and forth, denying Derian's words. He gave her a smug sneer that sent a shiver down her spine.

No, Kerric wouldn't come here on his own. She was about to demand an explanation from Amsden when Tia's voice echoed from inside the bowl again.

"How can you be so sure?" Tia asked and Kacie brought her attention back to the scrying bowl.

"I know Kerric." Derian shrugged as if that was all that needed to be said.

Kacie's brow creased as she listened. *Kerric's not that stupid.* She refused to believe Kerric would do something as foolish as come to the palace and try to get her out. She couldn't believe they would let him!

Beside her, Jozef scratched his nose. "I think we should find out where your other friend has gone." He passed his hand over the bowl and Derian and Tia's watery forms blended with the forest, swirling into a kaleidoscope of colors that darkened and began to reform.

Kacie's heart leapt to her throat. *NO! Protect him!* Every instinct in her body screamed to keep Kerric away from Jozef. Staring hard into the liquid images, she willed the vision to dissolve and to her surprise, a thick emerald haze rolled over the water.

Jozef tried to wave it away, but the green vapor only rippled around his fingers and remained impenetrable. He swore and tossed more powder into the water. The cloud thickened.

Jozef threw a sharp look at Kacie and drew back, vigorously rubbing his arms. "Very good, my Lady Emerald, but, you wouldn't have to work so hard at countering my spell if you would channel your energy instead of broadcasting it wildly about."

His quiet chuckle broke her concentration and Kacie realized she was holding her breath. She let it out in a rush, refilling starved lungs before meeting his amused gaze. "What do you mean, countering your spell? I didn't. I couldn't . . ."

"Of course you did." The edge in his voice stopped her cold. "And very nicely too. But, I refuse to have my blood itch every time you use your powers, so you will learn to control your energy." The smile was back, but it didn't quite thaw the glacial expression.

Kacie didn't hear anything past 'Of course you did,' before her mind started to buzz. *He thinks I countered his spell. Did I?* Kacie suppressed a grin. She dropped her eyes and pretended to study the floor. *I just countered the spell of a trained wizard!*

To hide her growing excitement, Kacie spun and flopped into a chair and crossed her ankle over her other knee. Her long skirts got hung up under her foot and she yanked them out, and then paused for a fraction of a second.

How did I do that? She thought back trying to figure out what exactly she just did, but her mind stayed blank. Glancing up at Jozef, she leaned forward again. "Look, I don't have a clue what I do or how I do it. How am I supposed to control it?"

"You make a good point," he admitted, taking the chair opposite her. "And that is exactly why you are here; to learn how to use your powers."

"So, how do we do that? How do I learn to use these powers you say I have?" *Please, teach me everything you know. Show me how to work magic that you can't detect.*

"Scrying is one of the simplest forms of magic to learn and use, and since its obvious you already know how to counter a scrying spell, let's see if you can conjure one." He stood and held out his hand to her.

Kacie looked at it and then up at the King as she put her hands on the seat cushion and slid to the edge of the chair. The artery in Jozef's neck began to pulse and his jaw clenched. Kacie stopped in mid motion and settled back into her chair. *Don't tick him off, Miller. You need his knowledge.* She forced a smile onto her face and swallowed her pride as she took his hand.

Jozef acknowledged her acquiescence to his will with a squeeze of her hand and led her back to the window. Kacie ignored the pain in her fingers and focused her attention on the scrying bowl.

It was probably just her imagination, but she swore the innocent little blue bowl grew into a giant blue bowl while she wasn't looking. Were those teeth sticking out of the rim? Sharp, pointy teeth that were just waiting for her to make a mistake so that they could dine on her tender flesh. She hung back, but Jozef propelled her forward with a firm hand in the small of her back.

"To use a scrying bowl or to make any kind of magic, for that matter," Jozef began her instruction. "You must clear your mind of all outside thoughts as you picture what or whom you want to see. Then, reach for the power within you. Let it build and when you feel it reach its peak, cast a pinch of powder into the water. Place your hand over the bowl, speak the spell and unleash the power.

"You've already seen your apartments, so why don't you start with them? I'll guide you through it the first time. Can you picture them?"

Kacie nodded.

"Good. Close your eyes and take a deep breath. Go on, close your eyes," he repeated when she continued to stare at him.

What the heck. Kacie closed her eyes and took a deep breath, filling her diaphragm with air. With Jozef's soft instructions to guide her, she cleared her mind as she exhaled and mentally reached down inside herself, searching for the center of her power.

Her stomach growled.

Kacie stifled a giggle. *If that's the center of my power, I'm in big trouble.*

Biting her lip to keep from laughing, she tried to concentrate on Jozef's insistent voice instead of her empty belly. But, it was food and not magic that was on her mind as she took a pinch of powder from the velvet bag. With super-human effort, Kacie dragged her mind back to the lesson, centered herself again and repeated the spell after Jozef. She did feel something building in the pit of her stomach, but instead of a pleasant energy, she felt a sick kind of sensation, dark and heavy. Kacie pushed aside the queasiness and wiped the perspiration from her forehead with the back of her hand before she tossed the powder into the water and unleashed the power.

Putrid, black smoke spewed into the air. Kacie snapped her head around and sneezed several times. Keeping her face as far away from the stench as her arched neck would allow, she rolled her eyes around and sneaked a peek. Her jaw dropped. Churning, spitting sludge oozed its way down the side of the bowl, puddeling at the base before it fingered across the table. Kacie touched the edge of the thick goo and brought it to her nose.

"Oh, yuck!" She yanked her hand down and pivoted on her heel, trying not to puke. The stuff smelled like raw sewage mixed with decaying bodies. Kacie stuck her head out the window and gulped in clean air. "What happened?" she asked when she stopped gagging.

Jozef fixed her with a withering glare, his eyes narrowed to slits. "I thought you understood the consequences of fighting me."

Kacie blanched and backed away a step. "No, I didn't . . . I don't know how . . . I . . ."

Jozef reached for her and Kacie flinched, her protest dying in her throat. But, he merely brushed her cheek with the back of his fingers, letting his thumb run along the ridge of her cheek bone. "Do not defy me again," he whispered in her ear as his knuckles traced her jaw line.

Kacie became a statue. It was the hardest thing she had ever done in her life. Her skin crawled at his touch and her palms itched to slap his hands from her face, but she endured it, pushing away the revulsion fermenting inside her. But, if he didn't get his hands off her, she knew she'd do something stupid, so Kacie made her eyes go wide and simply spoke the truth. "I don't know what happened. I was hoping you could tell me. I did everything you told me to do." She threw her arms up in a befuddled shrug, knocking his hands away as she did, and held her breath while Jozef continued to scrutinize her.

It felt like an eternity until Jozef finally nodded once and then turned toward Amsden. "Get someone to clean that up." He motioned to the scrying bowl that was still spewing its noxious contents onto the table.

While Jozef's attention was diverted, Kacie heaved a silent sigh of relief and slid into a chair before her legs gave out on her. She forced moisture into her parched throat so that she could swallow and wiped her trembling hands on her dress and then sat on them.

What happened? Kacie knitted her eyebrows. She really was trying to scry her room. *I followed his instructions to the letter. I emptied my mind just like he said. I found my power center and threw in that weird powder of his. I even said that silly spell. I didn't have a clue what I was saying, but I said it. And then I unleashed my power. Boy, did I unleash my power.*

Kacie looked at the slime that was now dripping on the carpet and gagged again as the stench grabbed an incoming draft, rode it across the room and assaulted her nose once more. *So, how come Jozef made pretty pictures and I conjured up the Goo From The Black Lagoon?*

Kacie's thoughts died as she felt Jozef's hard gaze fall on her again. He studied her for a long moment, pulling his earlobe in obvious thought. Kacie steeled herself.

"I have an idea," he said at last. "I think we should go for a walk. I have something I want to show you." Jozef offered her his arm.

"Excuse me?" Hidden under her legs, Kacie's fingers dug into the velvet fabric and bit her cheeks to keep from screaming.

"Let's go for a walk."

He wants to go for a walk? Aunt Mary, give me strength. She looked up into his serene face and realization dawned on her. *He wants me afraid and off balance. He's using it to control me.* One by one, she relaxed her fingers and released the pressure on her cheeks. *Well, not any more, dude. I'm on to your game.*

"I think a walk would be wonderful." She took his arm and allowed him to escort her out of the study. In the gallery, Kacie was very glad to see Amsden take his perpetually black clad, Snidely Whiplash self in the other direction.

****

Kerric rattled the iron bars of his cell for the tenth time that morning and they were just as solid this time as they were the previous nine times he'd tested them.

Seven colorful oaths matched the seven steps it took to reach the opposite wall and seven even more creative ones precisely matched the seven steps back. He wrapped his fingers around the bars and pressed his forehead against the cold metal.

"Railing against fate will get you nowhere, son," a deep voice said.

Kerric raised his head and squinted into the cell facing his. A form detached itself from the shadows and moved forward until it took shape as a man leaning casually against the bars of the opposite cell.

He was a big man, tall, broad-shouldered and lean. Kerric couldn't make out his features, but he appeared to be richly dressed. In the gloom it was hard to tell. The man's clothes could have been thread bare, for all Kerric could see. But, his accent and words spoke of refinement. His cellmate had to be a nobleman.

Now, what would a nobleman be doing locked up in Trion's dungeon? "It just irritates me when Tia's right," he said, instead of asking the question he really wanted to.

That produced a chuckle from the other man. "I can think of nothing worse than proving to the women in your life that they are right. Who is this Tia that you have proven correct? Your wife? Sister?"

"A friend." Kerric kicked at the bars securing his imprisonment. "She told me not to come to the palace alone. She said I'd get caught and thrown into the dungeon."

"And, what were you doing in Trion palace that got you thrown into its dungeon?" There was an edge to the man's voice that wasn't there before. "Are you a thief?"

Kerric bristled. "I could ask you the same thing. Why is a nobleman locked away in the dark of Trion's prison?"

Before the man could reply, the Earl of Amsden's gravely voice carried down the steep stairwell, followed immediately by the flicker of torchlight and the sound of boots on the steps echoed through the four cells of the square prison. The nobleman withdrew into the shadows.

A guard carrying a torch preceded Amsden down the narrow stairs until they reached the straw covered floor, then he held the light higher and stepped aside to let Amsden pass.

"Ah, Kerric Rouse." Amsden stopped when he reached Kerric. "Are you enjoying your stay in Trion? Are they feeding you well?"

"I'd enjoy it a lot better if they'd feed me your heart."

Amsden snorted at Kerric's empty show of bravado. "I'm beginning to think that keeping you as a hostage was a bad choice." He crossed his arms over his chest and shook his head. "You've been here all night and most of the day and no one's come for you. I'm disappointed. I thought Dahlen was a better friend."

Kerric moved away from Amsden and leaned with one leg propped under him, against the cold wall. "I told you he wouldn't come." He fingered through his hair to get it out of his eyes. "So, why don't you let me go and save us all a lot of trouble?"

Amsden signaled and the guard inserted a rusty key into the lock, jiggling it a couple of times before the lock yielded. The guard yanked the heavy door open and followed Amsden into the cell, clanging the door shut behind them.

Amsden stopped in front of Kerric and eyed him up and down. "I have a better idea. Why don't you tell me where Dahlen is?"

"Why would I want to do that?"

The guard kicked Kerric's leg out from under him, sending him sprawling. "Because it's polite."

Kerric's arms shot out and he twisted on his way down so that his right wrist and forearm absorbed most of the impact. He rolled onto his side and leaned on his left elbow as he rubbed his stinging wrist and glared at the guard towering above him. The man looked a lot bigger from this angle. "I don't know where Derian is." Kerric pushed himself up.

"That was the wrong answer," Amsden growled and the guard kicked Kerric in the stomach.

Kerric doubled over, coughing and taking in ragged gulps of air as he choked back the wave of nausea that gripped him.

"You always were stubborn." Amsden grabbed a handful of Kerric's hair and yanked his head up. "This is your last chance to be reasonable. Where is Derian Dahlen?"

Kerric stared at him.

"Have it your way." Amsden turned and started for the door, then turned back. "Oh, by the way, your friend, Kacie is settling in very well up at the palace. She and the King seem to have a special rapport. I think she likes him." Amsden sneered and motioned the guard forward again. "Don't kill him."

"How's your son?" Kerric asked Amsden's retreating back.

In a blur of motion, Amsden spun and kicked Kerric in the face. Pain exploded in Kerric's left cheek and the world went black.

When Kerric came to, he was alone and lying face down in a pool of his own congealing blood. He groaned and inched his himself into a sitting position. With gentle fingers, he wiped off the blood and probed his throbbing face. He got lucky. Nothing felt broken. Kerric drew his knees to his chest and dropped his forehead against them.

"Are you still alive?" The nobleman's deep voice pounded in Kerric's ears

"No," Kerric croaked.

The man laughed. "I'm glad to hear it. You were unconscious for a long time. I was beginning to worry about you."

"I appreciate your concern," Kerric mumbled, "but, can we chat later?" His face hurt too much to be polite.

"Of course," came the quick reply. "When you're feeling up to it. I have many questions for a thief who knows to ask about the Earl of Amsden's son."

Kerric didn't bother to answer. He slid to the floor and curled into a fetal ball as he lost consciousness again.

****

Guards snapped to attention and courtiers dressed in the finest velvets and silks bowed as Kacie and the King progressed through the palace. Kacie heard the curious whispers about her and held her head a little higher, taking her lead from Jozef who ignored them all.

Follow the yellow. . . She sang the rest of the song to herself as she followed Jozef through a maze of corridors, rooms and staircases filled with priceless art, plush carpets, polished marble and gilded everything. But, she was trying so hard to remember her way back that she didn't pay much attention the grandeur around her and by the time

Jozef stopped in front of yet another set of double gilded doors, Kacie was hopelessly lost. She cast a quick look about and prayed Jozef wasn't going to abandon her. *I knew I should have left a trail of bread crumbs.*

"Beyond these doors lies your heritage,"Jozef announced and pushed them open with a flourish that suggested he was about to give her the most wonderful present in the world and with a small bow, he ushered her into a wide gallery.

Sunlight streamed into the room from a bank of windows lining one long wall and Kacie breathed in the sweet fragrance of blossoming roses wafting in from the hundreds of bushes on the other side of the glass. She even noticed the pond at the center of the garden, surrounded by marble benches. But, the opposite wall captured and held her attention. Paintings covered every inch from floor to ceiling; portraits, large and small, of men, women and children.

My heritage is a room full of dusty old pictures? She looked back at Jozef to see if he was joking. The king wasn't smiling. He obviously expected her to be excited or impressed or something. *Okay, he's serious, so pay attention, Miller. He's up to something.*

"Impressive." Kacie nodded to the room in general for Jozef's sake and made a quick pass down the gallery, stopping only once to examine a portrait of her parents. *I wish I'd known them.* Aware that Jozef was watching her, she moved on to the next painting. There would be time for sentimental reflecting when she was alone. Kacie strolled to the end of the room, about-faced, and inched her way back, studying every picture.

"That frail gentleman,"Jozef pointed to a portrait half way up the wall, is your grandfather, Roland, the ninth Duke of Trion. And, up there in the corner, is his wife, Alexandra. She was a Princess of Lindria. As a matter of fact, Alexandra was the younger sister of my own grandmother, Queen Rosaleen. That makes us cousins."

"Does it? Wow." Kacie moved on to the next painting. *Cousin to an evil wizard. Jumpin' lollipops, my life is complete now.*

"This is my father, Gueran, the last Dragon King." Jozef stopped and gestured upward with a wave of his hand.

A dragon named Gueran! Kacie's gaze flew to the life-sized painting of a man in his early to mid forties, seated on a golden, jewel encrusted throne. Above his head hung the royal banner; a blood-red dragon, rampant, regardant emblazoned on a field of white.

Her mouth dropped open. *I know that banner.* She remembered her audience and closed her mouth, as her thoughts flashed back to the dream she had the night before she was thrown into this crazy adventure. She remembered seeing that same banner with the white field stained red – red with the blood of the dragon.

In her mind's eye, she saw herself lead a young man out of the shadows and place him on a throne. She glanced up at the painting. That throne. The Dragon throne.

She suppressed a shiver and forced away the images of the dream. This wasn't the time to think about that. Jozef was too observant and she didn't trust herself not to give something important away. So, she corralled her thoughts and continued examining the painting. That's when she spotted the broadsword resting across King Gueran's knees. Kacie stared at the ruby winking from the center of the silver hilt and a smile of delight light her face. "It's real?" She couldn't hide her excitement.

"The Medoran Sword of State," Jozef confirmed.

"I didn't really believe the sword existed." Kacie shook her head in wonder. How many times had she polished its counterpart at The Dreaming Tree and dreamed the sword was made of steel instead of wood? And here it was. Okay, she was still only looking at a painting, but it was a painting of a real sword. "Do you have the Dragon Sword?" She turned eagerly to Jozef. "Can I see it?"

Jozef compressed his thin lips in a hard line. "The Dragon Sword was stolen over twenty years ago and hasn't been seen since."

Kacie's excitement died and her heart sank

"But," Jozef continued, "Locked inside you, My Lady Emerald," he pointed at her, making her pay attention again, "is the key to finding it."

The hair on the back of her neck stood on end. *Find the sword; restore the king.* Reyna's words echoed in her mind. *Restore the King? Restore Jozef? No, that can't be what Reyna meant. What did Kerric say? There was a lost Prince out there somewhere.* Kacie rubbed her temples; she couldn't think. "Can we go outside? I'm getting a headache."

Jozef nodded and opened the door to the garden. Kacie stepped onto the gravel path and began to relax as the gentle breeze teased at her hair and ruffled her skirts. She tucked her hair behind her ears and picked a partially open rose bud and inhaled the light perfume before she drew the velvety petals across her forehead, letting their soft coolness caress away the tension behind her eyes.

"You said your father was the last Dragon King. Didn't you take the title when you became king?" Kacie asked, after they had walked a bit.

Anger flashed over Jozef's face again and then cleared. "A monarch cannot claim the Dragon title without the sword and as I am the Raven Wizard, my device has always been the raven. Even when the sword is returned, I will not take the Dragon title."

"Then why do you want the sword so badly?"

"The Dragon Sword is the Medoran Sword of State. It represents the power of Medora and the strength of her rulers. I would find it for the people."

What a crock. Kacie masked her disgust by sniffing at the rose bud.

Jozef stopped walking and searched her face. "Will you help me, Kacie? Will you help restore the symbol of Medora to her people?"

"Of course I will." Kacie looked down at the gravel beneath her feet and considered her next words carefully. "For the people of Medora, I will do my best to restore the Dragon Sword to their rightful king."

Heaven help me, what did I just do?

The full impact of what she just pledged hit her like a sledgehammer in the gut and Kacie staggered a step.

Jozef caught her arm and led her to the nearest bench and helped her to sit down. "Are you feeling well? You look as if you've seen a ghost."

Not a ghost, just my destiny.

CHAPTER TEN

Not a ghost, just my destiny.

The thought was so loud in Kacie's mind that she was sure Jozef had to hear, but he only looked concerned as he sat beside her.

"Are you feeling well?" he repeated the question.

Kacie resisted the urge to slide away from him and concentrated on the water cascading from the mouth of an alabaster cherub into a lapis tiled pool and nodded.

"I'll be fine." She scrubbed at her face. "I haven't eaten since yesterday afternoon and my head is throbbing." It was the first excuse that popped into her head and she grabbed it. She couldn't think with him breathing down her neck. "Can I go back to my room now?" She turned pleading eyes up to him and prayed he'd say okay.

Jozef nodded and escorted her back to her room. Leaving her at the door, he said, "I'll have food brought up to you."

Kacie watched him disappear around the corner before she closed the door and headed for her bedroom.

She sprawled across the bed and closed her eyes. *I've lost my mind. It's completely gone. If my mind was still functioning I wouldn't have ....* She couldn't make herself finish that thought. Instead, she worked her fingers through her hair to the scalp and tried to massage the tightness away. *What do I do now? I'm not Wonder Woman; I don't know a thing about saving worlds. Kerric, where are you when I need you?*

Kerric!

Her eyes popped open and as she jumped off the bed, her head spun and the world tilted. She stumbled to the vanity and dropped into the little chair, laying her head on the cool surface until the dizziness passed.

A moment later, when things steadied, Kacie turned her head and almost knocked Maya's pretty vanity bowl off the table with her elbow, sloshing water and rose petals over the side. Steadying the rocking bowl, she dipped her hands into the water and bathed her face and neck with the cool liquid.

"Where are you, Kerric?" she asked herself with a sigh, wishing she knew how to scry. Inside the bowl, the water rippled and an image began to form under the swirling flowers. "What the...." Kacie frowned and took a closer look. A picture was forming on the surface of the water under the rose petals. "Crimeny! Would you look at that? Kacie Miller can make pretty pictures in the water after all."

She beamed with pride and then bit her lip. *How'd I do that? I didn't say a spell or throw powder in the water. I just asked where Kerric was.* Her brows furrowed and then cleared. "Oh, who cares? Worry about that later. Right now, pay attention!"

She stared at the congealing picture and her heart almost stopped. Kerric sat on the floor of a small, dark cell, his head leaning back against the stone wall. Shadows from a smoking torch, ensconced outside his cell, flickered across his closed eyes and in the dim light, she could just make out the deeper coloration of a bruise on his left cheek.

"Kerric." Kacie reached out to touch him, realized what she was doing and drew her arm back, drumming her fingers on the table instead. "Where is he? Where is this cell? Show me." The water shimmered at her command and reformed into the outside of a square building. Kacie picked at the hem of her sleeve. This meant nothing to her. How could she get him out if she couldn't find him? Then, she remembered Jozef's trick for making the images move.

Oh no, I forgot about Jozef. Kacie hunched her neck into her shoulders and looked around the room. Was he watching her? Did he know she was making magic? She shivered at the thought of being spied on; ignoring the fact that that was exactly what she was doing to Kerric. *But, this is different; I'm trying to help him.* She stuck her tongue out at the ceiling and then regretted it and smiled sweetly just in case Jozef was watching.

Kacie looked back at the floating images and pursed her lips. *Well, Miller, what are you going to do? You've gotta figure out where they're keeping Kerric and you have to use magic to do it.* She slid another glance at the ceiling. *Oh what the heck, just do it. Cover the bowl with your body and if he says anything tell him you were*

131

practicing. Yeah, that's it; tell him you were trying to look for the Dragon Sword.

Kacie pointed at the water, and remembered what Jozef said about broadcasting her energy. "Okay, so how do I control my energy?" She thought about it for a minute and her mind flashed back to the books she'd read at The Dreaming Tree about expanding and contracting energy and auras and what not and decided to give it a try. *What have I got to lose?*

Kacie closed her eyes and took a deep breath through her nose like it said in the books, centered herself and then exhaled in a slow steady stream through her mouth. In her mind's eye she pictured a green energy field around her body and mentally drew it into her solar plexus, constricting it into a tight emerald ball. Drawing on a little at a time, she fed a thin stream of energy up through her body and out her finger.

Kacie didn't have any idea if it was actually working, but deep inside, it felt right. *If Jozef comes storming in here, I'll know I was way off base. Until then, on with the show.* She pushed her concerns aside and trailed her finger over the water's surface. She had to find Kerric and that was all that mattered.

The pictures shifted and Kacie saw that the prison that housed Kerric sat at the end of a two story brick building. Uniformed men went in and out and Kacie guessed it must be the garrison barracks. She continued scrolling across a wide cobblestone courtyard, ignoring the mounted soldiers practicing drills and allowed the images to flow until she saw an ivy covered wall separating the practice yard from a sloping lawn leading to a formal, box hedged garden. Kacie thought she remembered seeing that garden when she stuck her head out of the study window earlier.

She wound and rewound the images back and forth until she was sure she could find her way from the garden to the prison blindfolded. *Now how do I get back to the study?* Kacie started drumming her fingers again.

A noise in her sitting room alerted her to someone's presence and Kacie obliterated the images in the water and picked up Maya's brush and began to pull through her drooping curls.

"Your food, M'Lady."

Kacie turned and an elderly man in Jozef's red and gold livery bowed to her and stepped aside so that she could precede him into the sitting room.

"Thank you. You're a life saver." She grinned from ear to ear at the tray waiting on the low table beside the daybed. "I'm starving." Kacie took a deep whiff of the tantalizing aromas of meat and vegetables and sighed, thinking she'd died and gone to heaven as she snatched a piece of roast meat off the silver platter and stuffed it into her mouth, wiping the dripping juices from her chin with the back of her hand.

The butler looked horrified and Kacie guessed that wasn't how people of breeding ate in Medora. So, she sat and opened the white linen napkin that was provided at the side of the tray and dropped it into her lap, but ignored the knife and fork still in favor of her fingers.

"Will that be all, My Lady?" The poor man looked ready to bolt no matter what she said.

I don't think he approves of my manners. Well, tough tiddlywinks. Get over it. Kacie resisted the urge to laugh and nodded. "Yes, thank you," she said around a mouthful of roast.

The man bowed and was out of the door faster than she would have credited his old bones capable of moving.

Kacie dismissed him as soon as he was out of sight and turned her mind back to getting to Kerric. A second later she was on her feet and throwing the rest of the meat between two pieces of bread and heading for the door. *I love you, Kerric, but I'm not giving up my lunch for you.* She took a bite of her sandwich and stepped into the corridor.

"Okay, Miller, which way?" Kacie looked down both ends of the empty corridor and pretended to flip a coin. "That way." She pointed left and followed her finger to the end of the gallery. When she rounded the corner a palace guard stepped in front of her. Kacie rocked back on her heels and craned her neck up at the giant that blocked her progress.

"May I assist you, My Lady?" His deep voice vibrated all the way down her spine to her heels.

"Yeah, I want to go for a walk in the gardens below Duke Alexei's study. Can you take me there?"

The guard shook his head. "No."

"No? Why not?"

"The King's orders, M'Lady. You are not to go outside the palace unless the King or the Earl of Amsden escorts you."

Okay, Miller, now what? Arguing would get her nowhere. Kacie cocked her head the other way to ease the kink in her neck and tried another tack. "Do you know who I am?"

"You're the Emerald Sorceress, M'Lady."

"And you're not the least bit concerned that I could turn you into a frog if you tick me off?"

The horrid man laughed at her; a deep rumbling sound that shook his chest. "Everybody knows you can't turn people into frogs or anything else for that matter. And, the Emerald Sorceress would never hurt someone for just doing his job."

Kacie ground her teeth. *Don't bet on it.* She bit her lip. "What if I wanted to go to Duke Alexei's study? Am I allowed to do that?"

The guard nodded. "I can escort you there."

Well, halleluiah! "Then lead on, my good man." She motioned him down the hall. *I'll figure something out once I'm in the study.*

The guard retraced the route Amsden took earlier that day and soon they were standing outside of the study again. Only this time Kacie knew how to get there: Left out her door, straight down the next corridor, across the landing at the top of the pink marble staircase, then through the lapis columns at the end. Turn right into the hall of mirrors check you hair and makeup in one of the gold veined floor to ceiling mirrors. *Hair's flat - and you aren't wearing makeup, Miller. Oh well.* - Let the footmen open the humongoid mirrored doors then take the smaller, white marble staircase up two floors and it's the third door on the left. *Yep, got it down pat.*

Kacie left her escort at the door and went into the study alone. She kept one hand on the door as she flared her nostrils and took a tentative sniff, ready to run back out if the room smelled as bad as it did earlier. But only the musty scent of old books assailed her nose.

"So everything is just the way Alexei left them." Kacie circled the room, trailing her fingers over the rows of books, trying to feel his presence. She slid into the big, leather chair behind the desk and ran her hands over the glossy mahogany surface, imagining Alexei sitting in the same spot going over his ledgers and other affairs.

Kacie got up and pushed the chair out of the way so that she could look up at Alexei's portrait again. Tears trickled down her cheeks as she reached up and traced the shape of his face; touched his mouth, his nose, his eyes. She ran her hands along the broad expanse of his shoulders and down one arm, touching the tips of each finger as they rested on the hound's head. She laid her cheek against the canvas and sobbed for the father she never knew - the father the King of Medora tore away from her in his bid for power that didn't belong to him.

Kacie sniffed, wiped her nose on her sleeve and dried her eyes. "I will make him pay." She stared into her father's eyes. "I swear to you on . . ." Kacie scanned the room for something appropriate and spotted the golden Aideny crest hanging on the wall between the bookcases. She pulled a chair over and stood on the seat so that she could reach the sapphire eye of the phoenix. "I swear on the Aideny crest." She pressed the eye. "I swear justice for you." She pressed the sapphire in the first spike of the flaming crown. "And Maya, and Reyna and Medora." With each vow, Kacie pressed the gems in the successive crown spikes and then the eye of the phoenix one last time.

She almost leaped out of her skin when something bumped into the chair hard enough to rock her off balance. Kacie jumped down and moved the chair, allowing a four-foot section of the bookcase to swing open.

"A secret passage?" She flashed a grin at her father's picture. "How cool is this!"

CHAPTER ELEVEN

Curiosity drew her like a magnet. She'd never been in a secret passage. Wadding her skirts into a ball around her knees, Kacie ducked through the opening and closed the panel behind her, plunging herself into impenetrable blackness. She took a step backwards and pushed on the panel. It didn't budge.

"Okay, Miller, what are you gonna' do now?" Kacie refused to panic - yet. What good is a secret passage without an exit? "If you can get in, you can get out. I hope."

Turning around, she groped along the wall, looking for a handle or a lever or something that would release her. Inching her way forward, she didn't pay much attention to the tingling in her arm, at first. She just shook it out and continued on. But, the prickling persisted, creeping up her shoulder and across her chest. Kacie stopped and tried to rub away the pins and needles stabbing her body. It didn't help and she looked down at her chest and her jaw dropped open.

A faint green glow radiated through her dress, tingeing her skin just above the bodice of her gown.

Odds bodkins, Maynard! I've got a radioactive chest!

Kacie swatted at herself and hit the emerald signet ring hidden between her cleavage. She pulled on the chain around her neck and the ring popped free of the confining material, hitting her in the nose. Kacie rubbed the sore spot and heaved a sigh of relief when the tingling in her body eased and her chest stopped glowing.

She slid the ring off the chain and onto her finger and an unmistakable surge of magic coursed through her from the pulsing emerald, pulling her forward.

Kacie followed the ring's lead and continued feeling her way along the wall. Before long, another pinpoint of emerald light flashed in front of her. She leaned in to inspect the light and discovered the glow came from the wall itself. *Interesting.* She ran her hand over the wall and felt a slight depression.

"Oh what the heck." she touched the stone to the light. "This is what they do in the movies, right?" And just like in the movies, the ring slid into the depression like a key. A click and the rush of stale air told her a door had opened.

Ya gotta love Hollywood. Kacie grinned and then squinted, trying to see through the blackness.

"I could sure use some light right about now." She flicked her fingers in the general direction of the source of the stale air and a fat candle sprang to life just inside the doorway, beside her head. "Crimeny," Kacie yelped and jumped back, frowning at the circle of soft candlelight illuminating the closet-sized room.

"Where did you come from?" She stepped toward the tall mirror standing at the back of the room and caressed the head of the dragon carved into one side of the wooden frame.

"What an interesting place to find a Dragon mirror." She touched the wooden replica of the Dragon Sword carved on the other side of the frame and smiled. "Mirror, mirror by the wall, can you get me out of this hall?"

As if awakened from a long sleep, images of landscapes and cities panned across the mirror's surface, picking up speed until a blur of trees, rivers, mountains and farms flashed past. Feeling nauseous, Kacie looked away. "Whoa." She held out her hands. "Not so fast." The images slowed, but continued to change.

Kacie thought for a minute as she watched the Medoran countryside scroll by and then on impulse, asked, "Can you take me to Kiramer and the Emerald Palace?"

The endless parade of pictures stopped and was replaced by a rolling landscape dotted with brick houses on wide tracts of rich farmland. The scene in the mirror traveled across a pretty little town nestled at the foot of a small mountain. At the top of the mountain a fairy tale castle looked protectively over the valley.

"Is that the Emerald Palace?" Kacie almost drooled over the gleaming white castle with its slate-roofed, conical towers. "Crimeny. I'm surprised Reyna ever left there. It's gorgeous. Can you get me inside the palace?" she asked the mirror.

The mirror shimmered and Kacie saw a bright, sunlit room. From her vantage-point, she spotted a long, wooden table dotted with gold candelabras and a cast-iron brazier. Beyond the table, a fireplace dominated the back wall.

Kacie studied the room a moment longer. "Kerric said the Emerald

Palace was being protected by a spell and only the Emerald Sorceress can get in." She dropped her head onto her chest, took a deep breath, blowing it out in a gusty sigh. "How brave do you feel, Miller?" Kacie scratched her nose. "If you walk through this mirror and end up in that room...." A shiver of fear chased down her spine even as a spark of excitement tickled her belly.

"Oh, what the heck."

Throwing caution to the wind, Kacie stepped through the mirror. Unlike the first time, this was like walking through any other doorway. There was no dizziness, no throbbing head, no disorientation – nothing. *Awesome. How fun is that?*

She looked around the room and let out a whoop of delight. I did it! I'm here!" Kacie did a little kick ball-change step and sang "I'm the Emerald Sorceress. I'm the Emerald Sorceress," in time with a quick shoulder- shimmied three-step grapevine. *Fosse would be proud.* She laughed and did another kick-turn combination.

Half way through her turn Kacie froze.

She rushed forward and smacked the solid, white block wall in front of her. "Where's the mirror?" She frantically looked around the room. There was no mirror anywhere. "Great. I can get in, but I can't get out." *This isn't a palace, it's a giant roach motel. She* continued to beat on the wall where the mirror should have been, with the flat of her hand. "How do I get back?"

On command, the wall under her hand shimmered with a viscous silvery iridescence and Kacie almost fell through. She yelped and jumped back as the radiant quicksilver slowly cleared and the secret closet in Trion appeared.

"Curiouser and curiouser." She leaned forward and inspected the six-foot section of the wall that had turned itself into a portal.

Taking a tentative step forward, Kacie walked through the arch and was plunged into the darkness of the secret room back in Trion. "I guess that answers that." With a grin plastered across her face, she turned around and went back to the Emerald Palace. "Oh, this is way too much fun!" she said, stepping into the long room once again.

Metal utensils arranged around the cast iron brazier caught her attention and Kacie strolled over to the table. She picked up a nasty looking pointed implement with a short, curved handle and put it back down again. *Something tells me I'm glad I don't know what these are used for.*

With a shudder, she turned around and browsed over the books lining the wall behind her. The titles meant nothing to her so she pulled one down at random and leafed through the pages. It was a book of magic with some very interesting pictures. As the new Emerald Sorceress, Kacie knew she'd have to study all these books, but not now.

"Now it's time to explore!"

She put the book back and pushed open the door on the other side of the bookcase and stared open mouthed at the sumptuous pistachio and white bedroom. An over-sized white canopied bed dominated the room. She pulled back the bed curtains and threw herself across the green satin bedspread, bouncing up and down on the soft mattress before flopping on her back, so that she could look up at the fresco painted on the underside of the canopy. "Cool."

Kacie scooted off the bed and wandered across the room to the marble fireplace. She wiped her hand over the mantle and then inspected it. "There's no dust."

She fingered the green and white silk curtains framing the windows opposite the fireplace. "There's no dust."

She shook her head and pressed her nose against the windowpane. Squinting against the bright sunlight streaming through the glass, she peered several stories below her at the sloping palace grounds leading to a beautiful formal garden. It was too beautiful.

"Where are the weeds? This place has been deserted for the past twenty years. There should be weeds." She turned and leaned against the wall, her brow furrowed in confusion. "Kerric said nothing could get in but, I didn't know that included dust or weeds." A slow smile lifted the corners of her mouth. "I gotta' learn this spell," she grinned.

A door at the far end of the room beckoned and she obliged, strolling through a series of connecting rooms, each more beautiful than the last. But it was the ballroom that made her grin with pure delight.

Sun flooded the long narrow room from wide windows high along one long wall. The other three walls were painted a rich white and gold. Crystal chandeliers hung from the ceiling and there wasn't a mirror in sight. Beneath her feet, spread a parquet floor polished to a glass-like shine. Malachite fireplaces graced both ends of the room.

"Boy, would I kill for a pair of roller blades right about now. This would make a perfect roller hockey rink." Kacie spun, deeked left, keyed up and delivered a perfect slap shot through the number five slot. "She shoots. She scores! Kacie Miller wins the Stanley Cup!" *Hey, if there are alternate universes then I can take the cup.*

She laughed at herself and the sound ricocheted around the empty room before it bounced back to her. "Ooh," Kacie grinned and wiggled her eyebrows, a gleam of mischief sparkling behind the emerald eyes.

Pumping her arms, she ran a few steps to get up speed then flung her arms wide and dropped to her knees. A sustained high "A" rang loud and clear as she slid to the center of the room. Kacie bit the note off and held her pose, listening to the sound echo around her before she collapsed into a giggling heap.

Still laughing, she got to her feet and needlessly dusted off her skirt. Eyeing the two doors in the ballroom, she flipped a mental coin and pointed her feet toward the small camouflaged door beside the fireplace at the other end of the room.

It opened onto one of the whitewashed turrets. A narrow spiral staircase swirled its way up the next floor. Kacie mounted the stairs and reached the next landing wobbly-kneed and out of breath. The stairs were steeper than they looked. Massaging her quivering thighs, she pushed the door open with her shoulder and was surprised to find herself on the palace roof.

Before her a narrow catwalk stretched from the turret to a square tower with a conical roof. "I wonder what's in there? Looks like there's a room of some kind." She gave the rot-iron railing mortared into the catwalk a sharp shake. It felt secure, so with fingers crossed, she hurried across the catwalk to the tower landing.

Circling the landing, she peeked in the windows. It looked like a study. A wooden desk held court in the center of the room across from a brick fireplace. Two comfortable-looking chairs sat beside the hearth and a long, inviting couch rested under one window. An iron stair case lead to the open second level. Books lined the floor to ceiling shelves.

Kacie tried the door and like everything else so far, it opened easily at her touch.

She went inside and waved a small fire into the fireplace to take the chill out of the air. "I wonder if I'll ever get used to that?" She grinned at the cheery fire blazing in the empty hearth and grabbed the fire poker out of its bucket beside the fireplace. For a couple of minutes she teased the flames, delighting in sending them dancing high into the flume. Shaking her head at herself, Kacie put the poker back and stared up at the painting over the mantle.

A beautiful blond woman dressed in flowing sky blue robes handed a jeweled sword to a heavily muscled man wearing a baker's apron, kneeling at her feet. Kacie recognized Lara and Harvey and chuckled as her gaze wandered over the beautiful sorceress until she came to the round broach clasped to the left shoulder of Lara's gown.

"Wow." Kacie stared at the palm-sized emerald set into the center of a golden, seven pointed star. "That's one gorgeous pin," she said, as her gaze traveled to the Dragon sword in Lara's hand. Kacie studied the etchings along the length of the blade and then caught sight of the ring Lara wore. She took a step closer to the picture and held the ring on her own finger against the one in the painting. They were identical. "From Lara to Reyna to me." A smile touched her lips as a sense of belonging settled around her.

Kerric is gonna love this. Kacie turned away from the picture to inspect the big oak desk in the center of the room.

As she rummaged through the drawers, the emerald ring tugged on her finger and Kacie let the stone guide her. A moment later, her hand stopped under the desk by the front leg. Feeling around, she found a small depression in the wood and crawled under the desk to see what was up. It was only a nick in the wood.

"Someone must have scratched it at some point." She shrugged and moved her hand away, but the ring tugged again, pulling her back. Kacie looked from the scratch to the ring and shrugged. *Well, it worked last time.* She touched the stone to the notch and heard a soft click. She crawled out and found the side of the desk standing open. A large leather bound book rested inside the secret compartment.

Well, will ya lookie here? Kacie reached inside and took the book out. A quick inspection identified it as Reyna's journal. *Now why would Reyna need to hide a journal in her own castle?* Kacie opened the book and read:

> 'Prince Ian was killed today. A riding accident. Like Prince David, it happened the day after he announced his engagement. The King has been warned. I suspect Prince Jozef is behind this but as long as Jozef stays secluded in the Raven Tower, he cannot be touched. Every precaution must be taken to safeguard Prince Mylan. He and King Gueran are the only ones that now stand between Jozef and the crown of Medora.

Kacie stuck her finger between the pages and got to her feet and settled in the over-sized leather chair by the fire. Swinging her legs over the arm, Kacie thumbed through a few more pages, stopping at random.

> 'As we knew it must happen someday, Prince Mylan has fallen in love. The girl is Lady Liselle LeClair, the only daughter of the Duke of Rathborn. Mylan, aware of the fate of his older brothers, has kept the affair secret for sometime now. He married the girl in a secret ceremony last night. I have the wedding papers hidden to protect the girl as well as Mylan. She is to be set up in a house in Alorn close to the palace and passed off as the wife of Stephan Rouse, Mylan's body guard and friend.

Kacie skimmed the pages until the next words almost jumped off the page at her.

> 'Jozef has attacked!! King Gueran, Queen Magda and Prince Mylan have all been slaughtered along with most of the other people in the castle. Stephan brought the Dragon Sword through the mirror as soon as he could escape. Jozef may rule Medora now, but he does not do it as the Dragon King. And, now that I have the Eye of the Raven, he will not be

able to pervert the powers of the Raven Brotherhood any further.

'My first concern now is to get Liselle out of Alorn. Stephan assured me that she and the child she carries are safely hidden away from the palace.

'Mylan's unborn son is the last true heir to the Dragon Throne and must be protected at all costs. Stephan will bring Liselle here to Kiramer where I can watch over her and the child. I have arranged for them to live in a small farm in the valley, and persuaded Stephan to stay with Liselle and help me protect and teach the boy until he can take his rightful place on Medora's throne.

Kacie let the journal slip to her lap as she stared into the flames, her mind's eye conjuring bloody images of horrible carnage of that night.

"Jozef murdered his family to gain the throne." It finally sunk in. "Jozef is a power hungry monster who'll stop at nothing to get what he wants. And he wants my Emerald powers and the Dragon Sword. And he'll kill me in a heart beat as soon as he gets them." Kacie shuddered and huddled deeper into the chair as she picked up the journal and skipped down to the next entry.

'Liselle gave birth last night. He is a strong, healthy boy and they have named him Kerric. Medora has a prince. No, Medora has a King.

Kerric Rouse? Kacie's memory flashed back to Kerric's words: "I'm Kerric Rouse from Kiramer. I'm a farmer's son, not a king."
My sweet Auntie Grizelda.
Kacie snapped the book shut on her finger; covering her eyes she started to laugh. "He is SO gonna' hate this." Her laugh turned evil. *Paybacks, baby. Ya gotta love paybacks.*
"So, Your Majesty," she stood and practiced bowing to his imaginary form. "Now that you're the true Dragon King of Medora, what's your plan to save the world?"
Kacie shook her head. "This is gonna be fun," she said and opened

the book again.

> 'The boy will grow up safe and strong here in Kiramer under my protection and when he comes of age to claim his rightful place, I will lead him to the sword.

Kacie bit her lip and started picking at the hem of her sleeve. *Kerric really is the lost prince. And he's in Jozef's jail at this very minute!*

Panic seized her heart and Kacie jumped to her feet, letting the book fall, she waved the fire out in the hearth, retrieved the journal and thrust it back into its hiding place. Closing the secret compartment with her foot, she stepped out of the tower door.

Kacie grabbed her skirts and held them up around her knees as she ran, headlong across the narrow catwalk and back down to Reyna's workroom and the mirror.

"I've got to get him out of there!"

CHAPTER TWELVE

Kacie raced down the narrow spiral staircase, taking the worn steps two at a time.

"Hold on, Kerric, I'm coming." She rushed through the palace, retracing her path into the long workroom and slid to a stop in front of the shimmering portal.

Doubling over, she pressed her fist against the stitch in her side and took a couple of deep breaths. "I need to get inside Trion's jail," she told the mirror and crossed her fingers for luck.

The colors within the arch swirled, slowly darkening. "C'mon, c'mon." Kacie tapped her foot.

An eternity later, the kaleidoscope solidified into the half gloom of Trion's prison. "What a lovely place." She shuddered as she stared at the four cramped cells. Smoking rush lights stuck into chiseled holes in the brick walls sputtered in a pathetic attempt to illuminate the area.

"Where's Kerric?"

The scene in the mirror shifted and Kerric's bruised and bloody face swam out of the blackness. For one second she looked into his pain-filled hazel eyes before he dropped his head onto his bent knees.

"Oh, Kerric, what did they do to you?" Her throat constricted and she swallowed against the hard lump stuck in her throat. "I'm so sorry." She reached toward him and then let her hand fall to her side and set her jaw. "One more score to settle with Jozef Dearest." She stepped through the arch to Kerric's side.

"Kacie?" Kerric recoiled from her, his eyes wide and his mouth open.

"Well, that isn't exactly the reaction I was expecting." She looked down at herself. She was bathed in green light and out of the corner of her eye she caught sight of luminescent emerald fire spiking behind her and turned around. A rainbow of color in the shape of the arch in the Emerald Palace hung in mid air behind her, washing the cell in brilliant hues. As she watched, the shimmering portal shrank and winked out with a soft pop.

"Wow! Was that cool or what?" She turned back to Kerric and grinned.

He just stared at her.

"What?" She checked herself again to make sure she wasn't still glowing.

"H-how did you do that?"

Kacie rolled her eyes. "For heaven's sake, Kerric. You're the one always going on about me being the Emerald Sorceress. How do you think I got here? Magic, baby." She snapped her fingers.

"Magic?" He frowned.

She plopped down next to him, maneuvering her skirts so that she could sit cross legged. "Boy, they must have really done a number on your head. You Okay?" She felt his forehead for fever and then slowly shook her head as she trailed her fingers over his purple cheek. Oh, Kerric." She leaned forward and kissed his swollen jaw. "I thought you were smarter that this," she whispered.

Kerric draped an arm around her shoulder and squeezed. "It's not as bad as it looks." He dimpled and then winced. "What are you doing here?"

Kacie grinned. "I'm here to rescue you." She puffed out her chest.

Kerric looked around them. "From inside the cell?" He raised an eyebrow at her.

Kacie deflated. "Rats." She looked around the cramped cell and buried her face in the hollow of his shoulder. A muffled scream tore out of her throat.

Kerric laughed above her and Kacie pushed herself away from him and got to her feet. She stuck her chin in the air and calmly walked to the locked iron door standing between her and her glorious, heroic rescue of the true King of Medora from the bosom of the evil usurper . . .

With slow, precise movements, Kacie wrapped her fingers around the rusty bars and gave them a swift kick. "You are such a twit, Miller," she told herself, ignoring the sharp pain shooting up her leg.

Kerric laughed.

Kacie ignored him too. *Only you would attempt a rescue without a plan, Miller.* She laid her forehead against the bars letting them cool her burning cheeks. *Alright, you're here. So think. Kerric's a soldier and you're a sorceress, between the two of us we should be able to come up with a plan.*

"Well, well, where did you come from?"

Kacie looked up at the gray haired man leaning against the bars in the cell across from her.

"I didn't know anyone else was here." She turned to Kerric. "Who's he?" She looked back at the man. "Who are you?"

The man smiled. "I could ask you the same question. There aren't many who could suddenly appear in Trion's dungeon through a magical portal. Did I hear you say that you were the Emerald Sorceress?"

He remained leaning casually against the bars, but Kacie saw the clenching and unclenching of his jaw. His lips smiled, but the intensity of his unblinking stare made her swallow the glib answer she was going to toss him. "I am the Emerald Sorceress."

The man closed his eyes and hung his head. He scrubbed his face with shaking hands and sucked in a ragged breath. "Reyna, why didn't you tell me?" he whispered and when he looked up again his eyes were overly bright. "Forgive me." He wiped his eyes and cleared his throat. "If you are here than Reyna must be dead."

"She is," Kacie nodded. "Was she a friend of yours?"

"Yes." He said, studying her closely. He opened his mouth, then shook his head and Kacie thought she heard him say, "Let it go for now." Taking a deep breath, he began again. "Tell me, why is the Emerald Sorceress in Trion's dungeon with a thief?"

"I'm not a thief," Kerric defended himself.

"He's not a thief." Kacie said at the same time. "And you're in a fine position to be calling people names." She looked him up and down and wrinkled her nose at the tattered clothing that once upon a time were probably pretty expensive duds. "It looks like you've been here a while. Maybe you're the thief?"

The man laughed, a deep, rich sound. "Touché." He inclined his head to her. "I am not a thief either. I'm a Duke by birth."

"Let me guess, Jozef has it in for you, too."

"Yes, Jozef has a grudge against my family."

"It doesn't look like you've fared too badly." She nodded to the large bed piled high with thick blankets and fluffy pillows that dominated his double cell. A table and chair as well as a small bookcase stood against the back wall and he even had an oil lamp on the table.

"I have lived in this splendid luxury for twenty years."

Kacie didn't miss the sarcasm. "That sucks."

"As you say." He nodded, his eyes twinkling. "Now it's your turn. Why are you here?"

Kacie looked from the man to Kerric and back again.There was something about him that intrigued her. He looked vaguely familiar, but she couldn't put her finger on how or why. And it was obvious he was telling the truth. He had to be exactly what he said he was. The air of nobility and command fit him like a second skin.

A slight smile twitched at the corners of his full mouth as he watched her scrutinize him. He seemed amused by her inspection. Kacie's chin lifted a fraction. Who did he think he was anyway? He was the prisoner, not her. Their eyes met and held. A slight frown creased his brows for an instant and then was gone so fast that she decided it must have been just a shadow.

She shrugged and smiled. The man gaped, but he quickly closed his mouth and schooled his features.

"O.K. that's twice you've done that. What's the deal?" she demanded.

He waved away her question. "You were about to tell me how you came to be in Trion's jail." He steered the conversation back on track.

In spite of her growing curiosity, Kacie allowed herself to be turned and followed his lead. "I'm here to bust him out." She cocked her thumb at Kerric.

"From inside the cell," Kerric needled.

She jabbed him in the ribs with her elbow. "Yep, I just stepped through the arch in the Emerald Palace and here I am." She spread her arms wide.

"You were in the Emerald Palace?" Kerric grabbed her shoulders and spun her to face him. She smirked and batted her eyelashes. "Can you get us back there?"

Kacie hung her head. "No," she whispered. "Not from here."

The Duke threw back his head and laughed. "You are so like your mother."

"What?" Kacie whirled on him. "What did you say?"

"I said, so where are the others? You do have others to help with your escape plan, don't you?"

"Yes, Lady Emerald," Kerric stressed the title. "How are you going to get us out of here?"

She frowned at him. *I am so gonna' love torturing you, Your Majesty.* "Ya know, I've been thinking about this." She wagged her finger and drew her brows together. "And, it seems to me that it should be just as easy to open this lock from the inside as the outside." *Especially if you don't know how to do it from either side.*

"And once we're out, how do we get past the guards?"

Kacie planted her hands on her hips and glared at him. "Jeez, Kerric, do I have to think of everything? You're the soldier. You figure it out."

"The great rescuer," Kerric groused at her.

"Yeah, well, at least I . . ."

"Argue later, children," the Duke admonished. "Work out a plan now."

Without another word, Kacie grabbed the bars and took a deep breath, centering her attention on the locking mechanism.

"What are you doing?" Kerric broke her concentration.

"I'm trying to manipulate the lock with my mind," she said without taking her eyes from the lock.

"You're what?"

Kacie sighed and looked up at Kerric. "It worked in a novel I read once."

"You read it in a book?" Kerric glared at her, shook his head and began to pace the cell, mumbling to himself.

"I thought you said you were the Emerald Sorceress?" The nobleman teased.

"I am." She scrunched her face. "But, I'm like an apprentice sorceress. I'm still learning how to use my powers. Reyna died before she could teach me anything."

Keys fumbling in the lock of the heavy metal door at the top of the dungeon stairs echoed down to them. They all froze, listening.

"We have company," the nobleman warned.

Kerric pointed to the cell door. "Get us out of here."

The door above them scraped over the stone floor and Kacie's heart began to hammer.

"Just give me the torch," a high baritone voice drifted down the stairs. "I will talk to the prisoner alone. You stay here."

Kacie blanched. "It's Jozef!" She stared harder at the lock.

"Now, Kacie."

"I must agree with your friend. Jozef cannot find you here."

"Stop it, both of you. I don't work well under pressure." She shook her hands and rotated her neck, trying to relax before she gripped the bars again.

Jozef's boots scuffed on the steps as he descended into the dungeon. Panic gripped Kacie's heart. She couldn't let Jozef have Kerric and she sure as hell couldn't let him catch her here.

She shook the bars. "Open up. I need out of here now!"

A flash of emerald light shot out of her hands and traveled down the rusty iron and sparked in the lock for a second before it faded back into the blackness.

The cell door swung open.

"Crimeny, it worked." Relief washed through her, turning her legs to water.

Kerric grabbed her arm and propelled her out the door. "Faint later. We don't have time now."

"I wasn't going to faint." She stiffened her legs and rushed over to the other cell to release the nobleman too.

The glow from Jozef's torch splayed creeping tendrils of light along the dungeon floor and up the cell walls.

"Leave me," the man insisted.

"No." She grabbed the bars of his cell and began to concentrate.

The man covered her hands with his. "Kacie." His gentle voice compelled her to look up at him. "Jozef won't hurt me," he said, when he had her attention.

Kacie shook her head, still reluctant to leave him. Kerric took her arm again.

"Hide in the torture chamber. Through that door," the Duke told Kerric, pointing to the door at the end of the cell block. "Jozef won't see you there."

Kerric nodded and pulled Kacie after him. He pushed her into the back corner, behind an iron maiden and stuffed her voluminous skirts tight in behind her and stood in front of her blocking her from view.

"Hello, Alexei." Jozef's amiable greeting carried clearly to Kacie and Kerric.

Alexei? Her heart stopped. *No, it can't be.* She stiffened and Kerric put his finger to his lips. She nodded and craned her neck to see around his broad shoulder, holding her breath, not daring to give into the hope coursing through her soul.

"Jozef." Alexei inclined his head and moved to the other side forcing Jozef to turn away from where Kacie and Kerric were hiding. "It's been a long time. To what do I owe this pleasure?"

"I've come to take you back to the palace." Jozef ran a manicured finger down the stained lapel of Alexei's suit. "We have to get you cleaned up and into some better clothes."

"Why?"

"I'm going to introduce you to your daughter."

Kacie opened her mouth and Kerric clamped his hand over it before she could utter a sound. "Be quiet," he mouthed in her ear. Kacie's glare was mutinous, but she nodded. He cocked his head at her and raised an eyebrow. She forced herself to relax and nodded again. He removed his hand and she pushed him to the side a little so that she had a better view.

"My daughter is dead. You murdered her with my wife."

Jozef shook his head. "Maya is dead, yes. But, your daughter lives. She's up at the palace. Her name is Kacie." Jozef laughed. "She's quite a woman; spirited, like Maya."

The thin, hollow sound set Kacie's jaw. Kerric pinched her arm and shook his head. She unclenched her jaw, but she didn't relax as Jozef continued to talk.

"I've had a marvelous time with her these past couple of days. I can't wait for you to meet her."

Alexei paced his cell, his agitation apparent.

"She's shaping up to be an even more powerful Emerald Sorceress than Reyna."

Alexei stopped in front of Jozef again. "What do you want, Jozef?"

Jozef stiffened, anger present in every line of his body. "I want the

Dragon Sword and the stolen Raven's Eye," he snapped. "And you are going to persuade your headstrong daughter to find them and give them to me."

In your dreams, dude. I'll find the Dragon Sword, alright, but not for you. Never for you!

Kacie doubled her fists. How dare he try and use Alexei against her. There was no way she'd ever give Jozef the Dragon Sword. Oh, she'd find it alright. For Kerric. As far as she was concerned, Jozef could kiss the sword goodbye.

"And if I refuse?" Alexei said and Kacie strained to hear Jozef's reply.

"I'll kill her." Jozef shrugged. "And after you watch your daughter die, I'll kill you."

No! Touch him and I'll kill you here and now!

Kacie fought to get around Kerric, but he held her firmly in place, stopping her struggles by shear strength as his fingers dug into her arms.

"That's my father, Kerric," she whispered, tears welling in her eyes.

"You can't do anything to help him right now. Think." He tried to shake her into submission.

Kacie was beyond thinking. "I won't let him hurt my father." She twisted herself free from Kerric and ran out of hiding. "Leave him alone! Your fight's with me."

"Kacie, no!" Alexei shouted.

Kacie ignored him. All of her attention was focused on Jozef. An emerald aura crackled around her body. She gathered the anger inside her and threw a ball of energy at him.

Jozef flung out his arm and swept the Emerald magic away. "What did I tell you about focus?"

Kacie gritted her teeth and threw another ball of magic at him.

Again, Jozef swept it aside. "It's time you learn who is master here." He made a sign in the air and a sphere of blue energy formed in front of him. It hung in the air for one heartbeat before it shot forward and slammed into Kacie's mid section.

Oblivion overtook her before she felt the pain of Jozef's Raven magic.

CHAPTER THIRTEEN

Jozef laughed and nudged the unconscious heap sprawled on the dungeon floor with the toe of his boot. "Spirited, just like her mother." He opened the cell door and stepped back. "Pick up your daughter and carry her back to the palace," he told Alexei.

Wedged into the shadows of his hiding place, Kerric balled his hands into fists and sunk his nails into the flesh of his palms. His entire being screamed to rush forward and attack.

As if Alexei knew his thoughts, the Duke looked toward Kerric and gave an almost imperceptible shake of his head before he hefted Kacie over his shoulder and turned away.

The message was clear: do nothing. Kerric ground his teeth. Duke Alexei was right. He couldn't help them. Not now. So, for the second time in two days, he watched as the Emerald Sorceress was delivered into Jozef's clutches.

At the foot of the stairwell, Jozef looked back in his direction, seeming to study the shadows. Kerric melted deeper into the darkness until Jozef spun on his heel and followed Alexei out of sight.

Kerric hefted a mace from the wall and crept out of hiding and edged forward. At the top of the stairs he heard a grunt and quick shuffling of feet.

"Don't drop her, Alexei." Jozef's amused voice echoed through the dungeon.

Kerric froze.

Above him, the heavy iron door scraped against the uneven stone floor. He didn't move until the door banged shut. When he heard the lock slide home, Kerric breathed again.

Running his fingers through his hair, he counted to a slow one hundred to give Jozef time to get completely away from the building before he made his move.

His patience ran out at eighty.

Kerric took the narrow steps two at a time, being careful not to scrape the heels of his boots against the flagstone. On the landing, he flattened himself against the wall and peered through the grated window.

Two guards lounged at a rough wooden table playing a game of dice. Kerric's eyes narrowed as he watched the burly man closest to him turn and light a pipe. "You and I have unfinished business, friend." Kerric rubbed his bruised jaw.

One more slow look around the room confirmed that there were only two guards on duty. At last, something was going his way.

He ran back down the steps and started yelling and banging on the bars of the cells. It took a couple of minutes, but finally, the heavy door above crashed open.

"Quiet down," a rough voice bellowed. "Ye'r disturbin' the dead."

"When do I get fed?" Kerric yelled back, doubling his efforts on the bars. "And, the dead don't mind. They're starving too."

"Ye'r gonna join em if ya don't be quiet,"the man snarled as he rounded the corner.

It was his old buddy. Kerric smiled. "This really is my lucky day." Dropping the mace, he kicked the man in the groin. The guy dropped to his knees, retching. Kerric kicked him in the face and heard the satisfying sound of bone crunching. The guard fell face first into the matted straw.

Kerric retrieved the man's sword and slid it into his own belt. "Bullies always loose in the end." He patted the wide shoulder.

While surprise was still on his side, Kerric ran back up the stairs and burst into the guardroom. He crossed the room in three strides.

The second guard scrambled to his feet, knocking the bench over. Kerric jumped onto the table, his sword point circling dangerously close to the man's face. The guard jumped back, pulling his own sword and tripped over the bench. He sprawled across the cold stone floor. His rapier was knocked from his hand, just out of reach. He stretched toward his weapon, but before he could touch it Kerric leaped to the floor and planted his foot on the guard's outstretched wrist. The helpless man froze as the point of Kerric's sword touched his throat.

"Don't be a fool." Kerric kicked the weapon safely out of the way. It clattered across the floor and the guard relaxed, defeated. "That's better." Kerric stepped back. "Get up." He motioned toward the door leading to the dungeon. "Down there."

The guard got to his feet and did as he was told. On the landing, Kerric shoved him in the back and the man stumbled half way down the stairs. Kerric slammed the door shut, grabbed the keys hanging on a hook beside the door and locked it. He threw the large ring of keys into the fire and left the guard room.

A quick look outside assured Kerric the area around the jail was clear. He slipped past the door and edged along the back wall.

If his luck held he'd make it back to the summer house before the alarm was raised. He'd be safe in the tunnel until night when everyone in the palace slept. Then he could get both Kacie and Duke Alexei out.

"Duke Alexei alive. Who would believe it?" Kerric mused as he eased his head around the corner of the building and came face to point with the tips of two swords thrust at him.

Kerric swore. With one fluid movement, he jumped back and pulled his own sword.

"Kerric?" Derian gasped.

"What are you doing here?" Tia demanded.

"Me?" Kerric knocked both of their weapons aside with the flat of his blade. "What are you two doing here? I thought you were supposed to wait for me."

Tia sheathed her sword and grabbed his chin. "What happened to your face?"

Kerric shrugged and threw Derian a lopsided grin. "Amsden was anxious for Derian's well being."

"You got caught." Tia planted her hands on her hips and glared up at him. "I told you not to go alone."

"Well, I'm free now." He took her by the shoulders and spun her around. "But if we stay here none of us will be free for long." He pushed her ahead of him as he sprinted across the lane that ran between the barracks and the woods. They ran until the trees closed in around them and the shadows obscured them from sight.

"What's this about Duke Alexei being alive?" Derian asked as they slowed to a walk.

Kerric nodded. Duke Alexei is alive," he confirmed and ducked behind a giant oak, motioning Derian and Tia to do the same. The summer house was in sight, but he wasn't about to go charging into the open until he was sure it was safe. Placing a finger to his lips, he listened for sounds of pursuit. He heard nothing out of place and relaxed a bit.

"How can that be?" Derian asked, as they sprinted for the house.

"It makes perfect sense if you think about it," Tia chimed in. "Obviously, Jozef knew the Duchess of Trion carried the next Emerald Sorceress. He also knew Reyna hid the Duchess to protect the child. And, that the Emerald Child would emerge from hiding some day. What better leverage to use against her than the father she never knew?"

"Very good." Kerric closed the door behind them. "Jozef probably thought the new Emerald Child would be putty in his hands and he'd be able to mold her any way he wished."

Derian snorted. "I'll lay odds Jozef didn't calculate 'Kacie Miller from Santa Monica' into his plans." He snickered as he led them down the hall and into the back room.

"It would almost be worth it to leave Kacie there just to see Jozef try and mold her into anything," Tia agreed.

Kerric laughed and pressed the cherub's nose. Delightful visions of the battle of wills that would take place entertained him as he waited for the trap door to open.

"I don't suppose you brought a torch or lamp with you? No?" Derian answered his own question and sighed as he lowered himself down the dark opening.

"Sorry, they don't keep spares in Trion's dungeon." Kerric said, as he hunched his shoulders and followed Derian into the cramped tunnel.

There was a soft thud behind him as Tia jumped to the ground. "Tell us more about Alexei," she said, grabbing his belt.

"Jozef had him imprisoned all this time."

"How?" Derian wanted to know. "How do you imprison the most influential man in the Kingdom for over twenty years?"

"By telling everyone he's dead." Kerric shrugged and instantly regretted it when his shoulders scraped against the rough tunnel wall.

"That would do it. Who's going to question the word of a wizard king? Ouch. Watch your . . ."

"Ow." Kerric smacked his head on a low support beam.

"Too late," Tia laughed behind him. "Was he kept in Trion all this time?" She brought them back on subject.

"I don't know any details, but he was in the dungeon with me not more than an hour ago."

"Steps ahead." Derian paused and held out a hand to stop Kerric. "Where is Alexei now?"

Kerric grabbed Tia's hand and pulled her along with him as he mounted the first step of the spiral stairs that would take them to the Chapel. "Jozef has him and Kacie somewhere back in the palace."

"So, we're back to square one," Tia mumbled not quite under her breath.

"Except now we have two people to rescue instead of one." Derian's tone was anything but cheerful.

Kerric chuckled to himself as a string of colorful oaths drifted up to him. He made a mental note to remember some of the better ones.

Out of breath and slightly dizzy from the spiraling five story climb, they reached the top landing.

"Now what?" Tia whispered.

"Now we wait until everyone sleeps." Kerric sat on the steps with his back pressed against the cold stone wall as the others settled around him, trying to get as comfortable as possible for the long wait.

****

Pain.

Lots of pain.

Kacie tried to pull oblivion's sweet blackness around her again, but it danced just beyond her reach.

I hope someone got the license number of the truck that ran me over.

She willed her nauseated stomach to settle and forced herself to remain perfectly still so that she could take stock of her injuries in relative safety. She didn't want to alert anyone who might be watching that she was awake until she knew what kind of shape she was in.

She gave herself a quick once over and except for feeling like she'd been hit by a semi hauling manure, she felt surprisingly well. Her head pounded. That was to be expected and it wasn't hard to take care of. One by one, Kacie relaxed the knotted muscles of her shoulders and neck and the pain eased a little. She resisted the urge to sigh with relief as the pressure behind her eyes lifted enough that she could turn her attention to the raw nerve endings still firing with the left-over magical residue of Jozef's energy blast.

She had no clue how to stop the tingling pin pricks that snapped over her entire body, so she sent them a wash of soothing energy and mentally crossed her fingers, hoping they would calm on their own. At least she didn't feel as bad as the last time Jozef blasted her. When she saw that blue ball of energy coming at her in the dungeon – how long ago was it? She couldn't remember, but she thought for sure she'd wake up dead. Or worse.

The great Emerald Sorceress . . . I hate to break it to ya, babe, but you are no match for a fully trained wizard.

Not yet.

Kacie set her jaw in determination and opened her eyes a slit, peering around her through her lashes. She was lying on a settee in a room she didn't recognize. Peaking between her feet, she saw a set of double glass doors that opened onto a narrow balcony. Two men stood in the sun, leaning against the columned balustrade. She couldn't hear what they were saying, but they were close enough that she recognized Jozef immediately.

The other man faced away from her, his hands resting on the balustrade, his head bowed and his shoulders slumped as he listened to Jozef. But then, his head snapped up and his silver hair glinted in the sunlight. Lethargy melted away and his lean frame tensed as he straightened to his full height, which was several inches taller than Jozef. He was obviously agitated. Waving a hand toward the room he turned and Kacie got a good look at the square face and the set jaw. Her breath caught in her throat.

Alexei? Her heart began to pound and weakness washed over her as adrenaline pumped into her extremities. *I wasn't dreaming.* She sat up and willed the tears away, swallowing past her constricted throat. *Don't fall apart now, Miller. You're alive because Jozef still needs the Dragon Sword. And, Alexei is still alive because Jozef intends to use him against you. Well, fore warned is fore armed. Put your emotions on hold, and engage your brain, cuz now you've got your father's life to fight for too.*

Kacie scrubbed her face and took a deep breath and stood. The room tilted a bit causing her to weave just a little as she made her way to the veranda.

Alexei saw her and hurried into the room. He was almost at her side when Jozef stepped between them and took her arm. He led her to a hard backed chair and pushed her into it. Kacie's teeth jarred from the impact.

Alexei made a sound of protest and moved toward Jozef. Jozef threw him a scathing look and Alexei froze. Jozef nodded and snapped his fingers. Amsden detached himself from the shadows and came forward.

Where did he come from? Kacie suppressed a shudder as she realized that Amsden had been in the corner watching her the whole time.

Snidely Whiplash.

Alexei sank into the settee and Amsden clamped a restraining hand on his shoulder.

"Leave him alone." She glared first at Amsden and then Jozef.

Without warning, Jozef back handed her and Kacie's head banged against the hard wood chair. Across the room, Alexei lunged for Jozef. Amsden grabbed him and slammed him back into his seat.

"If he moves again, kill him," Jozef ordered, never taking his eyes off Kacie's face.

Kacie closed her eyes once and then deliberately looked away. She watched Amsden twitch his right arm and saw a dagger slide into his palm from the wrist sheath hidden inside his sleeve. With a nasty leer at her, he held the blade against Alexei's pulsing jugular.

Kacie bit the inside of her cheeks to keep herself in check as she turned a murderous glare on Jozef. He leaned in close and in a low voice said, "I rule here."

"What do you want?" Kacie managed through clenched teeth.

"Why it's very simple." Jozef straightened. "As you know full well, I want the Dragon Sword."

"And, if I refuse?" She could have kicked herself for baiting him.

Jozef shrugged and looked at Alexei. "I will kill your father."

"No you won't." She was pleased to see a look of surprise flash across Jozef's face. "If you kill my father, you will never have the sword. I will destroy it first," she vowed.

Jozef laughed; a frozen sound that raised gooseflesh on her arms and made the hairs on her neck stand. "My innocent little sorceress. There are things in this world that are far worse than death." He leaned in again, planting his hands on the arms of the chair, his face only inches from hers. "I promise you," he whispered. "If you do not find me the Dragon Sword, Alexei will beg for the relief death will bring."

Kacie forced herself not to move as his hot breath washed over her face. She pushed away the sick feeling in her gut and stared, unblinking into the ice blue eyes and laughed.

Jozef back handed her again. This time Kacie was ready for him. She absorbed the blow without so much as a flinch and her eyes narrowed to fiery emerald slits. An emerald aura crackled around her as she wiped the blood from her mouth.

Jozef snorted and his own energy field flared, blue and electric. "Try it and lose. You are no match for me," he warned.

It took every ounce of common sense she possessed to control the anger raging inside her and back down. Jozef was right. She wasn't a match for him. Yet. And, she couldn't afford a temper tantrum right then. She let the power fade. There would be time enough later.

"You are learning," Jozef smirked at her and then turned to Amsden. "Take the Lady Emerald to her quarters. She has work to do. Alexei and I will stay here and have a nice game of chess while we wait."

Kacie rose with as much dignity as she could muster and went to Alexei. Daring Amsden or even Jozef to interfere, she leaned down and hugged Alexei, kissing him on the cheek. "I'll figure out a way to get us out of here," she whispered.

"Be careful," he whispered back, kissing her cheek in return.

"Let's go, Snidely." Kacie motioned for Amsden to lead the way

"You have two days." Jozef's ultimatum followed her into the corridor.

CHAPTER FOURTEEN

Two days? Kacie wanted to throw up. How was she supposed to find that stupid sword in two days? It could be anywhere. Lost in thought, she blindly followed Amsden through the palace. When he moved to follow her into her rooms she growled at him and to her surprise, he closed the door behind her and stayed on the other side. Guards might be posted outside her door and she might be a prisoner, but at least she didn't have to put up with his sour puss. Dismissing Amsden, she plopped into a chair. Two days to find the Dragon Sword before Jozef made good on his threat. Her heart sank. How was she supposed to do that? She didn't even know where to begin – or how. Maybe if she was at the Emerald Palace.

"That's it!" Kacie sat up, excitement stirring. *The Emerald Palace. Of course. Reyna must have left something behind to hint at where she hid the sword.* Kacie knew her reasoning was a stretch, but it was all she had, so she ran with it. "Okay, I've got to get to the E.P. How?" She fingered the edge of her sleeve as she pondered a way to get past the guards and to the mirror behind Alexei's study.

"I sure wish Kerric was here. He'd know what to do."

Oh lord, I forgot about Kerric!

She sprang to her feet and raced into the bedroom. With all the stress of the afternoon she completely forgot about Kerric left in the dungeon. She sat at the vanity and scooped out the rose petals floating in the bowl of water beside the mirror. Taking a deep breath, she exhaled letting the pressures of the day drain away with the thin stream of air.

She peered into the water, ready to scry for Kerric when she remembered Jozef could watch her every move. "Not this time, Dude," she said to the room at large.

Being careful not to broadcast her magical workings, she pulled a thin stream of energy from her power center and pointed at the walls, drawing an imaginary line around the room. A curtain of emerald trailed behind her finger, bathing the room in a pulsing green barrier.

Closing the loop, she gave a little push with her hand and the energy sank into the walls creating a protective shield for her to work under.

"Ooh, good job, Miller." She patted herself on the back and grinned as she turned her attention again to the porcelain bowl.

"Where's Kerric?" The clear water swirled and colors blended together, darkening into the planes of Kerric's face. He sat on a stone floor, his head resting against a wall, his eyes closed. He was in total darkness.

Kacie frowned, puzzled. Was he still in the dungeon? No, he couldn't be. The dungeon wasn't that dark. "So where is he? Show me more."

She drummed her fingers on the vanity while the water swirled and reformed to show her a small chapel. *He's in church? Why is he in a church?* "Where is this chapel

A moment later, the corridor outside her rooms appeared in the water. The door directly across from her own was centered in the liquid image. *He's across the hall? What on earth is he doing there?* "More to the point, how do I get to him?"

At her command, the inside of the chapel shimmered in the water again and the picture traveled down the short center isle. Turning just past the right side of the quire, the image settled on a blank wall between the quire and the curtained alcove behind the alter. She frowned at the picture for a moment. *He's in the wall? That can't be. Of course! There's a secret tunnel! Ya gotta love this place.* "You are such a twit, sometimes, Miller," she laughed at herself.

Kacie fiddled with the gilded brush and comb lying in front of her while she decided what to do. She had to get to Kerric and she had to do it before he did his Knight-In- Shinning-Muslin thing and got himself captured again.

OK, so how do I get to him? She stared at herself in the mirror, trying to figure out how to get past the guards at her door. *Of course.* She snapped her fingers.

"You are down right brilliant sometimes, Miller," she told her reflection and pulled the protection shield around her so all of her movements would be blocked from Jozef's sight.

Hurrying through her apartment, she yanked the door open and jumped back a little when two nasty looking pikes crossed in front of her, almost scraping her nose. Kacie recovered quickly and smiled her most innocent smile and looked wide-eyed up at the iron muscled towering between her and her goal.

"Is it permitted for me to go into the chapel?" Her voice was soft and low as she pointed to the door across from them. "I have a huge task to perform for the King and the peace inside would help calm my nerves."

The guards exchanged glances above her and Kacie held her breath. At last one of them shrugged and the other nodded. "We can guard the chapel as easily as this room," he said. "And there's no other exit, so she can't escape."

That's what you think. She masked her triumph with a simple "Thank you." The spears were withdrawn and she forced herself to stroll the few steps across the corridor.

As soon as the heavy chapel door was securely closed behind her, Kacie ran down the isle and pounded on the wall. "Open up, Kerric. I know you're in there."

An instant later, part of the wall slid open. Before she could react, a hand clamped over her mouth and a strong arm circled her waist, dragging her into the tiny curtained off alcove behind the alter.

"Be quiet," Derian ordered.

"Are you trying to bring down the entire palace guard on us?" Tia added.

Kacie shook off Derian's hold just as Kerric stepped into the alcove. Relief washed over her. "Thank Goodness, you're safe." She flung herself into his arms and held on, thrilled to feel him alive, safe and breathing beneath her touch.

Kerric grinned down at her, both cheeks dimpling. "I'm glad to see you too."

All of a sudden, all of the fear and worry and frustration Kacie held bottled up, erupted in cold furry. She balled her fist and punched Kerric in the shoulder as hard as she could.

"What in blue blazes are you doing here? Do you have any idea what kind of danger you're in? I didn't risk my life and my father's life to get you out of that dungeon just for you to waltz back in here and throw it all away. And to make matters worse, you bring them along." She flung a hand at Derian and Tia.

163

"And you!" She rounded on Tia. "Why did you let these two hair brained idiots talk you into this. I counted on you to keep them out of trouble. They're men, they're stupid. What's your excuse?"

The three friends stared open mouthed at her. The looks on their faces said they thought she'd lost her mind. She didn't care. The lava was still flowing.

"I've only got two days to find that stupid sword before Jozef starts torturing my father and now I've got you three to worry about." She finished on a sob.

Kerric folded his arms around her and held her tight, rocking her gently back and forth.

I can't do this. Who am I kidding? I'm just a girl, I'm no super hero. I don't even belong here.

"Kacie?" Kerric's soft voice in her ear sounded worried.

Kacie sniffed and got control of herself. Her fears were her own. She had a job to do and she would do it. End of story. With another sniff, she tried to free herself. Kerric didn't let her go. He held her just far enough away so that he could see her face and feather her tears away with a thumb. He smiled down at her and raised a questioning eyebrow.

"I'm OK now." She pulled away, breaking his hold and standing on her own. Kerric would have enough to worry about pretty soon without her adding to it.

"Did you have to hit me so hard?" Kerric rubbed his shoulder and then rotated it to get the kink out of it.

She buried her face in her hands. "I am so sorry," she mumbled between her fingers.

"I think I'll live." He draped an arm around her shoulders and led her into the sanctuary sitting beside her on the front pew. Derian and Tia followed. "Now tell me about Jozef. You said he's given you two days to find the sword?"

"Yep, a whole two days. He must think I have magical powers or something."

"I'll bet he thinks you're the Emerald Sorceress," Derian said, straight faced.

"Didn't you tell him that you were just Kacie Miller from Santa Monica?" Kerric dead-panned.

Their teasing purged the last dregs of self pity from her and Kacie got down to business, telling them what happened while they listened without interruption.

"Where are you going to start looking for the Dragon Sword?" Derian asked when she finished.

Kacie shrugged. "For lack of a better place, I thought I'd start with the Emerald Palace. Maybe Reyna left some clues to where she hid the sword. I don't know," she spread her hands.

"You said you saw us by scrying in water," Tia began. "Can't you do that for the sword?"

Kacie shook her head. "I tried that once already. It wasn't pretty," she said, the stench of her first try at scrying still fresh in her nostrils. "I'm hoping I'll have better luck in the Emerald Palace."

"Well," Kerric slapped his thighs and stood. "I guess we have to get you to the Emerald Palace." He hauled her to her feet and started for the secret door.

Kacie hung back, making him stop and turn back to her. "Where does that passage lead?"

"To the palace grounds and then ultimately to the forest beyond."

"And then how long will it take to get to the E.P. from there?"

"The E.P.?" Derian questioned.

"Emerald Palace," she explained. "How long?"

"About a week?" Derian cocked an eyebrow at Kerric for confirmation.

Kerric agreed and Kacie shook her head. "I only have two days."

"What do you suggest?" Tia spoke up.

"There's a Dragon mirror in a secret room behind Alexei's study," Kacie told her. "We can use that to go through now."

Kerric ran his hands through his hair and pursed his lips. "Where is Alexei's study?"

Kacie made a face. "Two floors up in the north wing."

Tia swore.

Kacie agreed and then cleared her throat. "I've been thinking. I'd really like Kerric to come with me, but I think Derian and Tia should go back and wait in the forest until we figure out what's going on."

"No," all three of them chorused.

"We've come this far," Tia shrugged.

"You are not doing this without us," Derian agreed.

Kerric didn't say anything until he reached the chapel door at the other end of the sanctuary. "How many guards are out there?"

"Just the two outside my door. The guards at the end of the corridor aren't there any more."

"There were guards at the end of the hall before?"Kerric asked, a thoughtful frown on his face.

"They were there this morning. One of them even escorted me to Alexei's study just before I came to you in the prison. Why? Is it important?"

"I don't know," Kerric said. "Maybe."

"It sounds like Jozef is making it easy for you," Tia added.

Kacie looked from Tia to Kerric. "You guys think he's setting a trap?"

"Probably," Tia confirmed.

"What are we waiting for?" Derian grinned. "Let's go spring it."

"Maybe we should wait." Kacie wasn't so sure. "Is there another way?"

"Not unless you want to take the long way." Kerric put one hand on the door and the other in the small of Kacie's back. "Are you ready?"

"Ready for what?"

"To call the guards in here." Kerric opened the door and pushed her out.

"Kerric, wait," she hissed at him, but it was too late, she was already in the hallway and the guards were looking at her. *I swear, if we live through this, Kerric Rouse . . .*

"Umm, excuse me." She cleared her throat, thinking fast. "I wanted to light a candle and I can't find any. Can you help me?"

They looked annoyed, but one man came to her aid. *Yes! They bought it!* Kacie kept her features neutral and led him into the chapel. Before she could say,"Don't hurt him." Kerric smashed the pummel of his sword against the man's head. Tia took the spear from his nerveless hands and Derian caught him before he could fall and dragged him out of the way. Using the alter cloth and the man's tunic, Tia bound and gagged him. At her nod, Kerric opened the door again.

Sticking her head out the doorway, Kacie said, "I'm so sorry, but, your friend can't find the candles either." She was sweetness itself. "I know you can't leave your post to go find the chaplain, but could you come in here and help us look? I really want to light that candle."

The guard grumbled a few obscenities, but he came and was dispatched with the same precision as the first one.

Man, they're good. "Something tells me you've done this before,"Kacie observed to no-one in particular.

Kerric winked at her. "Let's go." He jogged the length of the gallery, flattening himself against the wall when he reached the end. When they all filed in behind him, Kerric poked his head around the corner. "All clear." He motioned them forward.

Just before they burst onto the landing above the grand staircase, they slowed to a walk. "Company," Tia said under her breath.

Kacie followed her gaze and saw a richly dressed man and woman entering the landing from the mirrored hall at the other end. *Rats.* She stepped around Kerric and took the lead. She smoothed her dress and straightened her shoulders, her manner regal. She inclined her head to the couple, then snapped back to the others. "Be quick. It won't due to keep the King waiting." Kacie ignored the curious looks the couple gave them, praying they would only see a noble lady escorting three servants to the King.

The couple nodded back to her and then paid the odd troop no more notice as they descended the wide stairs and resumed their conversation.

As soon as the four of them were safely through the lapis columns at the far end of the landing and alone in the hall of mirrors, Kacie sagged against the closed doors. Her heart was racing a mile a minute. "That was close."

Derian grinned and gave her a thumbs up. "Good job, M'Lady." He bowed to her. "Now can we go?" He waved a hand at the long hall they still had to traverse before they reached the smaller stairs that would take them to Alexei's study.

The four of them exchanged looks and then by silent agreement, broke into a run, their heels clattering in the empty hall. At the other end, Tia threw open the doors and they raced up the stairs.

"It's the third door on the left," Kacie told them when they reached the top. But, before they took another step, Amsden emerged from behind the first door, to block their path, sword in hand and ready.

I really don't like that guy. Behind her, Derian swore. Kacie ignored him and advanced on Amsden. "Get out of my way, Snidely." She tried to push past.

Amsden answered by lifting the point of his sword to her face. She stepped back just as Derian brought his own blade across Amsden's sword, forcing it down. With his free hand, Derian pushed Kacie behind him.

"Captain Dahlen,"Amsden sneered, making an insult of the title. "Aren't you dead yet?" He twisted his sword free and lunged.

Derian sidestepped, smacking Amsden across the shoulders with the flat of his blade. "Not before I settle with you," he said and attacked.

The sound of clashing steel brought soldiers running. Kacie swore. "We don't have time for this," she said, watching Tia draw her sword and engage a pair of soldiers. Beside her, Kerric drop kicked the man nearest him, knocking the sword out of his hand. Another kick to the man's head and he crumpled. Kerric slid the toe of his boot under the fallen sword and flipped it into his hand, whirling around just in time to block an attack from his right.

Then Kacie had no more time to watch as she was grabbed from behind. She stomped on her assailant's foot, then drove her heel hard into his shin. When she felt his grip loosen, she wrenched herself free and elbowed him in the throat. The man went down with a gurgled cry, clutching his throat.

Kacie grabbed his sword and was immediately engaged by another attacker. It took both hands on the weapon to defend herself from this new attacker and it soon became clear that she was way out of her depth. He hacked ferociously away at her defense, pressing her back, step by step, her hands stinging from the onslaught of his blows. One sharp twist and he sent her sword flying out of her hand. Kacie staggered back and tripped over a fallen soldier. Like a lamb to slaughter, she watched her opponent curve his arm back for the killing slice.

That was when Kacie remembered her magic. *For heaven's sake, Miller, you're the Emerald Sorceress!* She gathered the threads of her power into her gut and whipped her hand toward the man. A ball of emerald fire burst from her palm and exploded into the soldier. He was thrown across the room and slid unconscious down the wall.

"Very good." Kerric stood over her, smiling in obvious admiration.

"Better late than never." Kacie held out a hand and he hauled her to her feet.

"We've got to get out of here," he said, watching Tia tuck and roll under a man three times her size. He nodded his approval as she thrust her sword up, impaling her foe. She sprang to her feet and Kerric called her to him.

Tia nodded and whistled for Derian who was still engaged with Amsden. "Derian! Leave him. Let's go!"

Derian's attention was diverted for a split second, giving Amsden the opening he needed. He moved in close and ran his sword through Derian's side. Derian stumbled and pressed a hand to his side. With a stunned look on his face, he saw the blood gushing from his wound as he sank to the floor.

Tia swore and raced to him in time to deflect Amsden's killing stroke. Cursing, Amsden kicked her feet out from under her. But even lying on her back, Tia countered his attack, blow for blow until he kicked her hand, sending her sword spinning. With a feral grin, Amsden brought his sword toward her throat.

"Hold!" King Jozef commanded from the stair landing.

Amsden's sword hovered above Tia's neck for several long heartbeats. Kacie held her breath. Would he obey the King?

"Leave her," Jozef ordered again.

Amsden bowed to the King and finally lowered his weapon and turned away from Tia. He signaled the guards to surround her and Kacie began to breathe again.

As all eyes followed Jozef's progress down the corridor, Kerric took Kacie's arm and pulled her to the study. "Now's our chance, let's go."

Kacie knew he was right, but she still held back. She couldn't stand the thought of leaving Derian and Tia behind.

Kerric wrapped his arm around her waist and lifted her off her feet, carrying her with him. "I don't like this anymore than you do." He stood her on her feet and opened the study door. "We can help them best by finding the Dragon Sword," he said and pushed her inside.

"Alright, let's go." She ran to the Aideny crest and pushed the sapphires. The bookcase slid open and she shooed Kerric through, pulling the case shut behind them.

A wave of her hand opened the door to the secret room. Once again, she pushed Kerric through and closed the door. Another wave of her hand and the small fat candle on the floor lit, sending their shadows crawling up the walls.

"Now what?" Kerric asked.

Kacie patted the dragon's head on the mirror frame. "Now we go to Kiramer," she told him and the surface of the mirror shimmered and settled into the softly rolling hills of the Kiramer country side. "Yeah, that was my first reaction, too," she laughed appreciatively at his slack jawed expression.

Kerric closed his mouth and Kacie turned back to the mirror. "I want to go to Reyna's workroom in the Emerald Palace." Obediently, the mirror shifted. "Now, we walk through." She took Kerric's hand. "Don't hit your head," she warned as she bent and stepped through the mirror.

****

Jozef strode to where Derian and Tia sat huddled together, Derian's head in her lap. "How touching." Jozef crouched down and took Derian's chin in his hand and turned his face for a better look. Derian opened his eyes and stared at the King. "So, you're not dead after all. Good."

Jozef grabbed Derian's shirt with both hands and ripped it from shoulder to hem. He flipped back the bloody material, exposing the gash in his side. Heedless of Derian's pain, Jozef poked at the wound and surrounding area. "You'll live." Jozef stood and motioned to several guards. "Take him to my chambers. Alexei can bandage him up," he ordered and then pointed at Tia. "Put her in the dungeon."

Several pairs of hands grabbed for Tia, but she shook herself free. "No! I won't leave him." The guards secured her hands behind her back as Tia continued to fight.

Jozef moved in close to her and took her face in his bloody hands. "I could kill you now." He offered her another option.

Tia clamped her mouth shut and allowed herself to be led away, with only one last worried look back at Derian.

"You should have killed her, Sire."

170

"Not yet."

"What about the Emerald Sorceress? Should we go after her?"

"No." Jozef allowed the corners of his mouth to lift. "There is no need. She has gone to find a mirror that will take her to the Emerald Palace in search of the Dragon Sword, just as I told you she would if we left her alone." A real smile spread across his features as anticipation surged through him. His palms itched. Already he felt the power of the dragon's eye in the sword's hilt coursing through his body. Soon . . . Soon . . . .

CHAPTER FIFTEEN

Kacie helped Kerric through to Reyna's workroom, steadying him when he swayed slightly. She guided him to the couch and helped him to sit. "Relax a minute while I check on Derian and Tia." She turned back to the arched portal. "Show me Derian and Tia."

The space inside the arch shimmered and the colors swirled, fading in and out, showing confusing images, but not settling anywhere.

"Why can't we see anything?" Kerric asked.

"I don't know. I've never seen the portal do this before."

"Burr, it's cold in here." Kerric shivered and rubbed his arms.

A wave of her hand set a fire blazing in the empty fireplace. Any other time, Kacie would have marveled at the phenomenon. This time she hardly noticed as she tried to figure out what was going on.

Kerric stood and warmed his hands over the fire. "Maybe they were separated," he suggested.

"That's a thought. Show me Tia."

The swirling within the arch slowed and focused on Tia pacing back and forth in the same tiny cell Kerric occupied a few hours ago. She was swearing loud and long as she paced, stopping every once in a while to bang on the iron bars.

Kacie rolled her eyes. "I'd say she's okay." Kerric nodded and Kacie turned back to the mirror. "Now show me Derian."

The picture shifted to an ornate room within the palace itself. Derian sat on a red brocade chair beside an open window, angled to take advantage of the late afternoon sun as Alexei tended the wound in his side. Alexei gave the gauze bandage a final tuck and handed Derian a clean shirt to put on. Derian slipped it over his head and then took the glass of wine Alexei offered.

Kerric shoulders twitched as the tight muscles relaxed. "When I saw him go down . . ." He scrubbed his face, blowing out a long sigh between his fingers.

Kacie knew exactly how he felt. "Yeah, I was afraid of what we'd find too. But he looks fine." She waved the picture in the portal away.

"Where does this door lead?" Kerric headed for the door beside the bookcase.

"To Reyna's bedroom,"she told him. "You know,"she began, but Kerric had already disappeared.

She turned back to the portal just as the shimmering arch clouded over and turned a deep angry blue. From the murky depths, Jozef's face smirked at her. "Lady Emerald," he greeted, and his eyes shifted to the room beyond her.

"Jozef," she forced past her thudding heart as it lodged itself in her mouth. She cleared her throat and swallowed, her gaze darting to the room Kerric just entered.

Please stay away a little longer, Kerric.

One look at Kerric and Jozef would immediately recognize him as family. Then Jozef would kill him on the spot and pfffft, that would be the end of Kerric.

She moved to the work table, drawing Jozef's gaze as far away from the door to Reyna's bedroom as she could. "What do you want, Jozef?" She steadied herself against the edge.

"I assume you've checked on your friends?" He waited while she nodded. "Good, then you know that they are alive – for the moment." Jozef leaned into the picture, his ice eyes narrowing. "You still have two days to bring the Dragon Sword to me."

"How am I supposed to find the sword in two days? You couldn't find it in twenty years."

Jozef ignored her. "On day three, if the sword isn't in my hands, your friends will die."

Lovely. He thinks I can just conjure the stupid thing out of thin air. Maybe I could call Rent-A-Room and see if they have any spare Dragon Swords lying around. "I need more time. I can't do it in two days."

"Two days." Jozef held up two fingers. The arch shimmered and his image was gone.

Kacie stormed into the adjacent bedroom. "This just keeps getting better and better." She flopped across Reyna's big bed and stared up at the fresco above her. "I knew there was a reason I wanted you guys to stay in the forest. Now I have to figure a way to get Derian and Tia as well as Alexei out of Trion Palace."

"You mean you and me." Kerric pointed back and forth between them. "We will get them out of Trion."

All the blood drained from Kacie's face and she clutched the covers to keep from screaming as panic raced through her body. The thought of Kerric anywhere near Jozef made her sick to her stomach. If Jozef killed Kerric, Medora would lose her rightful king and all hope of a better life. All the sacrifices would have been for nothing.

"I can't let you do that."

Kerric looked shocked. "Excuse me? You can't let me do that?" He laughed at her. "My dear Lady Emerald,"

Kacie flinched at the anger in his tone, but said nothing.

"You may be a sorceress," he continued. "But all the magic in the world can't be in two places at once. You need my help."

Kacie crossed to where Kerric leaned against the mantle. Ever since she found out who Kerric was, she thought of almost nothing except how she was going to break the news to him. Oh, how she'd gloat. Turn about was fair play and she'd make him pay for torturing her about being the Emerald Sorceress. But now that it was time, the words wouldn't come.

So, Miller, now what?

She opted for plan B. "Come with me, Kerric. I have something to show you."

"My mind's made up, Kacie. We're in this together."

More than you realize, My Lord, King. She took his hand and led him through the palace to the tower study, refusing to answer any of his questions until they reached their destination. Once inside, she went straight to the desk and got down on her hands and knees, fumbling under the drawer for the release trigger that would open the secret compartment.

"What are you doing?" He sounded annoyed and she could tell his patience was wearing thin.

"Just go sit down." Kacie stuck her hand out and waved at the empty hearth, chuckling to herself when a cozy fire sprang to life. *Ya gotta love it.*

Kerric went to the sideboard and helped himself to a glass of wine before he followed her orders. A minute later, Kacie emerged triumphant, Reyna's journal clutched to her chest.

"What are you holding?"

"This is Reyna's journal." Kacie sat next to him, leafing through the yellowed pages. She was stalling and she knew it. Finally, she stuck a finger in the book to mark her place and looked up at Kerric. "It's a book full of wonders and a treasure trove of truths. I'm hoping she left a clue in here about the Dragon Sword." Kacie mentally took a deep breath and screwed up her courage. "Reyna wrote all about me in here, about what happened to my mother and how we ended up in Santa Monica."

"Ha!" Kerric crowed. "I told you."

"She wrote about you, too, Kerric."

His smile faded. "Me?"

"You. According to Reyna you are the only child of Prince Mylan and his wife Liselle." She saw denial in his eyes and hurried on before he found his voice. "It seems that you, my friend, are the lost prince and the rightful king of Medora. The crown and sword belong to you."

Kerric stared at her, obviously not believing her. When she didn't say anything else, he exploded to his feet and prowled the room. "No, you're wrong. For so many reasons. Not the least of which is that I know my father. I am a farmer's son, not a prince's."

"And I'm just a girl from Santa Monica." *Oh, Kerric, we're two of a kind, you and me. How can I make you understand that it won't do any good to fight what you are?*

"I'm not a king." Kerric returned to the sofa and sank down.

"I know your having trouble processing all this. And, I do know how you feel. Believe me I know what's it's like to have your world turned upside down by a few words." She handed him the book. "Read it, Kerric. Reyna explains everything." She started to hand him the journal then stopped mid-motion. "You can read, can't you?"

"I can read." Kerric snatched the book from her hands and started to read. Kacie stared into the fire and waited, hardly daring to breathe. Everything hinged on his reaction. He was right. She did need him. She needed him to be King. Without Kerric, Medora was lost. Only the two of them, working together, could defeat Jozef and heal Medora.

When she thought she couldn't stand another second of suspense,

Kerric closed the book.

He tossed the journal down. "This proves nothing." He stood in front of the fireplace and looked up at the portrait of Lara giving the Dragon Sword to Harvey.

He looked, but Kacie knew he wasn't seeing. Somehow she had to get through to him. *What do I say, Lara?* "You know," she began. "A few days ago, you asked me to trust you until I could believe what you were saying. I didn't want to, but I did. And you were right. As much as I would love to deny everything you said and walk away, I am the Emerald Sorceress. And, like Lara," she pointed to the painting. "I'm here to bring a king out of obscurity so that Medora can be made whole. You are that king, Kerric. And, I'm asking you to trust me until you can believe. Please."

He remained silent and stiff and Kacie gave a weak snicker. "How do you think Harvey felt when Lara told him?"

Kerric snorted. "Harvey was born to be king."

"Yep. He sure was," Kacie agreed. "And, so were you." She bowed her head to him.

"Don't you have a sword to find?" He snapped and raced up the circular stairs to the balcony two at a time.

Kacie let him go. He needed time to adjust and she had her own problems to work out at the moment. She picked up the journal and began her search for clues that would lead them to the Dragon Sword.

"Now, why would anybody want to do that?" She heard Kerric say a little while later. "Lady Emerald...." he called down to her. "Look at this." He held something over the railing.

Kacie squinted up at him. "What is it?"

"I was hoping you could tell me." He tossed a small golden object down to her.

"Like I would know." The object fit into the palm of her hand. It looked like a piece of jewelry of some kind that had been cut in half. This half was a golden four pointed sunburst radiating out from a large cabochon emerald embedded in mother of pearl that had also been cut in half. She ran her finger over the smooth, straight edge along the bottom of the emerald. "How weird. Why would someone want to cut this in half? Where'd you find it?" She looked up, but Kerric was gone.

Lifting her skirts so that she wouldn't trip, Kacie ran up the stairs to look for him. He was secluded in a tiny alcove pouring over a big leather bound book.

"What are you reading?" She edged in beside him to get a look at what had him so engrossed.

"I'm not sure," he said without taking his eyes off the book.

The Renberg coat of arms was embossed at the top of the page. Below the white shield bearing the rampant regardant red dragon, was a genealogical chart of the Royal House of Renberg. Kacie skipped down to the last entry and saw Kerric's name. Maybe it was a trick of the light, but she swore Kerric's name glowed when she looked at it. "I told you so," she said quietly and nudged his shoulder.

"It's a coincidence." He stalked back down the stairs and stretched out on the couch and closed his eyes.

"Of course it is." She followed him down the stairs. "You just keep telling yourself that." She patted his shoulder and yawned. "I'm exhausted." She laid the gold piece on the desk. "I'm going down to get some sleep. I'll keep looking for clues to the sword tomorrow when I'm not so tired."

As she opened the study door, she caught a glimpse of Kerric reaching for Reyna's journal. She smiled and closed the door leaving him to come to terms with his destiny.

****

Kacie stood high on Mount Danua, beside a tall white tower. A shooting star blazed across the night sky. As she watched, a small piece broke off and fell to earth, landing at her feet. She bent, but the hands that retrieved the glowing mass weren't her own and the hair gently blowing in her face was flaxen.

Lara stood and took the fist sized chunk down the hillside to the old wooden shed beside the calm waters of Lake Zegari. She heated the solid mass in the fires of the shed's forge until it turned molten, and then shaped it into a long sword. From a pouch on a shelf behind her, Lara sprinkled a handful of finely crushed emerald powder into the liquid metal and then plunged the sword into the icy lake, speaking the words that would give the sword power. The waters churned, and through the cloud of hissing steam, the great sword rose, sending a beacon of emerald light high into the sky. Inside the emerald fire a rampant dragon clawed the night. With a roar he turned his great head, his fierce eyes staring into hers. Lara bowed to the powerful creature. He returned her salute and sunk back into the blade with a blaze of white light. When the waters calmed again, Lara took the sword and returned to her tower. As she crossed the threshold, her blue robes turned to gold and her silky flaxen hair became thick chestnut waves.

Sword in hand, Reyna climbed the inner steps of the tower. At the top, she pushed open the heavy door and crossed the floor ignoring the inlaid seven pointed star and being careful to skirt the six foot oval emerald recessed at it's heart. She went to the gilded throne sitting at the apex of the star and laid the sword across the arms of the throne. Turning, she stretched out her arms and raised her hands. At her command, the emerald flashed and rose from the floor becoming an altar. Reyna retrieved the sword and placed it on the stone. She murmured an incantation and the sword sank into the gem. A whisper of emerald power rippled through the altar sealing the sword within. Reyna trailed light fingers across the emerald and then turned to lower the stone back into the floor, hiding the sword from sight before she retraced her steps to the foot of the tower. Outside, once again, she closed the carved door to the tower and stood back.

The spring breeze blew a strand of jet-black hair into her eyes. Kacie looked up at the Emerald's tower standing at the top of Mount Danua.

****

Kacie woke from the dream with her heart thudding against her ribs."I think I know where the Dragon Sword is!"

She scrambled out of bed and ran into the workroom, rocking to a halt in front of the arch. The rainbow of colors shimmered in the early morning light. She stared at them for one excited heartbeat then took a deep breath. "Show me the Emerald's tower."

The kaleidoscope swirled, picking up speed as the colors pulsed and flashed deep within the heart of the arch. Kacie folded her arms across her chest and tapped her bare foot on the cold stone floor. "Come on, come on," she urged. After an eternity, the colors settled and focused on a tall mountain. As the picture zoomed closer to Mount Danua, the tiny speck at the top of the mountain grew into a tall white tower.

Kacie gasped. "It's real," she whispered then let out a whoop.

Without a second thought, she stepped through and found herself standing beside the white tower. She petted the sun heated stones and a smile lifted the corners of her mouth.

A light breeze ruffled her hair and Kacie lifted her face to the soft air, basking in the warm sun. Orange, red and yellow poppies dotted the lush carpet of grass covering the mountain top. Wiggling her toes in the satiny stuff, she bent and picked a bright orange poppy and sniffed its spicy scent before tucking the blossom behind her ear.

Ignoring the tower for the time being, Kacie followed her dream and Lara's path down the gently sloping hillside. Excitement tickled her insides when she came to the old shed. One peek inside confirmed that the forge was there. *Yes! It was a true dream!* She danced the rest of the way to the banks of Lake Zegari. Tears trickled down her cheeks as she knelt at the edge of the small lake and scooped up a handful of the crystal clear liquid and sipped.

The legend is real.

The cold water trickled down her throat, quenching a thirst she wasn't aware of having. As she swallowed, a sense of peace and belonging washed through her, leaving her content as never before. She stretched out on the grass and watched the cotton candy clouds drift past.

I could stay here forever.

Reluctantly, Kacie got up and turned her feet back up the hill. There would be time for daydreaming when this was all over. Right now, she had a sword to find.

She approached the tower and circled the base until she found the beautifully carved door.The designs carved into the body were incredible and the workmanship was superb, but she couldn't figure out how to get in. The door didn't have a knob, a handle, a rope - nothing.

"I knew finding that stupid sword couldn't be this easy." She stood back and examined the door again, following the swirls and curls with her eyes until she found a plain uncarved circle slightly above eye level. "That's weird." She put her hand in the center of the circle and felt the unmistakable tingle of magic, but no revelations came to her.

Kacie pushed a little harder and her hand slid through the circle up to her elbow. She yelped and jumped back, her heart beating out

Morse Code for "What the heck was that?" She took several deep breaths to calm down and then grinned.

"Of course!" She smacked her forehead. "It would have to be a magical door, wouldn't it? All I have to do is walk through it." She pushed on other parts of the door to test her theory. Each time, her hand slid easily through the solid wood.

"Oh, I am so good," she smirked and stepped through the door.

"Where were you?" Kerric demanded. "If you're going to go roaming through that thing, I wish you'd at least tell me." He grabbed her arms and pulled her away from the arch.

Kacie screamed and pushed him away from her. "Don't do that. You scared me half to death."

"I scared you? I've combed this entire castle looking for you."

"How did you get here?" She frowned at him, confused. What was Kerric doing in the Emerald's tower? Her frown deepened as she looked around her and recognized the old worktable and the potions cabinet beside the fireplace. She crossed the room and sank into the couch. "How'd I get back here?"

"Where were you?" Kerric followed her to the couch and stood, glaring down at her.

"I was on Mount Danua. I walked through the door of the Emerald's tower and ended up here. How can that be?"

"You were on Mount Danua?" Kerric furrowed his eye brows.

"Yes, I was." Kacie took the flower out of her hair and twirled it between her fingers. "That's where Reyna hid the sword."

"How do you know?"

"I saw it in my dreams last night."

"You dreamed it." He ran a hand through his hair. She could see that he wanted to believe her, but for all his belief in magic, he was a soldier. Dreams and visions were not part of a soldier's life.

She could almost hear his flawed logic and resisted the urge to snort. "My dreams are true, Kerric. The Dragon Sword is there." Kacie narrowed her eyes in thought and pushed herself up. "Now all I have to do is figure out how to get into the tower." She strode to the arch. "Take me back to Mount Danua," she demanded and was instantly rewarded with a clear view of the sun drenched white tower. "Wish me luck." She winked at Kerric and stepped through the arch.

Once more, she stood beside the carved door. "All right, you stupid tower, let me in," she demanded and walked through the door and collided with Kerric in the workroom.

"Rats." She kicked at an imaginary dust bunny and tilted her head up. "What happened to you?"

"I tried to go after you and ran into the wall instead." He rubbed his scraped nose.

Kacie stifled a giggle, then frowned. "I don't understand it. Why can't I get into the tower?"

"Maybe because there's a spell on it?" Kerric settled himself on the table and watched her pace the room.

He was so good at stating the obvious. "Of course there's a spell on it, but I'm missing something. I have to be," she muttered to herself. "But, what?" She stopped and pinned Kerric with a penetrating stare. "Maybe if you went with me. . ."

"Me? What could I do?"

"I don't have a clue. But, it's your stupid sword. Maybe Reyna keyed the door to you."

"I don't want the stupid sword."

"Yes, you do." She took him by the hand and tugged him to the arch and took him through.

Kerric looked up at the tower and then back to Kacie.

"Try touching it," she ordered.

Kerric placed his hand on the door, and the tower flashed a brilliant green. For a single heartbeat, time stopped and she saw the sword lying inside the stone, high in the tower room. The stone pulsed once and time resumed.

"Did you see that?" she cried.

Kerric dropped his hand. "See what?"

"The tower. The sword. Do it again. Put your hand back."

Kerric did as he was told and the tower flashed again showing her the sword. She was ecstatic. "The tower recognized you! I saw the sword. It's there! I told you, you were the key."

"Then let's go get it."

Kacie took his free hand and together, they pushed through the door.... and ended up back in the workroom.

"Aaagghh! I don't believe this!" Kacie kicked the leg of the worktable. "Why can't I get in?"

"Relax." Kerric took her by the shoulders and guided her to the couch and pushed her down. "You won't get anywhere ranting like a lunatic."

Kacie leaned her head back and pounded her fists on the cushions.

"Why don't you try calling the tower room? He suggested.

"I did."

"No. You called up the tower, not the room inside."

"Oh for heaven's sake." Kacie ran to the arch. "I need to get inside the room at the top of the Emerald's Tower," she told the portal.

Nothing happened. The arch remained dark. Kacie tried again. Nothing. She didn't kick the wall because she didn't want to hurt her foot, but boy, was she tempted. "I'll be honest, I'm out of ideas," she told Kerric.

Kerric put an arm around her shoulders. "Well, I think better on a full stomach. Let's eat breakfast and maybe something will come to us."

"That is a wonderful idea," she agreed, her mind still hashing over her dilemma.

"I almost hate to bring this up," he said. "But is there any food in this place?"

He sounded so pitiful that Kacie had to laugh. "There's fish in Lake Zegari."

Kerric grinned and hauled her to her feet. "Let's go get some."

The simple act of fishing restored Kacie's perspective so that she hardly flinched when they walked through the tower door and ended up in the workroom. After foraging the castle for plates and utensils they took their catch up to Reyna's study to cook. Kacie still believed the key was there somewhere. But Kerric forbid her to do anything until she had eaten, so she sat at the desk toying with the gold piece he found the night before, while she ran over the morning's events in her mind.

Still deep in thought, Kacie hardly noticed what she ate, and half way through, she pushed her plate aside and came around to stretch out in the big chair. She slouched back and stared up at her predecessor. *Come on Lara, help me out here.* Kacie sighed and rubbed her temples. Abruptly, she stopped mid-motion and sat up goggle eyed.

"Kerric look." She jumped up and grabbed the gold piece off the desk and held it up to the picture. "It's her brooch."

"Half of it, anyway."

"It's the key. I know it is."

"Slow down, girl," he cautioned. "Even if it is, it's still only half."

Kacie refused to be daunted. She rushed down and would have jumped through the arch if Kerric hadn't bellowed for her to wait. Impatiently, she waited for him to catch up and together they went through.

With an air of triumph, Kacie placed the piece into the uncarved circle in the door. She flashed a grin at him. The piece fit like it was made for it.

"Now all we have to do is find the other half."

"You just love pointing out the obvious, don't you?"

CHAPTER SIXTEEN

Kacie sat in front of the fire in the tower study, twiddling the brooch half between her fingers. Kerric was sprawled out on the couch with Reyna's journal perched on his chest, searching for a reference to the other half of the brooch.

Kacie shut out the soundof turning pages and stared into the flames. Something in the back of her mind was nagging at her memory, but she couldn't quite coax it to the surface.

It was frustrating to be this close to retrieving the Dragon Sword and not be able to get to it. But if they couldn't get into the Emerald's Tower, the silly thing might just as well be in another universe.

One whole day was almost gone and they were no closer than when they started. Somehow they had to find a way to get the sword out of the stone. *Why couldn't my name be Merlin? I bet he'd know what to do.*

There was no doubt in her mind that Jozef meant what he said. If the sword wasn't in his hands by tomorrow – well, she wasn't going to think about that end of that story.

Kacie dug her finger nails into her palms and concentrated on not giving in to despair. *What am I going to do?*

"Have you found anything yet, Kerric?"

"Not yet."

Kacie ground her teeth. "For about two cents I'd tell Mr. Weatherby at the Dreaming Tree to send me some dynamite so that I could blow that stone to pieces." Her jaw dropped open. "That's it! Another universe. Mr. Weatherby!" She beamed at Kerric.

"What are you talking about?"

"Mr. Weatherby has the other half of the brooch."

Kerric was looking at her like she'd lost her mind.

Nothing new there.

"Who is Mr. Weatherby?" Kerric wanted to know.

Kacie grabbed the journal from his hands and slid down beside him, thumbing through pages. "Here." She found what she was looking for and handed the book back. Niles Weatherby was sent to my world from here to watch over Maya and me," she said while Kerric read. "What could be safer than to send the other half of the brooch to another world? A world that Jozef couldn't get to." Kacie jumped up and started dancing on the couch. "He wears it as a belt buckle,"she laughed, delighted with her discovery. "Now all I have to do is figure out how to contact him."

Kerric pulled her down beside him again. "Use the mirror."

Gee, why didn't I think of that? Kacie hugged her hands between her knees. "I don't know if I can. I've never tried anything like that before."

Kerric rolled his eyes at her. "She creates fire out of thin air, but she's afraid to call up a picture in a mirror." He hauled her to her feet and out of the room. "What have you got to lose, Lady Sorceress?"

"That's right," Kacie snapped her fingers. "I'm the Sorceress and you're the King," she taunted then fled.

With Kerric hard on her heels, she raced to the workroom and skidded to a halt in front of the arched portal. Glancing up at him, she crossed her fingers for luck. "Here goes nothing. Show me The Dreaming Tree."

The arch seemed to take forever to slow its swirling, and Kacie thought she'd have a nervous breakdown before the silly thing cleared and reformed itself into the crystal room at The Dreaming Tree. She let out a whoop and did a short victory dance, before Kerric's raised eyebrows made her assume a more dignified attitude. She cleared her throat and ducked her head. "Let's just hope he's there." She couldn't resist one last heel-toe.

"How will we know?"

Kacie thought about it for a minute. *I guess I could ask* "Is Niles Weatherby there?"

She ignored Kerric's snort, throwing him a look of triumph when the picture changed and they saw a man hunched over a desk absorbed in paperwork. Kacie smiled at the familiar white ponytail swishing across the middle of his bright purple paisley shirt as he moved from one stack of papers to the next.

"Mr. W...." she called and his head came up searching for the voice.

"Mr. W, it's me, Kacie."

"Kacie?" He spun around as if expecting to see her standing behind him.

"Yes, it's me. Go to the mirror, I have to talk to you."

Kacie exchanged an amused glance with Kerric as they watched him leap to his feet and hurry through the store. He closed the doors to the crystal room behind him and then Kacie was staring into his twinkling blue eyes and smiling face.

"Well Child, I see you survived after all. And, you've made it to the Emerald Palace as well. Congratulations."

"Thank you," she preened. Kerric elbowed her in the ribs and she held up her half of the brooch. "I need your belt buckle."

"Ah." Mr. Weatherby nodded once. "Give me your hand, and help me through."

Kacie stretched her hand through the mirror and flinched a little when it was clasped in a warm strong grip. Remembering her own trip between the worlds, she said a silent prayer and drew her hand back. Mr. Weatherby stepped into the room without any ill affects and she sighed with relief.

"I told you he wore it as a belt buckle." She grinned at Kerric and pointed to Mr. Weatherby's belt. "Mr. W. may I present . . ."

He held out a hand to stop her and bowed low to Kerric. "Niles Weatherby, Baron of Ridgley, ever at your service Your Majesty."

Kerric froze for one awkward second. "Kerric Rouse." He half bowed, stopped, and thrust out his hand.

Kacie chortled. If looks could kill Kerric would have murdered her on the spot. "Kerric's having a little trouble adjusting to his new status," she explained.

"Something you can fully appreciate," Mr. Weatherby said and Kacie had the grace to blush. He patted her arm, then turned back to Kerric, studying his face and baring. "There can be no mistake, Lad. You are the image of your father." He motioned for Kerric to sit on the couch, while he dragged a chair over and made himself comfortable.

"Your father was a particular favorite of mine. In fact, I was Mylan's godfather."

"I didn't want to believe any of this,"Kerric admitted.

Boy, can I relate to that one.

186

"Not even after I read Reyna's journal,"he continued.

"But it is true," Mr. W. affirmed. "Mylan Renberg was the second son of King Gueran of Medora. The man who raised you, Stephan Rouse, was Mylan's closest friend."

Denial flashed across Kerric's face. He started to protest, but Mr. Weatherby shook his head.

"It's true, Lad. I was witness to Mylan's marriage to Liselle. I helped Stephan bring her to Kiramer after Jozef murdered King Gueran and the rest of your family. I was also there to witness your birth. You have a birth mark on your left shoulder, as well as your mother's hazel eyes."

Kerric's shoulder twitched as if an unseen hand pressed against it.

Mr. Weatherby smiled and looked up at Kacie. "And now, if I'm not mistaken, you two are on the trail of the Dragon Sword."

"We are," Kacie said.

"Then I believe the time has come for you to assume you full powers as the Emerald Sorceress."

Kacie's knees turned to jelly. *I'm not sure I'm gonna like this.*

Mr. Weatherby removed his belt and detached the buckle, but instead of handing it to Kacie, he held out his hand for the other half. Kacie gave it to him and her heart leaped when he fit the two halves together, forming a brooch with a golden seven pointed star.

A faint glow reflected deep within the heart of the emerald when the two halves touched and their sigh of peace echoed through her blood.

"No!" Kacie blanched, and held her hand out in protest when Mr. Weatherby separated them again. she slumped back, as a sharp pain stabbed through her head. "I can't stand it." She rubbed her throbbing temples. "They're in pain. I have to heal them."

"Not yet." Mr. Weatherby laid a gentle hand on her knee.

Her hands dropped back into her lap and she took a deep, steadying breath. Suppressing the urge to sob, Kacie shut her mind to the cries of the separated brooch and forced herself to sit up. "What is it? I mean, I know it's a brooch. But it's more than that."

Mr. Weatherby nodded. "This is the ancient seal of the Emerald Sorceress and it holds the key to all Emerald magic. The brooch is passed in ritual from Emerald to Emerald."

"What kind of ritual?" Kacie focused on the word. "Are we talking baby sacrifice or water sprinkling?"

"Where do you get these ideas?" Kerric gaped at her.

"Well....?" She persisted.

Mr. Weatherby laughed out loud and shook his head. "Somewhere in-between, I should think." He stood. "Get some rest. I'll be back later tonight."

"Tonight?" Kacie jumped up and followed after him. "Where are you going? You can't leave now."

"We can't do anything until midnight, and I've got a date." He handed the brooch pieces to Kerric. "Don't let her touch these until I return. Now, give me your hand, Kacie and help me get back."

Speechless, Kacie extended her hand. Mr. Weatherby took it and stepped through the portal and back into The Dreaming Tree. He turned to the mirror and shook his finger at Kacie. "Remember, don't touch the brooch. Get some rest, and no food or wine. You either." The finger swung and pointed at Kerric. "I'll be back here at 11:00. Wish me luck." He winked and was gone.

Kacie stared at the dark arch until Kerric placed a finger under her chin and pushed up, closing her mouth. "How am I supposed to know when it's 11:00?" She whirled on him.

Kerric chuckled softly."We'll figure it out."

ΛΛΛΛΛΛΛΛ

Kacie was wrenched from a fitful sleep by the fear that she'd missed Mr. Weatherby. She crept through the darkened bedroom and eased the door to the workroom open.

Kerric slept soundly on the couch, his face serene in the glow from the fire. The arch showed that the book store was still dark. Kacie relaxed.

A date at his age. She grinned and then sobered. She couldn't decide whether she was excited or terrified about what the old coot had in store for her. It wasn't that she thought Mr. W. would hurt her. She didn't. Really. But, she had no doubts that he wasn't beyond making her extremely uncomfortable.

Well, whatever happened, happened. She had to have the Dragon Sword and the only way to get it was to possess her full powers. And that required the brooch.

Kacie's gaze was drawn to the desk where the golden pieces glinted in the firelight. Being careful not to disturb Kerric, she tip toed across the room and knelt beside the desk. She rested her chin on her folded arms just inches from the divided brooch and studied the pieces.

She felt their pain; heard their soft cries, begging her to rejoin them. A hurt deep in her chest spread through her body. Her throat constricted around a silent sob. Everything drained from her mind except the burning need to heal their pain. She unfolded her arms and inched her hand closer to the brooch pieces.

"Don't touch them." Kerric grabbed her hand and pulled her to her feet.

Kacie stiffened, arching back to the split seal, fighting him as he drew her away from the desk and pushed her into a chair by the fire. "It's like having a piece of my own body ripped in two." Her voice shook.

Kerric followed her mesmerized stare and stepped between her and the desk, breaking her eye contact with the brooch.

"They cry to me." She drew a ragged breath and slumped back into the chair.

A piece of cloth lay close at hand and Kerric quickly moved back to the table. Snatching it up, he dropped it over the brooch pieces before returning to Kacie's side. "We'll heal them soon."

"Hello, is anybody there?" A hallow voice called from the mirror.

"It's about time," Kerric muttered and then looked back at Kacie. "Are you up to this?"

Kacie nodded and stood to help Mr. Weatherby through the arch.

"It's like tomb in here." Mr. W. frowned around the dark room. "Hit the lights, Kacie. Let's get this show on the road."

Kacie waved a hand in the air and the candles blazed. The bright, cheery light chased the echo of pain from her mind as well as the shadows from the room. She sighed with relief and gave Mr. Weatherby a mischievous look.

"So, did you get lucky?" she asked with a perfectly straight face.

"Impertinent child." He looked shocked, but his eyes twinkled before he turned his back on her. "Kerric, do you have a knife? Good."

"A knife? Why does he need a knife?"

"Hush." Mr. Weatherby placed a finger on her lips to still them. "Now, we need a bowl, a couple of pieces of silk and a light of some kind." He ticked the list off on his fingers. "I have the silk and you can light our way," he told Kacie. "But we still need a bowl. Ah, Kerric, you found one. Good." He stuffed all the items into the bag looped over his shoulder. "Now, my dear, if you will be so good as to call up Mount Danua, we'll be on our way."

"Don't I have to put on a white robe or something?" Kacie asked.

Mr. Weatherby looked over his nose at her. "Why? Are you uncomfortable in what you have on?"

"Never mind. Show me the Emerald's Tower," she told the arch.

Mr. W. scooped up the brooch from under its cover and slid it into his bag before going through the portal. He found a spot he liked beside the tower and took Kerric's knife before sending him down to the lake to fill the bowl. Kacie started a small fire and Mr. Weatherby placed the blade in the flames. From his pouch he produced a tin of tobacco and began sprinkling it on the ground in a large circle, closing it off when Kerric returned with the water. Next, Mr. Weatherby pulled an abalone shell and a stick of sage from his pouch. He crumbled the sage into the shell and light it, offering a prayer to the four directions before he ran the pungent smelling smoke over each of them and the bowl and knife.

When the smoke from the sage leaves died out, Mr. Weatherby repeated the process with a mixture of sweet smelling copal and lavender.

Kacie watched with a raised eyebrow, but she didn't have the courage to ask what exactly he was doing. She might have worked in a metaphysical book store for a year, but she never bothered to read many of the books. A job was a job. She needed the money for school and the Dreaming Tree had an opening. Done deal. Now she thought she probably should have paid more attention because she had no idea what he was up to and it made her a little nervous.

Mr. W. saw her frown. "An American shaman taught me this ritual," he explained, slipping the two halves of the brooch into the water and then sent Kerric's knife hissing after them. "I find the sage works very well for purifying an area to work in and for protection."

OK, if you say so.

Mr. Weatherby replenished the incense and motioned for Kacie and Kerric to sit close to the fire. He reached for the knife and placed it against Kacie's right index finger. "Your blood will heal the brooch and release the magic."

With her mouth suddenly too dry to speak, Kacie nodded and Mr. Weatherby slid the knife across her finger and squeezed, encouraging the blood to flow.

Kerric leaned over the bowl and used one piece of silk to fish out the brooch halves and lay them on the other piece of silk in front of Kacie. Being very careful not to touch the seal, he fitted the two halves together.

At Mr. Weatherby's nod, Kacie picked up the brooch and traced her finger along the crack. Her blood mixed with the gold and the stone, sealing the breach and fusing the two halves together. Emerald fire exploded behind her eyes. White hot flames raged through her body searing the very essence of her being.

Kacie screamed. Her body was and inferno. If she stayed she'd be incinerated. Like the phoenix rising from it's own ashes, she broke the chains binding her spirit to her body and rose. Soaring. Free. Never to be tied to earthly restraints again.

High above her a finger of emerald light beckoned. She soared toward the ever brightening beacon until the unceasing brilliance blinded her.

When her vision cleared, she stood on the threshold of a large circular room. Inside the room, Reyna sat on a gilded throne. She wore a deep emerald robe and on her head rested a golden circlet studded with three cabochon emeralds the size of a child's fist.

On either side of the throne, fifteen more women stood in a circle around the room. Each of them wore matching gowns of light green and wore plain golden circlets on their brows.

Kacie brought her attention back to Reyna who smiled at her and came forward to take her hand and lead her into the center of the room. They crossed the seven pointed star inlaid into the floor, and when Kacie stood on the oval emerald at the heart of the star, the women began to chant.

Reyna took the brooch from Kacie's hands and stepped back into the circle of chanting women. Kacie swayed as the chanting washed through her, carrying her on a wave of heart soaring bliss. Beneath her, the emerald thrummed to the rhythm of the chant.

Kacie watched it for a moment and then a tall woman with long auburn curls detached herself from the circle and moved toward her. In her hands, the woman carried a light green gown. "Welcome, Sister," she said and slipped the gown over Kacie's head and returned to her place in the circle.

Kacie looked down at herself and realized she was now dressed like the others. Looking up again, she recognized Lara's flaxen hair as she stepped forward, her hand extended. Kacie blinked back her tears and took Lara's hand.

"You have joined us at last. We had almost given up on you," Lara teased with a low, musical voice and helped Kacie to kneel.

Taking both of Kacie's hands, Lara traced a seven pointed star on her palms and then placed an emerald in the center of each star. The emeralds sank into her palms, making them tingle. Next, Lara drew the star on Kacie's forehead, placing a third emerald between her eyes. The chanting grew louder. Kacie swayed and the Universe expanded.

Between one heart beat and the next, Kacie knew the secrets of the cosmos. She saw everything and everyone. She was as big as the Universe and totally invincible.

The chanting stopped and Kacie drew back into herself. Once more, just a girl. No, she would never be that again. The Emerald Power was hers to command. She was The Emerald Sorceress.

Kacie looked into all the answering emerald eyes in the circle and understood each of them. She contained within her the knowledge and awareness of all of them. She belonged to the Sisterhood. Tears sprang to her eyes. his was her destiny. This was her home. This was where she belonged. Lara smiled and raised her, leading Kacie to where Reyna stood beside the throne.

Reyna draped the velvet robe around Kacie's shoulders and Lara fastened it with the brooch. Then, Reyna removed the circlet from her own head and placed it on Kacie's. Together, Reyna and Lara led her up to the throne and seated her as the reigning Emerald Sorceress.

"You will be the greatest of us all," Reyna said, hugging her tight.

They bowed respectfully and stepped back into the circle of sorceresses who had gone before and they began to chant again. Kacie closed her eyes and joined the chanting, becoming one with them. Peace stilled within her and time slipped away.

Taking a shuddering breath, Kacie opened her eyes and found herself lying on the grass at the foot of the Emerald's Tower. *Wow, that was one wild dream.*

The palms of her hands still tingled and the magic sang within her. Power was there, just under the surface, waiting to be called. *No, I didn't dream this.* She hugged the memory close.

She squinted and turned her head away from the glare of the morning sun, dislodging the brooch resting on her stomach. Kacie retrieved it and ran her fingers over the surface, feeling the power of centuries of magic surge through her. Smiling, she tried to sit up.

"Stay there." Mr. Weatherby put a restraining hand on her shoulder and forced her to lie still until Kerric returned from the lake with water.

Kerric knelt beside her and helped her to sit up and placed a cup to her lips. Kacie drank, grateful for the cool liquid that trickled down her parched throat. Kerric took the cup from her and tried to make her lie down again.

"Kerric, I'm fine," she protested. "In fact, I've never felt better," she grinned at the two men.

"What happened?" Kerric asked.

"I'd tell you, but then I'd have to kill you." She winked at him and sprang to her feet.

"What?" He was very confused.

Kacie laughed at him and said, "I'll tell you later. Right now I've got a sword to retrieve." She left them and ran to the wooden door. She slid the Emerald's brooch in place and crossed her fingers for luck before walking through.

"It worked!" she whooped and raced up the stairs to the room at the top of the tower. The door swung open at her touch and Kacie stopped in her tracks. She stared in wonder at the golden star on the floor and the throne on the far side of the room.

"This is where the initiation took place," she whispered, rubbing her itching palms on her thighs. She skirted the emerald at the heart of the star and walked to the throne. She caressed the soft velvet of the ceremonial robe draped over one of the arms and then reverently lifted the circlet off the seat and put it on her head, once again feeling the magic of the ritual.

Cocking the circlet over one eye, Kacie pushed up her sleeves and turned back to the emerald, palms outstretched. *OK, Miller, let's see what ya got.* She raised her hands and the recessed stone began to glow from within as it rose from the floor, revealing the Dragon Sword at its heart. Kacie held her breath until the emerald slab stopped moving.

"Crimeny." She gaped at the stone altar and the prize inside. "This thing's like a giant box of Cracker Jacks. Just stick your hand in and pull out the prize." She did just that and cracked her knuckles against the solid stone. "What the heck?" She reached for the sword again and came up short. "Abracadabra?" She tried once more and smacked her hand. "Guess not. Hmmm. . ."

Stumped, she retreated to the throne and plopped down. "Why won't you let me in you silly hunk of green rock?" She pushed the circlet back on her head and made a face at the uncooperative emerald. "You don't have to protect the sword form me. I'm the new Emerald Sorceress. Really. I was here last night. You remember, Lara, Reyna, women dressed in green. I stood on top of you, for heaven's sake."

She got up and walked around the stone, inspecting it from every angle trying to figure out what she was missing. Nothing came to her. She reached for the sword one more time and came up short again. "Look, I'm taking the sword to Kerric, okay? He's right outside." Her eyes widened and she smacked her forehead. "Kerric, Of course! I am such a twit sometimes. Don't go away, I'll be right back," she told the emerald and raced down the stairs. She grabbed Kerric by the hand and tried to pull him along with her. "Come with me."

Kerric yanked back, almost knocking her off her feet. "What happened up there?"

"You're about to do your 'Arthur' bit." She hauled on his hand.

He yanked her back again. "What are you talking about?"

"Oh, for heaven's sake. Don't argue with me, just come on." Kacie raced back up the stairs with Kerric in tow. She slid to a halt in front of the stone and pointed. "okay, Arthur, pull the sword form the stone."

"Have you lost your mind?" Kerric looked from her to the sword locked in solid stone. "How am I supposed to get it out of there?" He moved in for a closer look and the emerald blazed, showering him with its radiance.

"Look, it recognized you." Kacie almost shouted with joy. Kerric started to back away, but Kacie's hand in his back stopped him. "Take it," she ordered, her voice low and insistent, all humor gone now. "The emerald will yield. Take the Dragon Sword, Kerric. It is yours."

Kerric stared at her for a long moment and then reached out as ordered. His hand slid through the solid stone like water. Penetrating the emerald, he grasped the hilt of the Dragon Sword and pulled it free.

Sword in hand, he turned back to Kacie. "Sire." She bowed to him.

Kerric turned on his heel and left the room.

"Oh no you don't. You're not running away this time." Kacie clattered after him, chattering the whole way. "I told you were King. You never listen to me. Didn't I tell you? Yes, I did. Now maybe you'll listen when I tell you something. I'm the Emerald Sorceress, you know, I know things."

"Shut up."

"As you command, Sire." She grinned and linked her arm with his.

Mr. Weatherby fell to his knees when he saw the sword in Kerric's hands. "Your Majesty." He bowed his head.

"Not you too," Kerric groused. "Please don't do that."

"But you are the King. Lesser subjects will always bow to you."

"Even my friends?"

Mr. Weatherby nodded. "In public, even your friends. However, in private, you will make your own rules." He smiled and got to his feet.

Kacie bit her lip to keep from gloating. *This is great.*

Kerric saw her. "Don't say a word," he warned.

"Who, me?" Her eyes were wide and innocent. "Never crossed my mind – Sire." Kacie spun away from him, clearing her throat a couple of times to keep from laughing out loud. *He's so easy to tease, now.* She removed the brooch from the tower door and held out her hands to Mr. Weatherby and Kerric. "We have a lot to do before we give Jozef the Dragon Sword."

CHAPTER SEVENTEEN

"You can't give Jozef the Dragon Sword," Kerric said as soon as his feet touched the workroom floor. His voice as sharp as the blade clutched white knuckled in his hand. "He'll kill them all as soon as he has the sword."

"He'll try," Kacie agreed and leaned against the long table. "You do realize that he's after the ruby in the hilt not the sword itself?"

Kerric looked confused. "Why would he want the Dragon's Blood?"

Mr. Weatherby put his hand out for the sword and then held the hilt up so that Kerric could see the stone. "This ruby is the Raven's Eye. It belongs in the Raven Wizard's signet ring and holds the key to full initiation into the Raven Brotherhood. Reyna and Mykal switched the stones before Jozef murdered Mykal and usurped his powers."

"Jozef could care less about the sword," Kacie added. "He just wants the rest of his powers."

Kerric ran his hands through his hair. "We can't let him obtain any more power."

"No, that would be bad." Kacie took the sword from Mr. Weatherby and laid it on the table. Using Kerric's knife, she loosened the prongs holding the Raven's Eye and pried the thumb nail sized ruby out of its setting. When she finished, Kacie set the ruby aside and held the Dragon Sword out to Kerric.

"Take the sword," she told him, her voice low and filled with power. Kerric saw the emerald fire crackling in the air around her and hesitated. "Take the sword, Sire," she repeated.

Kerric swallowed hard and did as he was bid. He wrapped his hand around the hilt and Kacie looked into his eyes, holding them spellbound.

"From this moment forward only the true Dragon King of Medora shall wield the Dragon Sword. If used by one who is not rightfully born King of Medora, The Dragon Sword will shatter."

A jolt of energy sparked from Kacie's hands to the blade and traveled up Kerric's arm and over his body until both he and the sword were bathed in a shimmering emerald aura.

"It is done," she said.

The aura vanished and Kerric staggered back a couple of steps before he regained his balance.

Behind them, Mr. Weatherby chuckled. "Oh, she's good."

Kacie turned around to see a delighted grin stretching across his face.

"Medora's going to be a lively place with you two in charge," he continued.

Kerric grunted and turned his back on them, sinking into the couch.

"And on that positive note, I think I'll go home," Mr. Weatherby turned to the arch.

"You're leaving? You can't leave now." All of Kacie's new found confidence hopped on a jet bound for Fiji.

"I promised Millie we'd go surfing today."

"I thought you were staying to help us defeat Jozef?"

Mr. Weatherby put an arm around her shoulders and drew her to the arch with him. "You don't need me to defeat Jozef. Just trust your instincts, Lady Emerald." He bowed his head to her. "And remember, if you truly need me I'm just on the other side of the mirror." He winked and then bowed low to Kerric. "Your Majesty," he said and stepped through the portal.

Surfing at his age. She snorted. "Watch the undertow off Santa Monica pier." Kacie looked around the room and sighed. He was really gone. The one person in the whole place that actually knew what was going on just vanished into another universe.

Now what?

Now you grow up and stand on your own two feet.

She stilled the panic doing the Boston Shuffle in the pit of her stomach and forced herself to relax. As she calmed she felt the wealth of the Emerald magic coursing sure and strong through her being, just waiting to be tapped. Her doubts fled. Mr. W. spoke the truth. She did know what to do.

The first order of business was to forge a link between herself and

197

the Raven's Eye. She retrieved the ruby and her seal from the table and took them back to the fireplace. Sinking cross-legged onto the floor in front of the fire, Kacie placed the ruby against the face of the emerald, she cocooned them between her hands and let the outside world recede. She slowed her breathing and drifted into a light trance, focusing her power on the stones. The talismans grew warm and a shaft of ruby light shot into the emerald. An answering flash flared within the emerald and twined itself around the red beacon, spiraling back to the ruby. Kacie's heart picked up the rhythm of the pulsing stones and she merged her energy with theirs, completing the link.

"That's done." She scooted back and leaned against the couch beside Kerric's feet.

"What did you just do?"

"I connected the Raven's Eye to the Emerald Seal. That way if Jozef does get his hands on the ruby I'll be able to follow it to wherever he is and I'll know when he begins his power ritual."

"How do you plan on keeping the Raven's Eye from Jozef?"

"That is a very good question. And the answer is I don't have a clue." Kacie waved a hand at the arch. "Show me Tia."

The shimmering rainbow within the portal turned to slate. Shadows flickered behind the dull surface, but she couldn't make out any details. The harder she tried to penetrate the haze, the darker the arch became.

"I don't like this. Show me Alexei."

Nothing happened. The murky gray fog still undulated over the surface.

"What do you think is going on?"

"Nothing good, that's for sure." Kacie fingered the hem of her sleeve as a sliver of foreboding seized her. "He's blocking them from me."

"Why?"

"My guess is he's setting up for his power ritual."

Kerric frowned. "That's taking a lot for granted. How does he know you'd even be able to find the Dragon Sword?"

"Oh, he knows."

Kerric sat forward, his arms resting on his knees. "What about Derian?" he asked and ran a hand through his hair.

Kacie shrugged. "I don't know. Let's try. Where is Derian?" she asked and held her breath until the darkness began to clear and rainbow colors swirled again. "Thank goodness. And he's alone." She smiled up at Kerric as the shifting colors settled into an image of an elegant room within Trion palace.

Derian prowled the small confines, never taking his eyes off the gilded door to his left.

"Is he?" Kerric frowned. "Where's Jozef? Why would he block Tia and Alexei and then leave Derian open? It has to be a trap."

"I agree. It probably is a trap, but Kerric, we have to get Derian out of there before Jozef shields him too and I can't reach him."

Kerric shook his head. "We can't just charge in. There's too much at stake."

"Yeah, there's a whole lot more at stake here than rescuing Derian. But, if we can get him out that would be one less lever Jozef could use against us.

"Show me Jozef," she told the arch.

The arch went dark again.

"How did I know that was going to happen?" She twisted around to face Kerric. "So what do you think?"

"I don't like it. Jozef could be standing on the other side of the room and we wouldn't now it."

Kacie agreed with him, but that didn't change anything. "Kerric, I have no idea where Tia and Alexei are or what Jozef has done with them. They could be dead for all I know. If Jozef shiclds Derian he'll be lost to me too. I won't be able to find him. And if that happens we may never get him back. With luck we can jump in, grab Derian and be back here before Jozef knows what's happening." She stuffed the emerald brooch and the Raven's Eye into her pocket and held out her hand.

"I know I'm going to regret this." Kerric stood and picked up the Dragon Sword.

"I'm totally open to any other ideas?"

He took her hand and they stepped through the portal and into the middle of the room Derian occupied.

Derian spun around to face them, his hand reaching for the sword at his side. When he grabbed air where the sword should have been, he jumped behind a chair.

"Derian, it's us." Kacie held up her hands to show him they were unarmed. "Come on, we've got to get you out of here."

"Go back. You shouldn't have come." Derian's gaze darted to the gilded door.

Kerric looked toward the door. "Derian, what's going on?"

"Will you two chit chat later? We've got to get out of here, now." She grabbed Derian's arm and tugged.

"Don't rush away on my account." Jozef's cold voice in the doorway behind them stopped them dead.

"I told you it was a trap." Kerric tightened his grip on the Dragon sword.

"Let me deal with this." Kacie spun, an Emerald aura crackling over her body.

"Don't do anything stupid." Jozef leaned back and pulled Alexei to his side. Threads of pulsing gold protruded from Alexei's heart and wove themselves around his chest. Jozef held out his hand to show her the ribbons of Alexei's life wrapped around his fingers.

Kacie blanched and clamped her mouth shut, stifling a cry at the sight of her father bound by Jozef's magic. *Don't fall apart now, Miller. You can't help him if you go to pieces.*

Jozef gave her a sadistic grin and twitched his fingers. Alexei gasped for air, his eyes glazing.

Kacie glared at Jozef, hate burning in her eyes. *I swear, if you hurt him the entire Universe won't be big enough to hide you from me.* "Alright, I get the picture." She let her power fade.

"That's better." Jozef relaxed his fingers allowing Alexei's heart to pump unimpeded again.

Kacie's jaw clenched and unclenched as she fought the urge to blast Jozef to oblivion. But, while he held Alexei's life literally in his hands, she was helpless and he knew it.

"Where is the Dragon Sword."

"Here's your sword!" Kerric circled the blade above his head and lunged for Jozef.

"Kerric, No!" Kacie yelled and Jozef whirled to face the threat, using Alexei as a shield.

"You dare threaten me?" Jozef challenged. His thin lips compressed into a hard line as he took a long look at Kerric's face and bearing. "Well, well, well," Jozef said at last. "You cast a wide net, Lady Emerald."His gaze flicked to Kacie and then back to Kerric. "I never dreamed that you would find a Renberg bastard to help you in your quest. I thought I killed them all. Careless of me. "He shrugged looking Kerric up and down. "You have the look of my brother Mylan. Are you Mylan's bastard, boy?"

Kerric didn't move a muscle, but Kacie recognized the angry smolder in his hazel eyes and prayed he wouldn't do anything stupid.

"I am the son of Prince Mylan Renberg and his wife Liselle LeClair, eldest daughter of the . . ."

"Duke of Rathborn, yes, yes. I know Medora's peerage." Jozef looked up at the sword still poised to attack. "And now, you've come forward with the Dragon Sword in hand to claim the throne of Medora?" He snorted and returned his gaze to Kerric's face. "If this wasn't so pathetic it would be amusing." His eyes narrowed and he stepped closer to Kerric. "But, you have to go through me to get to the throne. Your father wasn't strong enough to stand up to me. Are you, Nephew?"

"Kacie," Derian whispered, edging closer to her without attracting Jozef's attention. She raised a questioning eyebrow and he rolled his eyes at Alexei.

Kacie followed his gaze and saw nothing. Derian continued to insist, so she shifted slightly to a better vantage point and saw Jozef's hand conjure a ball of magic behind Alexei's back where Kerric couldn't see. Kerric wouldn't even know he was in danger until it was too late.

She had to distract him from Kerric. "The Raven's Eye isn't in the sword. I removed it."

Kerric spun the sword so that Jozef could get a good look at the hilt. "What have you done with it?" Jozef demanded.

"Oh, it's safe. It isn't here, but it's safe," she said, never taking her eyes off the growing ball of energy.

"Give me the Raven's Eye."

"No," she said and Kerric chose that moment to attack. He sprang, Dragon Sword arcing toward Jozef's head.

Jozef sidestepped, pulling his hand away from Alexei.

"Kerric watch out!" Kacie yelled and Kerric dropped to the ground. Kacie threw an emerald shield of protection around him a fraction of a second before Jozef unleashed his killing attack.

"That was stupid,"Jozef hissed at her, slowly closing his other hand. "We end this now. Give me the Raven's Eye or your father dies."

Alexei's eyes bulged and he clawed helplessly at his chest as life was torn from him.

Kacie threw a desperate look at Kerric. She didn't know what to do. She couldn't give up the Raven's Eye, but she couldn't stand by and watch Jozef kill her father, either.

Kerric nodded. "Give him the stone."

Jozef continued to constrict his hand. "Time is running out."

Kacie hung her head and prayed she wasn't dooming Medora for her own selfishness. She pulled the ruby out of her pocket and tossed it to Jozef.

Jozef snatched the Raven's eye out of the air and held it in the palm of his hand for a moment. Kacie knew he was feeling for the power in the stone.

"It's the Raven's Eye," she told him.

"So, it is," he acknowledged and eased the tension on the threads of Alexei's life force.

Alexei gasped, pressing the heel of his hand against his chest and sagged against Jozef's side, but he was breathing.

Kacie began to breathe again as well. "You have what you want. Let him go."

"No." He pulled Alexei into the next room with him. "Nephew, we will meet again, soon."

Through the open door, they saw the room beyond flash an inky blue and then go dark.

Kerric and Derian ran into the room after Jozef and straight to the mirror. "Let's go," Kerric urged.

Kacie stood at the doorway, her hand gripping the frame, white knuckled. "We can't," she said, in a choked voice. *I'm sorry, Alexei.*

Kerric spun around and glared at her. "What do you mean we can't? He just took your father and he's still holding Tia. Let's go after him."

"Don't you think I know that?" Kacie heard the shrillness in her tone and made herself calm down and speak normally. Yelling at

Kerric wouldn't make up for her failings. "Even if I knew where he went," she squinted at the mirror, seeing the bands of blue energy criss-crossing the mirror's surface. "Jozef blocked the mirror. No one can get through." She knew they couldn't see the magic surrounding the mirror, but to her those thin blue bars were as good as a pad lock – better. She could pick a pad lock.

"Can't you break his magic?" Derian asked.

"Given time, but we don't have time."

Kerric was still staring at her. "So, what do we do now?"

"We have to get to Alexei's study," she told him. "We need another mirror."

CHAPTER EIGHTEEN

Kacie hurried Derian and Kerric out of Jozef's apartments and through the palace. The odds were that Jozef went through to the Raven's Fortress. And while they were twiddling their thumbs, he was preparing the ritual that would give him the full magical powers of the Raven Wizard. She reached out with her senses and felt the pull of the Raven's eye. Good, the bonds still held. They would lead her to Jozef. But, would she be in time to stop him? Kacie started to run.

With Kerric and Derian right behind her, they burst into the study. Derian closed the door behind them and stood guard in front of it.

Kacie went straight for the server and poured water from a silver pitcher into a crystal goblet. She took a deep breath and centered herself. Drawing on her bond with the Raven's Eye, she peered into the water. "Where have you gone?"

The water churned within the cup and a blue haze obscured the vision. Only a pinpoint of red light pierced through to the surface.

"Show me." Kacie blew across the cup and the mist billowed up, spilling over the rim. The ruby beacon grew stronger and she followed it down to a stone fortress hidden in a narrow valley. Tall, craggy mountains loomed high, their shadows hiding the entrance to the valley.

The image in the water rippled and focused on a dark room in the fortress itself. Wall sconces showed that the room was empty except for a stone bowl and a gold cup sitting in the middle of the floor. Kacie looked closer and saw that the cup was half filled with a wine-like liquid.

Moving her finger over the water, she shifted the picture and saw Alexei and Tia bound and gagged in a corner. They were either drugged or under a spell, because when Jozef held the cup under Tia's hand and sliced a knife across her forearm, squeezing the flesh above the cut and catching the flowing blood into the cup, Tia didn't even flinch. Horrified, Kacie watched Jozef perform the same procedure on Alexei and then himself. Swirling the contents of the cup, he drank.

Kacie almost retched.

He just bound their energies to him. Their lives are now his to use as needed and then discard. She swallowed the bile lodged in her throat and forced herself to continue watching.

With a satisfied smirk, Jozef set the cup down and picked up the bowl. He passed his hand over the opening and a blue flame sprang up from the depths of the shallow vessel. Kacie watched his lips move in a silent spell before he dipped his fingers into the fire and retrieved the Raven's eye from inside. Cupping the jewel in his hands, Jozef closed his eyes and grew very still.

Kacie withdrew, letting the images fade. "Jozef went to the Raven's Fortress. He's started the power ritual."

"Then, let's go get him," Kerric repeated his earlier suggestion.

"It's not that simple."

From the doorway, Derian groaned. "Somehow I knew you were going to say that."

Kerric looked back at Kacie. "Why can't we go after him?"

"The Raven's Fortress is warded. Just like the Emerald's Tower, no one gets in without permission."

"What do we do now?" Kerric paced in front of the fireplace. "Do we just wait while Jozef assumes more power?"

"Not on your life." A ghost of a smile touched her lips. "Now we get permission to go after him."

"Who's going to give you permission?" Derian put in. "I can't see Jozef letting you inside so you can ruin his plans."

"Of course I'm not asking Jozef." She crossed to the Aideny crest and pressed the gems in the Ducal crown that would open the secret panel. "I'm going straight to the Raven Brotherhood."

"The Raven Brotherhood?" Derian asked. "I've never heard of them."

"The Raven Brotherhood is the fraternity of Raven Wizards past and present. They hold the culmination of the Raven Wizard's powers. Normally, the current wizard would pass on this knowledge and magic to his apprentice before he dies. But in this case, Jozef is trying to steal their power. I know they'll help me stop him."

Kacie grabbed the candelabra off the desk and shooed Derian and Kerric into the secret passage. Lighting the candles, she closed the panel and led them into the tiny mirror room.

Kerric crossed to the mirror and rested his arm on the frame. "Are you saying that you're going to go ask a bunch of dead wizards for help?"

"They aren't dead, Kerric," she said.

"I don't know," Derian began. "They sound dead to me."

"Don't help, Derian." She glowered at him. "Their essence lives and their knowledge can help us."

"I still don't like it," Kerric persisted.

"Enough, both of you." Kacie ended the conversation. "Unless either of you have a better idea, we do it my way." She waited for one of them to speak up. The silence was deafening. *I didn't think so.*

She settled herself on the floor. "Sit down, guys. We need to talk." She patted the ground next to her. "In order to reach the Raven Brotherhood, I have to go into trance. It's nothing dangerous, but it leaves me vulnerable to outside attack. I need the two of you to make sure I'm safe."

Without a word, Derian scooted over to rest his back against the door and Kerric pulled the Dragon Sword, resting it on his knees. Kacie smiled and continued. "I'll ward the room and block the mirror so you won't have to worry about a magical attack."

She raised her hand and drew a circle in the air above their heads three times. After the last time, the walls of the room blurred a little and shimmered with a faint green aura, wrapping them in a cocoon of protection. "It's done. We're warded. One more thing," she pinned them with a hard look to make sure she had their attention. "I may be out for a while. Don't get nervous. And whatever you do, do not touch me."

When she had their assurances, she pulled the Emerald Seal out of her pocket. Using the stone as a focal point, she let the world slip away from her. She inhaled deeply through her nose and exhaled through her mouth. Centering herself, she let her consciousness merge with the energy of the emerald. A moment later she saw the ruby beam. Withdrawing her essence from her body, Kacie stepped onto the Emerald spiral that still twined around the ruby thread, climbing higher and higher until she came to a landing guarded by a giant black raven. His ruby eyes flamed in the darkness as he stared at her.

In a voice deep and commanding, the raven asked, "Who seeks audience with the ancient Brotherhood of the Raven? What is your purpose?"

Kacie bowed to the guardian and then straightened to her full height, letting the Emerald Power radiate from her. "I am the Emerald Sorceress and I have come to ask the Raven Brotherhood for their assistance."

I can't believe I'm talking to a giant bird.

The guardian moved away from the double iron doors baring entrance to the hall of the Raven Brotherhood and bowed his ebony head to Kacie. "Enter, sister and be welcome."

Kacie stepped onto the landing and pushed on the doors. They swung open on soundless hinges. The room stretching out before her was long and brilliantly lit by a source she couldn't see. At the end of the hall, someone cleared his throat and Kacie realized that several men sat watching her. She stopped gawking and strode forward.

"You have come seeking entrance to the Raven's Tower," the elderly man sitting in the center chair told her. "Why would the Emerald Sorceress have need to enter the Raven's Tower without an invitation form the Raven Wizard?"

"I've come to the Raven Brotherhood because there is no true Raven Wizard. And, there hasn't been one since the apprentice Jozef murdered the Wizard Mykal."

"I am Mykal," the man identified himself. "I was the last Raven Wizard," he confirmed.

"Then it is your aid I seek, my Lord Raven. I come to you on behalf of the true Dragon King, Kerric of Medora. Jozef grasps for power that is not his. And, with this power he will do more harm to Medora and her rightful King. As protector of Medora and the Dragon King, I cannot allow this."

Mykal spread his hands. "Continue."

"Jozef has the Raven's eye." Her words sent a buzz of whispered comments from the assemblage. "My quest, my Lords," she cut across the noise and they quieted. "Is to stop Jozef from using the Raven's Eye to obtain the full powers of the Raven Wizard."

Mykal's expression saddened. "Jozef has always wanted what was not his. As the youngest son to the King, he had to yield everything to his elder brothers. Jozef spent his whole life proving that he was their equal in every respect. He could never be content with their leftovers or being last in anything. It was the same when he came to me. Jozef had to be first and he could not wait for the knowledge to come to him in the natural order. He always took what he wanted, when he wanted it."

So, he murdered you and his entire family to prove he was just as good as the rest of you? My heart bleeds peanut butter and jelly for him. She couldn't believe what she was hearing. "Are you making excuses for Jozef?"

Mykal shook his head. "Not excuses, no. But I thought it would help if you knew why . . ."

What a crock. "I don't care why he did any of it. My job is to put him down. Jozef is in the Raven Tower as we speak preparing for the ritual that will allow him to destroy even you, my Lords. Will you help me or not?"

"We cannot," Mykal said, simply.

"What?" She felt like the ground under her feet suddenly turned to quicksand and she was sinking fast. "You cannot?"

"I'm sorry." Mykal shrugged in a helpless gesture. "We have no powers. All of our powers reside in the current Raven Wizard or in this case in the Raven's Eye."

Kill me now and put me out of my misery. "Are you telling me I'm on my own?"

"You are the Emerald Sorceress, vested with your full powers," Mykal began. "You are more than a match for an upstart wizard with only half his magical powers."

An upstart wizard with delusions of grandeur and about twenty years more experience. Somebody help me here, I'm in deep doodoo.

"My lady Emerald." Mykal brought her out of her wallowing self-pity. "Are you prepared to battle Jozef to stop him?"

Don't really have a choice, do I? "I am."

He rose and came to her. "Then go with our blessing and stop him." He placed his hands on her head in benediction.

From the doorway, icy laughter reverberated around the hall. Kacie whirled to see Jozef standing before the open doors. "Yes, stop me if you can, little sorceress." He strode forward, his cold stare boring into her. "This time I will kill you."

"You can try." Kacie returned his stare. *OK, Miller, you get one shot at this. Don't screw it up. And don't worry about the pressure, it's not like the whole world is depending on you or anything.*

"I will squash you like an insect under my foot." He pointed his hand at her and a killing stream of blue energy shot from his fingers.

Kacie threw a shimmering wall of green up in front of her, blocking his attack. "Better watch what you step on," she advised, bringing her palms together. "Some insects have deadly bites." *Did I just call myself an insect?* She spread her hands and flashed her palms at him. The air around him blazed with emerald fire.

Jozef managed to deflect most of the blast, but the tail of the lash stung him. He shouted a curse at her and Kacie flew backwards, crashing against the wall. *That hurt.* She fought to catch her breath as Jozef advanced on her, chanting.

Blackness feathered the edges of her vision. *NO! You will not win.* Kacie closed her eyes and ears to his voice and drew the Emerald Power around her like a protective mantle. His spell slid away from her, harmless.

She got to her feet and brushed herself off. Power sang in her veins. "Good try, though," she said and flicked her fingers at him.

Jozef flew through the air. He landed across the room, gasping in pain. She gathered the threads of her power together and wove a net of emerald fibers, binding him. He fought to free himself, but the more he moved the tighter the net constricted. He shouted the beginning of a spell. Kacie made a fist and his words choked in his throat. Helpless, he watched her come towards him.

Kacie knelt by his side. "You see, I have all of the Emerald Powers." She smelled the fear on him, strong and acrid. His face paled when she placed her hands on his temples.

Kacie exerted her powers and his mind opened to her. She saw images of a younger Jozef placing his own hands on Mykal's temples, just as she was doing, and strip away what was left of Mykal's magic. She felt Jozef's rage when he learned that Mykal and Reyna had given Mykal's powers back to the Raven's Eye. She saw Mykal writhe in agony as Jozef tore his mind to shreds before he allowed Mykal to finally die.

A cold fury burned within her as she sought and found the center of Jozef's powers. And just as Jozef did to his master so many years before, she ripped the magic from him, letting it flow into herself.

Jozef screamed and slumped over, unconscious, the ruby still clutched in his slack fingers.

Kacie bent and retrieved the Raven's eye. "I take back what was never yours."

The magic binding the stone to Jozef broke and Jozef was yanked back to the Raven's Tower and into his body.

Kacie held the Raven's Eye in her open hand and took a breath to still the anger inside her and concentrated on the stone. Finding the bond that was forged between them, She allowed Jozef's stolen magic to flow along the ruby path, back into the jewel. The Raven's Eye flashed, bathing the hall in a brilliant ruby light. Kacie withdrew her consciousness from the bond and the ruby pulled the light into itself once more.

Kacie handed the Raven's Eye to Mykal and bowed to the Brotherhood.

Mykal took the gem, clasping her hand in both of his. "Thank you."

"Keep it safe until a new Raven Wizard can be found," she said and pulled her hand free. "Now, I must finish this."

CHAPTER NINETEEN

Kacie turned from the Raven Brotherhood and descended the emerald spiral leading back to her body. She drew her essence into the center of her being and opened her eyes looking around the tiny mirror room.

Derian still guarded the door and Kerric stood over her, sword ready. She smiled at them to let them know she was back.

"Jozef's magic is gone," she announced and got to her feet. "Take me to Jozef," she ordered the dragon mirror.

Kerric moved to her side and searched her face. "What do you mean, Jozef's magic is gone? Are you all right? What happened?"

Kacie placed a hand on his arm to stop the questions. "I mean I stripped his magic from him. Look, I'll explain everything later, but right now, we have to get to the Raven Tower." She pointed to the candle-lit room where Jozef sat slumped against the wall, his head lolling on his chest.

But, before they moved an inch, Jozef raised his head. He pushed the heels of his hands hard against his temples and the agonized scream that ripped from his throat made the hair on the back of Kacie's neck stand on end. For just a second, his glassy eyes seemed to stare directly at her; hatred etched in every line of his body, before his gaze darted to Tia and Alexei, bound and helpless across the room.

Jozef rushed toward them, his hand dropping to his belt. Something flashed in the dim light as his hand slashed toward Alexei's throat.

"No!" Fear squeezed the breath out of Kacie's lungs. She grabbed Kerric and Derian's hands and pulled them through the mirror with her.

The moment her feet touched the stone floor, she threw a ball of energy at Jozef. It exploded against his chest, sending him hurtling through the air. He crashed into the wall with a dull thud and slid to the floor.

Kacie gathered herself for the killing blow. Emerald power crackled along her skin waiting to be unleashed.

"No!" Kerric roared and rushed to Jozef's side, checking for a pulse.

"What?" She couldn't have heard him right. Kerric wouldn't dare stop her. Rage chased the adrenaline shooting through Kacie's veins. "After everything he's done to my family and yours? You want me to stop?" Kacie shook her head. No, she couldn't let Jozef get off that easily. It was her job to finish him and Kerric wasn't going to stop her. "Move away, Kerric," she ordered.

"No." He stood between her and Jozef. "You cannot kill him."

Kacie swallowed the urge to blast Kerric out of the way. "Give me one good reason why not."

He started to touch her arm and obviously thought better of it and let his hand drop back to his side. "Jozef is a traitor. He must stand trial for his crimes." Kacie opened her mouth to protest, but he held up his hand. "I will not start my reign as King with his murder on my hands. The people of Medora need to see him punished. It will help them heal."

She chewed on the inside of her cheek while she listened to him, reason warring with rage. *I only asked for one good reason.* The emerald glow faded from her skin and Kacie slumped a little as the energy drained away.

"I hate it when you're right," she grumbled not quite under her breath as she turned her back on him.

Kerric chuckled and picked up Jozef's knife and tossed it to Derian who had plastered himself out of harm's way the second they arrived.

Derian plucked the blade out of mid air and peeled himself away from the wall. Kneeling between Tia and Alexei, he cut them free.

Kacie forced herself to forget about Jozef for the moment and turned her attention to Tia and Alexei as well. Other than lack of circulation to their hands and feet, neither of them seemed worse for their encounter. They were both aware of their surroundings and talking to Derian.

"How do you feel?" Kacie asked, giving them a quick scan for residual magic.

"Fine." Tia leaned against Derian as she rubbed the circulation back into her wrists.

"Quite well, surprisingly." Alexei agreed and stood.

"Good. Taking away Jozef's power must have broken the effects of his magic." She smiled at them but, to her horror, her knees started to shake when she thought how close she came to losing Alexei before she ever got to know him. Tears stung her eyes as relief flooded over her and she looked away not wanting anyone to see her cry, but Alexei saw and the next thing she knew, she was being folded in her father's arms.

Kacie buried her face in Alexei's shoulder and Alexei crushed her to him. She sniffled back the tears and grinned as a chorus line of butterflies tap danced in her stomach. *I have a father!*

"Did he say start his reign?" Tia's question brought Kacie back to the matter at hand.

Uh-oh. Kacie cringed, very glad she didn't have to be the one to explain.

"That's what he said," Derian confirmed. "A lot's happened since we saw you last."

"But, I don't - Kerric look out!" Tia cried.

Kacie broke Alexei's hold, whirling around in time to see Jozef pull another knife from his boot and throw it at Kerric's back.

At Tia's warning, Kerric twisted out of harm's way and the blade only sliced through the sleeve of his shirt.

The next second, Jozef was on his feet and charging at Kerric, sword in hand.

Kerric side-stepped the attack and Kacie raised her hand to attack Jozef again, but Kerric warned her away. "Don't interfere." He whipped the Dragon Sword from his scabbard and held ready, poised to draw blood. "This is between the two of us."

"Yeah, well, if he kills you, all bets are off," Kacie informed him as Alexei moved her out of the way. "The people of Medora will just have to find another way to heal."

Kerric circled Jozef, studying him. "If he kills me you have to rule Medora. I just made you my heir."

"Then you better win, son," Kacie said. "Cause I am not doing your job, too."

Jozef sneered at them and lunged for Kerric. "I am the King of Medora."

"You are the murderer of Medora and your reign is over." Kerric leaped sideways as the flashing blade arched laterally, missing his stomach by a breath. He circled around slashing at Jozef's knees, forcing him back.

With his back to the wall, Jozef pivoted to his left and sliced at Kerric's neck. "Mylan was arrogant too," he sneered. "He fancied himself a master swordsman." Jozef snorted. "I killed him in three moves."

"I'm not my father." Kerric ducked under the sword, moving in close enough to knee Jozef in the groin. Jozef doubled over, gasping and coughing.

Kerric flexed his fingers into a better grip on the unfamiliar Dragon Sword as he raised it to strike at Jozef's unprotected back. But Jozef managed to slip away and Kerric's stroke whistled harmlessly through the air.

"You'll have to do better than that, nephew." Jozef recovered and whirled on Kerric, weaving a net of ringing steel around him that Kerric was hard pressed to match.

Kacie sucked in her breath as Kerric jumped back. He obviously didn't see the stone bowl still on the floor behind him. She shouted a warning.

It came too late.

The heel of Kerric's boot landed in the middle of the bowl. His ankle twisted, throwing him off balance as he slipped on the blood and wine pooling under his feet.

Kerric sprawled on his back, the Dragon Sword flying from his hand. Jozef pounced, sword raised for a killing stroke, triumph written on his face.

Kacie gathered herself; ready to take Jozef out. Alexei grabbed her arm, breaking her concentration.

"Don't interfere," he warned when she stayed poised for attack. "Watch." Alexei nodded to Kerric. "He's not out of it yet. Wait."

Kerric lay perfectly still, watching Jozef advance. He looked beaten, but Kacie realized that his muscles were coiled, ready to strike.

"Alright." She'd wait. For now. But, she didn't go through all this to stand by and watch Kerric die.

Kerric didn't move as Jozef's blade whistled through the air. He waited until the last possible second when he was sure Jozef couldn't check his swing and then, with a growl, Kerric lashed out. He kicked Jozef's sword hand deflecting the killing blow and rolled away. With a lightening movement, Kerric snatched the Dragon Sword up and swung it under Jozef's hacking weapon. The tip of Kerric's sword caught Jozef's flesh at the waist. Using all his strength, Kerric dug in and sliced Jozef open from waist to shoulder.

"Is that better, Uncle?" Kerric sneered, jerking the Dragon Sword free.

Jozef's eyes widened in surprise for a split second before the light went out of them and he crashed to the floor dead.

Kacie rushed forward and bent over the body, checking for a pulse just as Kerric did a few minutes earlier. "I thought you said you wanted him alive?"

Kerric rolled his eyes. "I'm fine, thank you for asking." He sank back on his heels and hung his head, slowing his labored breathing before he got to his feet. Using the hem of Jozef's tunic, he wiped the Dragon Sword clean.

Kacie watched the silver blade slowly disappear into the worn scabbard at Kerric's hip.

It was over.

CHAPTER TWENTY

Jozef lay at Kacie's feet, his dead eyes staring into oblivion.

A smile passed between Kacie and Kerric as the enormity of their accomplishment washed over them. "Let's go claim your throne, Sire." Kacie called up the portal that would take them back to Trion.

"Hold a moment." Alexei put out a hand to stop them. "It's not that simple."

"What do you mean?" Kacie frowned at him.

"If we just appear in Trion carrying Jozef's dead body his guards will kill us instantly."

"Alexei's right," Derian agreed and Kerric nodded.

"What do you suggest?" Kerric asked.

Alexei thought for a moment. "Take us to the Emerald Palace, Kacie. We can make our plans there."

Kacie shook her head. "No way. I do not want him smelling up my house while you guys decide what to do with him."

"It's a castle, not a house," Derian pointed out. "I don't think he'll smell up the whole place."

"Whatever. He's not going there and that's final." She folded her arms across her chest and glared from Alexei to Kerric.

"We aren't going to leave him there," Kerric said.

"No." Kacie set her jaw and narrowed her eyes at him.

Alexei almost masked a bark of laughter behind a cough. "Oh ho, I know that look. Her mother had the same one. I advise you give in, Kerric. This is one battle you won't win," he shook his head and draped an arm around Kacie's shoulder. "Very well, daughter, what do you suggest?"

Kacie drew herself up straight and slowly let her gaze fall on each of them, looking them in the eye and holding their gaze. "You all seem to forget who I am." She raised her arms and a ring of emerald fire sprang up around her. "Kerric is in no danger with me at his side."

"She's got a point." Derian took a step away from the pulsing aura, pulling Tia between himself and Kacie.

216

"We'll take him back to Trion. We might as well make our stand there. With Jozef's body in tow there won't be any doubt that we mean business."

Kerric grinned and bowed. "As my lady Sorceress commands."

"You are such a pain in the butt." Kacie turned her back on the evil twinkle in his eyes and called up the portal. "Take us to Jozef's sleeping room."

"Nothing like walking into the lion's mouth," Tia muttered as the colors swirled and settled into the image of Jozef's bed room.

Derian mumbled an agreement as he and Alexei hefted Jozef to their shoulders and stepped to the portal.

"Wait." Kerric motioned them back and lifted Jozef's dead hand, working the Raven's signet ring off his finger. "This ruby belongs in the Dragon Sword."

Alexei nodded approval and he and Derian carried their burden through the portal, followed by Tia.

"After you, Sire." Kacie motioned for Kerric to proceed before her.

"Put him on the bed, Derian," Alexei said as Kacie stepped into Jozef's bed chamber.

Across the room, Tia eased one side of the double doors open and peeked through the crack. She quickly shut it again. "Keep your voices down," she hissed. "There's a lot of people in the next room." Tip toeing away from the door, Tia motioned Kacie away from the others. "Is it true?" she whispered, when they were out of ear shot. "Is Kerric really the King of Medora?"

"It's true," Kacie confirmed. "Kerric's the lost prince everybody's been looking for. He's the son of Prince Mylan, Jozef's older brother and the true heir to the Dragon Throne."

Tia frowned. "I knew it was too good to last."

"I give. What was too good to last?"

"Never mind." Tia waved Kacie's question away and went to watch Derian and Alexei situate Jozef. But Kacie was sure she heard Tia mumble, "Just my luck; the one thing I've been trying to escape."

And they think I'm weird. Kacie rolled her eyes and followed Tia. "So, now what?" She waved at Jozef and Kerric.

"Now we tell the world the King is dead," Alexei answered.

"Long live the King," Tia muttered to no one in particular.

"How do we do that, Alexei, with out getting ourselves killed?" Derian raised a questioning eyebrow at them.

"The King will return soon." Amsden's sandpaper voice carried clearly through the door. "I want a fire and mulled wine waiting for him."

Everyone froze, their gaze riveted on the slowly moving door handle.

Alexei's curse broke their immobility. Kerric and Tia shot across the room and flattened themselves against the wall on either side of the door while Alexei pulled the heavy bed curtains closed, hiding Jozef's body just as Amsden stepped inside the room.

Two steps inside, Amsden spotted Derian and Kacie standing beside the bed and stopped mid-stride. "What are you . . . Guards!" he called, drawing his sword.

Kerric shoved him farther into the room and Tia slammed the door shut behind him, using her body as a blockade to keep anyone else out.

Amsden whirled on Kerric, his sword threatening. Kerric's hand dropped to the hilt of the Dragon Sword, ready to oblige.

"No, Kerric." Derian stopped him. "He's mine."

Without a word, Kerric inclined his head and stepped back.

Derian drew his sword and moved toward Amsden. "You have a nasty habit of blundering in where you aren't wanted."

"We don't have time for this, guys," Kacie said, but she should have saved her breath. Both combatants smelled blood and they weren't about to listen to her.

"We end this now," Amsden sneered, charging Derian with a two handed attack.

Alexei grabbed Kacie's arm and yanked her out of the way as Derian spun, narrowly missing her head. Kacie yelped and turtled her neck as far into her clothing as her collar would allow.

Derian sliced at Amsden's mid-section and a thin line of red trailed behind his blade. Derian smiled. "That was for Rebecca and my son."

Amsden hissed in pain and jabbed at Derian. "How does if feel to know that your son carries my name?" he taunted.

Derian danced out of harm's way. "How does it feel to know that everything you own will belong to my son when I kill you?"

Amsden swore and flicked his wrist. A hidden stiletto appeared in his hand. He ran in close, trying to stab Derian in the neck. Derian side-stepped and knocked the knife out of Amsden's hand with the hilt of his sword.

"Enough!" Kacie yelled and made a yanking motion with her hand. Both swords jerked out of their hands and flew across the room, crashing against the wall and clattered to the floor. "I said, we don't have time for this," she said into the stunned silence.

"That's one way to get your point across,"Kerric said, placing his sword to Amsden's throat, holding him motionless.

A smile touched at the corners of Kacie's mouth. "Whatever works."She shrugged and turned to Derian. "Find something to tie him up with. Now, Derian," she commanded when he hesitated. "There's been enough killing today."

Derian glared at her, but obeyed and pulled a drapery cord loose and bound Amsden's hands behind his back.

"You'll never get away with this," Amsden spat at her. "The King will have your head."

"Or not." Kacie flung open the bed curtain, exposing Jozef's body. "Jozef's dead and the *King* is holding a sword at your throat."

Amsden's stare darted to Kerric. "Rouse?" He began to laugh, shaking his head in denial. "This is treason. Guards!"

Kerric hit him on the side of the head with the hilt of the Dragon Sword, stunning Amsden into silence. "The name is Renberg." Kerric stared, into Amsden's eyes until the man finally looked away.

"I could use some help here." Tia leaned her whole weight against the door, her body bouncing from the pounding on the other side. "I can't hold them."

Kacie bit her lip, thinking furiously and then snapped her fingers and turned to her father. "Alexei you and Derian guard Amsden. Kerric, come stand by me." She waited for them to change positions and then nodded at Tia. "Okay Tia, let go and beat feet over here."

Tia didn't need to be told twice. She straightened and darted to Derian's side just as both double doors flew open and armed guards and nobles burst into the room.

"Seize them. They've murdered the King," Amsden shouted.

"Hold!" Kacie drew a line in the air, pointing from one side of the room to the other and a wall of shimmering emerald fire sprang up in front of them. Screams erupted as palace guards and Medoran nobles crashed into the magically charged barrier. The barrier flared and the men fell to the ground, unconscious, green energy crackling over their bodies. Those behind, pulled up short, crowding into one another, trying to avoid their comrades' fate.

"They murdered the King. What are you waiting for? Arrest them," Amsden continued to yell.

Kacie frowned at him. "You really are getting on my nerves. Somebody shut him up."

Derian was only too happy to obey. He tore a strip from Amsden's shirt and crammed it into his mouth, ignoring Amsden's gagging.

Angrily, the men protested Amsden's rough treatment. Kacie let them grumble.

"I assume by now you all recognize who or rather what I am," she spoke softly and they quieted to hear her.

"You're the Emerald Sorceress," someone said, stepping forward.

Kacie recognized the mountain-sized guard she threatened to turn into a toad and smiled. "That's right, I am."

"What's going on here?" The man asked her.

"Jozef is dead. But.... " Another uproar met this announcement. "But," she said again and they quieted. "Beside me stands your true King." She nodded to Kerric. "Kerric Renberg, grandson to King Gueran. Son of Prince Mylan and his wife Liselle LeClair, daughter of the Duke of Rathborn. His birth and legitimacy witnessed and recorded by the Emerald Sorceress, Reyna and his godfather, Duke Alexei Aideny the ninth Duke of Trion." Kacie pointed to her father.

Alexei stepped forward and the buzz started again.

"We were told you were dead," a nobleman in front said.

"Jozef said you and your lady wife and child died in an attack on Trion castle by mercenaries trying gain a foothold in Medora," added another voice by the door.

"Jozef attacked Trion castle in retribution for my lack of support. My wife was killed." Alexei cast a quick look at Kacie before continuing. "I was taken prisoner and held at Desar for the past twenty years. But, Reyna saved my daughter and with the help of the Baron of Ridley, raised her in secret just as she also safely raised Medora's true heir." He pointed to Kerric and all eyes followed.

Kerric stood motionless under the scrutiny. His head high, his stance wide, his manner calm as he looked into the eyes of every man there.

To Kacie's mind, his very essence shouted royalty. Harvey, himself couldn't have looked more regal that long ago day when he claimed the Dragon Throne.

"He has the look of the old Dragon," a deep voice to their right said.

"I knew Prince Mylan,"someone else said. "And, he's the image of the prince."

Nods and mummers of agreement rippled through the crowd until one of the guards said, "Is that the Dragon Sword he carries?"

Kerric held up the sword for everyone to see. "I carry the Dragon Sword of Medora," he spoke at last. As decreed by the Emerald Sorceress two hundred years ago, only the true Dragon King may wield the Dragon Sword." He suddenly slashed the blade through the air in front of him.

His audience gasped and took a collective step backwards. In the front line, the guards shifted their stance, the threatening spears dipping a little.

"Jozef may have sat on the throne, but he was never able to find the Dragon Sword. Jozef committed treason when he murdered my grandfather and father so that he could steal the throne and begin his reign of terror."

Kerric began to move forward and Kacie took a calculated risk and casually flicked her fingers. The emerald barrier vanished. No one noticed. Kerric held them as completely as if he were the one with magic powers.

"My Lords," he continued as he began to move among them. "Jozef bled Medora dry and held all of you hostage."

Kerric strolled through the outer sitting room and into the long audience chamber as he spoke. Kacie stayed on his heels, alert for any trouble, but she didn't need to worry. They parted like water before him. The silent crowd of nobles hanging on his every word as they filed in behind.

"Jozef has paid for his treason as all traitors do – with his life." He moved to the daiz steps and turned to face the room full of people.

"Now, My Lords, the time has come to heal our land. With your support and the help of the Emerald Sorceress we will succeed."

He waved a hand at Kacie and she realized he was reminding them of who stood at his side. *Good move, Sire.*

"As your King," Kerric sat on the throne, resting the Dragon Sword across his knees. "I pledge this to you."

Kacie held her breath.

The entire room erupted in cheers and one by one, every person knelt in homage.

Kacie breathed again.

Under cover of the cheers, Kerric motioned Kacie closer. "We did it." He beamed up at her.

Kacie grinned. "You bet your Twinkie we did it!"

Reyna would be proud of them both.

"You know," Kerric continued. "There is still a lot to do before I can formally take the Throne. Will you help me?" He held out his hand to her. "Will you stay?"

Kacie looked over at her father standing on the other side of the throne and smiled. *Are you kidding; miss all the fun?* "I'll stay. But," She batted his hand away and wagged her finger at him. "I'm telling you here and now, I'm sending to Mr. Weatherby for some jeans. Have you ever tried to do anything with fifty yards of silk wrapped around your legs? And music. I've got to have my CDs. And my roller blades. Have you seen my ball room at the Emerald Palace? It's perfect for roller hockey. I'll teach you how to play. You'll love it!"

ACKNOWLEDGEMENTS

I'd like to send a huge thank you to my wonderful critique partners. Miriam Pace, Jackie Hamilton, Sydney Sterling, Pamela Moran, M. A. Taylor, love you all! Your help from start to finish was invaluable.

And a very special thank you to my friend, Peggy Wu - I couldn't have written this without you.

www.ingramcontent.com/pod-product-compliance
Lightning Source LLC
Chambersburg PA
CBHW032155190626
46808CB00020B/408